THE LIAR
NEXT DOOR

BOOKS BY NICOLA MARSH

The Scandal
The Last Wife
My Sister's Husband

NICOLA MARSH

THE LIAR NEXT DOOR

bookouture

Published by Bookouture in 2021

An imprint of Storyfire Ltd.
Carmelite House
50 Victoria Embankment
London EC4Y 0DZ

www.bookouture.com

ISBN: 978-1-80019-844-9
eBook ISBN: 978-1-80019-843-2

Caitlyn and Simon, thanks for being great neighbors and nothing like the twisted liars in this book.

PROLOGUE

I don't make friends easily. I never have. I'm inherently suspicious of people: their motives, their lies. That's what I hate the most, the monstrous untruths people tell in the name of self-preservation.

Though I'm a hypocrite. I'm guilty of lying myself, but I have a conscience and I despise myself for the charade. Keeping up the pretense is hard. I'm not sleeping well. I'm edgy. Lamenting the mistakes of the past and trying desperately to keep a grip on the present.

This sham I'm perpetuating won't end well. I know this. I have a plan. It's complicated and risky, but aren't all good things in life worth taking a risk for?

I can see my future so clearly. I deserve to be happy. But one false step will bring my carefully constructed façade tumbling down and I'm incredibly nervous.

I hear sirens and foreboding trickles down my spine. Silly, because I haven't hurt anyone. Not really. They can't be coming for me.

But as the wailing intensifies and flashes of red and blue light illuminate the room, every muscle in my body tenses, ready for flight.

I take a deep breath, blow it out, and do it again, calming myself before I cross to the window and peek out. Three police cars pull up next door and the sirens are barely cut before the doors fly open and officers exit the vehicles, twelve in total. Some wear uniforms, some are plain-clothed detectives.

My gut twists with dread as I watch them stride up the path—thankfully not toward my front door—and I'm instantly remorseful for such a selfish thought.

Something bad has happened. That many officers wouldn't show up for a simple disturbance or grievance, and certainly no detectives. I hope nothing's wrong with one of the children. There are several youngsters in our cozy enclave. I see them playing in the park and it brings a simple joy to my complicated life.

I can't see who opens my neighbor's door no matter how hard I crane my neck. An officer notices me peering out my window and our gazes lock for a moment before I back away and draw the curtain so I'm out of sight.

While I hope my neighbors are fine, particularly the children, I don't want to draw attention to myself. It's the last thing I need.

I must relax and try to distract myself with mundane tidying, web surfing, even mindless reality TV. But I'm still on edge and when I hear a scream, a chill ripples over me, raising goosebumps.

Is it the anguished cry of a mother whose child is in jeopardy?

Or the shriek of someone who's lost everything?

CHAPTER ONE

FRANKIE

I believe in love at first sight.

The moment I laid eyes on 8 Vintage Circle in Hambridge Heights, I fell hard. It came as a shock because after living in Manhattan for so long I never envisaged moving to Brooklyn. But Andre and I needed a fresh start—our marriage depended on it—so I took the plunge and put in an offer on the delightful brownstone, knowing in my gut I'd made the right decision.

It seemed like fate when we got the house and moved in five years ago, a sign. Andre had begged for another chance and I relented. Nobody's perfect. We all make mistakes. We'd been married for eight months when he cheated on me. A slip-up, he said. A drunken one-night stand that meant nothing; a stupid lapse in judgment that wouldn't be repeated. He'd made a lot of trite excuses at the time, and eventually I grew tired of hearing them; his genuine remorse got to me after a while. I didn't want to absolve his sins but I had a few of my own to hide so I forgave him. Luna was born eight and a half months later and the moment I glanced at her squished face after an exhausting sixteen-hour labor I was glad I gave him another chance.

My daughter is my world and I didn't want to be responsible for blowing hers up. I wanted to preserve our family, to give my daughter the stability of having two parents in the same household, parents who could work through problems rather than running away. Even though I'd forgiven Andre quickly after he cheated, once Luna was born I became intolerant of his idiosyncrasies. Silly things, like the way he chewed peanut brittle with his mouth open so I could hear every annoying crunch, and leaving a trail of clothes to the bathroom when he showered. I didn't have postpartum depression, but my haywire hormones made my irrational anger escalate and I had to do something about it. Turns out, because I'd forgiven him so quickly for the sake of the pregnancy, I still harbored antipathy toward him and needed to deal with it. It took four weeks of therapy before I finally let my resentment go, and that's when we bought this place and moved here.

Andre and I have been solid since then. Luna is a happy, well-adjusted five-year-old, my career as a lifestyle vlogger is thriving, and Andre's graphic design business sees him working from home more days than he's away.

We're happy. I'm happy.

Yet as Luna and I cross the road in front of our house and enter the community garden, a sliver of foreboding makes me pause.

"What's wrong, Mom?"

My gorgeous, sweet daughter is staring up at me with big blue eyes so like her father's. With her blonde hair, dimple in the right cheek and easy smile, everyone says she looks like me. But the shape of her eyes, the unique blue that I'm certain turns indigo when she's emotional, is all her father.

"Nothing, sweetheart. Are you looking forward to the party?"

A stupid question as she starts hopping from one foot to the other, not even looking at me, and I follow her gaze to find her attention fixed on two long tables draped in white linen, covered in a variety of pink and blue cupcakes, candies and lemonade.

"Duh." Her eye-roll is cute and I struggle not to laugh.

I have no idea where she's heard that, probably one of those cartoons she watches when I need to keep her occupied. I love the flexibility of working from home—being a full-time mom and earning a great wage—but it has its challenges, like Luna wandering into the kitchen when I'm doing a live stream.

"What are we waiting for, Mom?"

"Nothing," I say with a smile, and with that she's off, running to join a group of children clustered near the cupcakes.

I'm more reticent. I wouldn't say this to anyone but I've never really understood the point of a gender reveal party. It usually means the most to the parents. And this one is particularly odd, as our new neighbors, Saylor and Lloyd Abernathy, only moved in two weeks ago. Why invite the whole neighborhood?

We're a close-knit community, thirty houses surrounding a square of garden that is perfect for kids and parents alike, and we congregate here on major holidays like Fourth of July and Christmas Eve, each family bringing a plate and sharing food and conversation.

Maybe the party is Saylor and Lloyd's way of trying to fit in? If so, I applaud them, but I'm also wary. Not their fault, mine, because having a high profile online means I'm cautious with strangers in general. Some people equate popularity with ownership and I regularly receive a plethora of emails and DMs from men and women, who feel like they know me, want to date me, or want to be me. It's disconcerting, having fans reach out like I'm their best friend. Some gush, some ask for advice, and some tell me personal stuff I'd rather not know. It scares me, being so well known, when I've spent most of my life fading into the background.

I hadn't expected my vlog to take off. I started it a few months after I had Luna as a fun way to pass an hour or two when the rest of my day was filled with feeding, diaper changes and rocking her to sleep. Never in my wildest dreams had I anticipated earning a six-figure income from my ramblings about motherhood, home cooking and decorating, let alone have millions of daily hits. Viewers had told me they'd been drawn to my honesty initially, when I'd show them my disasters in the kitchen, like the time I was pureeing organic squash for Luna, hadn't screwed the blender lid tight enough and ended up wearing orange goop. Or the time I'd been so exhausted because I'd been up half the night with a teething Luna and had forgotten to add baking soda to my sponge and it had turned out flat as a pancake.

But as Luna got older and I grew more comfortable in front of the camera, I became more competent. I'm obsessed with perfect pictures online, so I try to emulate some of the stylists by presenting pretty food and wearing cutesy matching outfits to match my theme of the day. Luckily, my viewers like my new image as much as they liked my food-splattered one and my vlog has thrived since.

But I worry that my amazing job might vanish at any second. It's crazy, because my followers grow daily, but I'm aware I'm making a living from an unpredictable job. What kind of world do we live in when people hang on the words of a stranger— me—and treat me like a guru? I'm no expert, far from it, and it's my inherent fear of being labeled a fraud that feeds into this insecurity. What if I lose everything? What if something happens and I lose my major brand partnerships? What if my content isn't interesting and my followers disengage? Having a steady income stream of my own is important to me and I can't afford to lose it, which means I need to be careful, keep smiling for the camera, pretending I'm well put together and in control when I'm nothing like it on the inside.

I spot Andre chatting with Ruston, a guy who lives across the park. He's leaning close to Ruston, attentive to some anecdote that has him flinging back his head and laughing loudly in the next second. I can't help but smile when I hear his laugh. It's spontaneous and natural and one of the things I love about him.

I may seem happy most of the time, but deep down I'll always harbor doubts about us. Namely, will he cheat again? Not that he knows I struggle with suspicion at times. I'm good at pretending for Luna's sake, but I lost my ability to trust the day I learned about his betrayal. I'm so tired. Exhausted down to my soul. Faking it—for my followers, for my friends, for my husband—is taking its toll.

For Luna's sake, I hope if something has to give, it's not my marriage.

I make a beeline for the gift table. Like me, most of the neighbors have ignored the "no gifts please" addendum on the cutesy stork invitation Saylor had slipped into our mailboxes, and brought something. Mine's nothing fancy, a set of body lotion for mom and baby, but my wrapping—all pale blues, pinks and lemons from the paper to the silk ribbons—makes it stand out. I'm all about the presentation, ask anyone. I'm known for it in the neighborhood.

Frankie Forbes, you are divine. You're flawless. I love your look.
What brand of foundation do you use, Frankie? You look eighteen.
Your clothes are to die for. Which designer is your favorite?

I get comments like this on a daily basis and because anything I recommend sees an instant uptake in sales for the retailer I get a lot of free stuff sent to me. Some days our stoop is piled high with deliveries. Luna thinks it's wonderful, Andre is tolerant yet bemused and I'm grateful that people listen to what I have to say.

It wasn't always like that.

In my previous life, Francesca Mayfair was invisible.

I much prefer being Frankie Forbes.

After finding room for my gift and placing it down, I turn away from the table to find a woman standing too close behind me. I stiffen, hating the invasion of personal space.

Sensing my annoyance, she holds up her hands like she has nothing to hide. "Sorry. I'm not sneaking up on you, it's just that the tag is poking out and your dress is so adorable I was trying to sneak a peek at the label."

Self-conscious, I muster a smile and tuck the label in. "That's what happens when you're running late and grab the first thing from your closet."

Her eyebrows shoot up. "If how you look is the result of you running late, what's your secret?"

She doesn't seem to know me and that's refreshing.

"No secret. It's all in the accessories." I point to my earrings, chandelier-style turquoise feathers hanging from a gold hoop, and then to my espadrilles in the same color.

"You look amazing." She screws up her nose and points to her jeans and paisley peasant top. "This is dressed up for me. My daughter's the fashionista."

"I hear you there. It feels like Luna has been color-coordinating from the cradle."

"Luna's a gorgeous name," she says. "Is your daughter here?"

I nod and point to the cupcake table. "She's the one in the pink polka-dot dress marshaling the kids."

The woman glances over and smiles. "Violette is the one hanging back at the end of the line."

I see a girl about Luna's age standing apart from the other kids, five rambunctious boys. She's wearing an impractical white dress, Mary Janes and a dainty pink bow in her hair, a few shades darker than Luna's.

"We should introduce the girls," I say.

She nods and casts me a shy glance. "I'm new to the neighborhood, so maybe we should introduce ourselves first?"

I laugh and stick out my hand. "I'm Frankie Forbes, number eight."

"Celeste Reagan, number ten."

She shakes my hand and hers is surprisingly icy on this warm day.

"You're my neighbor?"

She laughs at my obvious shock. "Looks like it."

Number ten has been vacant for months and I haven't seen any moving vans recently. Besides, I would've heard signs of life next door and I haven't, which is weird.

"When did you move in?"

"Last night." She presses a finger to her lips. "Under the cover of darkness to avoid the busybodies."

I chuckle as she intended. "We're actually a great bunch, as you can see from the turnout here today." I gesture toward the crowd milling around. "Saylor and Lloyd only moved in to number six a few weeks ago, so I guess this is a get-to-know-you kind of party as well as a gender reveal."

Her nose crinkles slightly. "Can I be perfectly honest?"

I like that she feels comfortable enough around me already to be upfront, something I value. "Absolutely."

She points to the giant helium balloon filled with either pink or blue confetti tied to a stork. "What's with the gender reveal thing? When I had Violette I wanted a surprise and I sure as hell didn't want everyone else knowing my business."

I admire her honesty, pleased to have found an ally in my skepticism. "Same. Guess we're in an old-fashioned minority because these parties are all the rage now."

We laugh in sync and I realize I've been enjoying chatting to my new neighbor so much I haven't really looked at her. I think she's around my age, but on closer inspection she has carefully concealed wrinkles underlying her eyes and threads of gray through her auburn hair. She could be closer to forty than my thirty and there's a look in her eyes, like she's seen more of life than I have and it hasn't been kind.

When a slight frown appears between her brows I realize I've been staring. "Let's introduce our girls now."

"Violette would love that." Her frown deepens. "And I would too, because she's shy and it would be great for her to have friends around her age. How old is Luna?"

"Five."

"Same as Vi, great." Her eyes light up. "They might end up at the same school."

"More than likely. Hambridge Heights has the best."

"That's one of the reasons I moved here. I did a lot of research online."

I warm to her more. As a mother, I can identify with her wanting the best for her daughter. Giving Luna the opportunity to thrive is my major motivator to slather on make-up, put on a bright top, and step in front of the camera when I'm feeling lackluster and blah with a distinct case of PMT.

"It's a great place to raise kids," I say.

"Living opposite this park must be a bonus." She gestures at the lush green space around us. "You must be out here all the time."

"We like it." She hasn't mentioned a husband or partner and I can't quite see if there's a ring on her finger. "Is it just you and Violette?"

"Yes," she mutters, sharp to the point of rudeness, and I can't help but wonder if there's a story behind her brusqueness.

"Okay then."

My smile is apologetic for probing and she winces. "Sorry. It's just that Vi's father hasn't been there for me or her and it's a sore point."

"Don't apologize, I'm one of those nosy busybodies you were hoping to avoid."

We smile at each other and once again I'm struck by the shifting shadows in her eyes. Celeste definitely has a story to tell.

Then again, don't we all?

CHAPTER TWO
CELESTE

I spotted Frankie Forbes the moment she set foot in the garden.

Who wouldn't? She stands out like a graceful gazelle in a herd of clumsy hippopotami. Several women are wearing sundresses but the simplicity of Frankie's, combined with perfect accessories, make her eye-catching. The aqua sheath dress has bold slashes of emerald swirled through it, like the rainbow ice cream Violette often asks for but rarely gets. All those artificial colors aren't good for my baby. Nothing but the best for my Vi.

But it isn't just her dress that makes Frankie stand out. She's one of those enviable women who have a hint of class, like they stand head and shoulders above everyone else.

It surprised me to see her standing alone though. I expected her to be surrounded by adoring worshippers. I'm glad she'd been by herself. It made it easier for me to strike up a conversation, to establish a rapport. I don't know why I pretended not to know her. Inferiority? Shyness? It's silly because she's nothing but pleasant and I enjoyed chatting with her.

As we head toward our girls I feign interest in her general chitchat as she points out who's who from the neighborhood, when I'm only focused on one thing. Meeting Luna. Moving can be stressful for kids and Violette's not great with change at the best of times, so I'm hoping she makes friends and that will help her adjust to living here. From our chat, Frankie seems just as keen to foster a friendship between the girls, which is great. From what I've seen at today's turnout, there are a lot of young boys. Maybe there aren't many girls Luna and Violette's age who live around here.

I feel like I already know Luna. Frankie doesn't stop talking about her beautiful daughter during her live videos, waxing lyrical as she prepares the perfect child-friendly vegetable lasagna or banana bread that hides zucchini and carrot too. It's "Luna-this" and "Luna-that".

Why doesn't Vi tell me knock-knock jokes off-camera like Luna does, making Frankie laugh uproariously? Does Luna really go to bed at seven p.m. on the dot and not wake for a full twelve hours, or does she sneak into Frankie's bed like Vi likes to do with me, afraid of her own shadow?

I know I shouldn't watch Frankie Forbes. Her competency and perfection make me feel bad about myself. But I can't look away, drawn in by her charisma like the rest of her millions of viewers. Her proficiency intimidates me and I expected to dislike her because of it. When the realtor mentioned her name as I inspected the house before signing the rental agreement I thought it would be daunting to live next door to someone so perfect. But Frankie in person surprises me. She's… nice. Normal. Almost reticent, with a hint of vulnerability I never expected.

We're almost at the cupcake table when I spy Luna already chatting with Vi and my daughter is more animated than I've ever seen her. I breathe a sigh of relief, short-lived when a man detaches himself from a couple and joins us, and ridiculously, I'm nervous.

"Hey, beautiful, glad you could finally make it." He slides an arm around Frankie's waist and plants a resounding kiss on her mouth. "What took you so long?"

Before Frankie can respond, he says, "Let me guess. You were getting the gift wrapping just right."

"Nothing wrong with good presentation." Frankie arches away from him slightly, as if uncomfortable with his overt display of affection. "Andre, I'd like you to meet Celeste Reagan. She's our new neighbor. Celeste, this is my husband."

He's tall, with dark blond hair in a ruffled surfer-cut, dark blue eyes bordering on indigo and a wide smile. They make a good-looking couple.

"Pleased to meet you," he says, barely glancing at me. "Would you ladies like a drink?" Frankie and I ask for sparkling water and he bounds away like an eager puppy, his long, loping stride indicative of a man who likes to go places fast.

"If our girls start hanging out together, you'll see Luna has inherited his energy," Frankie says, her laugh self-deprecating, but I detect a hint of weariness rather than admiration.

"How long have you been married?"

"Six and half years, but sometimes it feels like forever."

"Don't all wives feel that way after two years?"

"That long?" I laugh at her sarcasm and she smiles. "Don't mind me. I'm tired and I've got a lot of work to do after this."

"What do you do?"

Her eyebrows rise slightly and I'm glad she believes my act. After pretending I didn't know her earlier, I'm too embarrassed to admit I watch her religiously, usually at the end of a day after Violette's in bed and I'm curled up on the couch with a glass of wine.

"I'm a lifestyle vlogger."

I feign confusion. "I'm a bit of a dinosaur, so, similar to all this gender reveal stuff, I don't really know what that is."

"I make videos and post them online, mostly about mother-hood. I talk about my daily life, activities, interests, funny stories, cooking, decorating. A bit of anything and everything, really. People seem to enjoy it."

I hear a squeal and glance over to see the kids, Violette included thank goodness, engaged in a game of tag. Frankie and I share an indulgent smile, pleased our daughters are holding their own with the rowdy boys. "That sounds… different."

She laughs at my naivety. "It started out as a bit of fun and has grown so huge I don't know what to do most days. It's exhausting trying to come up with new stuff to talk about."

"You film at home, right? Must be great."

She nods, pensive. "It is, but sometimes I envy those mothers who get to walk out the door and compartmentalize their home life as separate from their work life, whereas my worlds are constantly colliding."

She sounds sad and for a second I pity her. Before I remember she probably doesn't have a clue what it's like to have it tough, to raise a child on her own, to want to feel safe and protected.

I might tell her what that's like one day but for now, I'll take it slow until we know each other better. I don't have many friends. None I can count on, and while I think this whole gender reveal is stupid, I like the camaraderie among the neighbors.

Surprisingly, I feel like I almost belong here.

CHAPTER THREE

SAYLOR

My back aches, my feet are swollen and my head is on the verge of exploding. Enduring congratulations from a bunch of strangers isn't my idea of fun but I decided to throw this party to establish rapport with our new neighbors. I need to fit in, to be accepted, to become one of them, because I only moved here for one reason.

To get what I'm owed.

"You okay?" Lloyd's hand rests in the small of my back, giving it a gentle rub, and I stifle a moan.

"Better now you're doing that."

"I told you not to wear those heels."

"Stop nagging, more pressure," I murmur, sighing with pleasure as his strong fingers dig into my back. "That feels so good."

He leans down and whispers in my ear, "Maybe we should ditch this party and continue this massage in private?"

"Pervert," I say, grinning at him, loving that he still finds me as attractive at twenty weeks pregnant as he did when we married nine months ago.

Our trajectory from dating to parenthood has been swift. My religious parents approved of my pregnancy so soon after we married because they introduced me to Lloyd in the first place. They knew him through their church, a modern blend of Methodist and Presbyterian. He'd been a visiting youth minister and his ease talking with kids is one of the things that caught my eye. I saw him preach once, in the early days, and anyone who can captivate a bunch of kids must be doing something right. He'd been using an old parable about forgiving your neighbor for any wrongdoing and relating it to a kid who'd stolen his friend's bike the week before. Making the story relatable ensured the kids could identify and I'd been impressed.

Lloyd is trustworthy, exactly what I needed at the time after having my heart broken by a guy who was anything but. A guy who'd been the love of my life. A guy who wouldn't know the meaning of dependability even if it bit him on the butt.

My parents had seen it. They'd disapproved of him from the moment he strutted into my senior year at high school. I'd fallen hard, they'd done everything in their power to keep us apart. They deemed any boy who didn't go to church not worthy of me. Throw in the rumors about alcohol and drug use, and our romance had been destined for failure.

I should've been happy to see the back of him. But there's a vast difference between logic and the heart, so when I saw him last year, I did something incredibly stupid.

I'm dealing with the consequences now.

Lloyd and I married in a quiet ceremony presided over by my folks. I hadn't wanted any fuss or attention. I'd been eerily composed standing outside the church, mentally counting the red bricks above the doorway to stay focused and quell the urge to bolt. My father had been reciting some passage from the Bible about love, but I'd tuned him out too, breathing slowly and deeply, filling my lungs with the familiar scents of damp moss and oak, comforting smells that evoked memories of attending services every Sunday for as long as I could remember.

Marrying Lloyd had been the best decision I've ever made. Some guys have dependable stamped in invisible ink on their foreheads and Lloyd is one of them. I'm so lucky. His adoration, his steadiness, calms me. I wish I could be a good person like him, so I could be honest and tell him why I really wanted to move to Hambridge Heights, why I insisted on it. He's clueless and I intend to keep it that way. I need him, as more than a husband and a father. He'll never know how much.

"We should introduce ourselves to our next-door neighbors." He points to an attractive blond couple talking to a woman in dowdy jeans and an ugly paisley top. "Frankie and Andre."

"They sound like a pop duo."

"Pretty enough to be one too." He bumps me gently with his hip. "Don't go getting any ideas about swapping me for that blond himbo."

"Don't you mean mimbo? As in male bimbo?"

"Whatever the terminology, you're stuck with me." He presses his palm to my belly that's only just beginning to protrude. The ob-gyn said the baby is small for five months but he's not worried so neither am I. I may be able to control some things in my life, like where we live and how I'll get the money to support my baby, but the size of the life growing inside me isn't one of them.

"We're lucky to have you." I cover his hand with mine and we stare into each other's eyes. Lloyd's are brown, mine are hazel, and I wonder if our baby will inherit the same color or something entirely different.

I know next to nothing about Lloyd's family. His parents died a few years ago and that's when he found his way into the church. My parents adore him and I can see why. He's never given me any reason to doubt him, which makes my deception worse.

But everything I do is for our baby. It's justified. Maybe if I keep telling myself this, I'll start to believe it?

I keep referring to our "baby" when I know it's a boy, as everyone at this gender reveal is about to discover. I've already started decorating the nursery in pale blues and greens, with a border featuring tiny boats and dolphins. I love the idea of having a boy the image of his father. Lloyd had been ambivalent about discovering the sex but I'd been adamant. I had to know. I'm done with surprises.

Someone snaps a photo of us on their cell and we blink, breaking our stare and we laugh. I turn and see it's the small pretty blonde whose husband is a himbo according to Lloyd.

She's brandishing her cell and smiling. "Sorry for the intrusion. I'm not usually snap-happy but the two of you standing there with your hands on your baby bump is the cutest thing I've ever seen. Thought you might like a memento."

"Thanks." I slip my hand into Lloyd's and we move toward the small group. "I know it's weird to meet like this but I'm Saylor, this is my partner Lloyd and this," I pat my belly, "is Bump."

"Frankie. Pleased to meet you." She gestures at the gorgeous guy by her side. "This is my husband, Andre, and our neighbor on the other side, Celeste."

No wonder Lloyd scoffingly warned me off. Andre's stunning, his beauty marred by a scar running from his right eyebrow to his hairline. It adds a toughness to his features, making him breathtaking.

"Hey," Celeste says, her gaze lingering on my belly a tad too long, making me uncomfortable, but I force a smile and return her greeting with a "Hey."

As Lloyd and Andre shake hands, I see something over Andre's shoulder: more precisely, someone.

It can't be.

What is *he* doing here?

I feel the blood drain from my face and I'm grateful Lloyd has his arm around my waist.

Ruston is standing by the food table, alone, serving salad onto a plate. As if sensing my gaze, he looks up and his shock mirrors mine.

Like always, I feel the eye contact with Ruston all the way down to my toes. Neither of us look away. Stunned, I can't breathe, my lungs constricting in horror. This can't be happening.

After what seems like an eternity, he arches an eyebrow and finally turns away, leaving me flustered. My palms are clammy, my fingers tingling, and I'm lightheaded with nerves. It's hard enough pretending daily that everything's fine so Lloyd doesn't notice I'm on edge. Secrets have a way of festering and growing, until it's too late to contain and they explode in a gory mess. I don't want that. Now this?

As if sensing my unease Frankie touches my arm, her smile genuine, her big blue eyes guileless, and I'm glad for the distraction. I wish I could tell Lloyd everything. But I can't.

Not yet.

CHAPTER FOUR

FRANKIE

THEN

The afternoon of my eighteenth birthday, I'm heady with excitement and come home early from the hairdresser's, eager to try a few new make-up looks before the party tonight. I jog up the path to the front door and am about to open it when I hear a crash coming from the garage. Hoping it's not a present for me that's fallen—my folks have always hidden large birthday and Christmas gifts in the garage since I could walk—I let myself in the side door to check out the noise.

To find my dad having sex with my mom's best friend.

They don't see me because I back out of the door as fast as humanly possible, those few seconds I witnessed more than enough. It's the most hideous thing I've ever seen but not the most shocking.

The shock comes thirty minutes later when I confront Mom at work after running the whole way there to tell her what I'd seen.

And she shrugs.

My gorgeous mother—with her flawless skin, big hazel eyes and long auburn hair—who I've wanted to emulate my entire life, actually shrugs, like what I saw is inconsequential.

"Francesca, I haven't raised you to be a prude and now you're eighteen perhaps it's time you understand the ways of the world?"

As if by some miraculous changing of my age from seventeen to eighteen I should find it acceptable that my father is cheating on my mother. "What the hell are you talking about, Mom?"

Remorse deepens the lines bracketing her mouth, and she takes a deep breath before responding. "Your father and I have an open marriage and have for years." She gives a little shake of her head, like she didn't want me to discover the truth. Too late for that, Mom. Way too late. "I think you're old enough to know that now."

My mouth drops open as I stumble to the nearest seat and collapse into it. I thought open marriages were a thing of the past, in the sixties and seventies when key parties were all the rage. I'd read about them online while doing a history project on feminism at school last year and had found more detail than I would've liked. Now, to discover my parents indulge in partner swapping... I want to vomit.

"I know this must come as a shock, and I'm sorry you had to find out that way, but do you have any questions?"

Embarrassment heats my cheeks. Hell no. I don't want to ask anything about their sordid affairs. "I don't get it. I've grown up idolizing you and Dad, and can't fathom you being blasé about something so..."

I'm about to say sacred but stop myself at the last second. Will she even understand? And after what I've learned today, my parents obviously don't understand me. If they did, Dad would've taken greater care to hide what he was doing and Mom wouldn't calmly pronounce their life choices like I'm the one with the problem.

"Francesca, I've been married to your father since I was your age. He's my one, true—"

"Don't say love, because if he was, you wouldn't be cheating and calling it an open marriage."

I've always admired my parents' relationship—I thought they were committed to one another. They're so affectionate, touching each other on the shoulder and hip as they pass in the kitchen, holding hands when we go out. I catch them looking at each other sometimes and their level of devotion makes me equally uncomfortable and envious. How could they still be so in love after nineteen years of marriage?

To discover it's all a lie is devastating.

The last few years, I've wanted to find a guy like my dad, a man who adores his partner. A boyfriend I can rely on, to make me feel special, like I'm the only woman in the world for him.

Discovering what my parents are really like is disillusioning, like the day I learned there's no Santa. Now, like then, I have the same queasiness in the pit of my stomach and the tightness in my chest, like nothing will be the same again. Tears of disappointment burn the back of my eyes and I blink to keep them at bay.

"He is my one true love, and I won't have you disparaging that. Perhaps you're still too young to understand."

I don't like her condescension. "As you just pointed out, I'm the same age you were when you married Dad, so I'm not too young to judge my parents and find them lacking."

Hurt flickers in her eyes and I almost feel bad, before the image of my dad in the garage flashes in my head.

"We got married too young and that's something I wouldn't wish on you. I want you to take your time. Date different boys. And don't settle."

Confusion makes my head ache and I press my fingertips to my temples. "I don't understand. You just said Dad's the love of your life and that's why you married young, now you're telling me to do the opposite?"

She nods, sadness bracketing her mouth. "People change over time. Rather than drift apart, as was starting to happen a few years ago, we embraced a different lifestyle."

"Is that what you're calling cheating these days, a different lifestyle?"

I lash out, disappointed to discover the people I idolize the most in this world aren't who I thought they were.

"When you fall in love, you'll understand how you'll do anything to keep that love alive."

I don't say what I'm thinking, that when I fall in love I won't lose my self-respect. That I'll find a man who adores me so much he won't look elsewhere. That I'll build a solid relationship with that man, far from here.

I need to get away, to distance myself from my folks. I hate them for ripping off my rose-colored glasses. But I love them too. They're my parents and we've been close for so long.

"This changes nothing, Francesca. We're still your parents. We love you. And we're looking forward to your party tonight."

Mom's wrong. Discovering their proclivities changes everything and the last thing I feel like doing is pretending this is the best day of my life.

"Cancel the party." I stand, eager to get away. I've heard enough.

"Darling, that's impossible." She looks at her watch. "The caterers will start dropping off food in an hour."

Like a bunch of stupid hors d'oeuvres is so damn important when I've had my life upended. "Doesn't it bother you at all what I saw?"

Her expression is guilty as she nods. "I'm sorry you had to walk in on your father. He should've been more circumspect. But it's done and I can't change it. But what can change is your attitude. I want tonight to be special for you. We've invited all your friends and you deserve to have fun."

Mom has the best intentions but she leaves out one salient fact. She's invited a bunch of my parents' friends too, family friends we socialize with regularly, friends with kids my age. I used to think it so cool I got to have a wide circle of friends that extended beyond school. Now I wonder if those people only come around because they share in my parents' liberal views on marriage.

"You're a young woman now, Francesca. And while I wish you'd learned the truth about us in a different way, it's done. So let's focus on the party, huh?"

Mom takes hold of my hands and I stare at her long crimson manicured talons, the flashy gold rings adorning almost every finger, the bangles jangling at her wrists, and close my eyes against a horrific image of her grabbing at every one of the men who we class as "family friends".

"Baby, are you okay?"

She releases my hands to place a finger under my chin and tips it up. I have two choices. Make a big deal of this and ruin my eighteenth or try to forget it. I open my eyes and give a little nod.

"That's my girl."

However, as Mom bundles me into her arms and I screw my nose up against the overpowering waft of the rose fragrance she favors, I know one thing for sure.

I'm not her girl.

And I'll make it my life's work to be nothing like my mother.

CHAPTER FIVE

FRANKIE

NOW

I may have forgiven Andre for his infidelity years ago but I developed a bad habit not long after we reconciled.

I watch him.

Not in a creepy way—I don't stalk him or follow him. I just watch when we're at a party or a special occasion or at a work function; like now, while I'm getting a drink, and he's surrounded by neighbors, the center of attention and loving it.

I watch to see how he interacts with women, wondering if I'm missing something, feeling like a gullible fool despite him being a devoted dad and husband since his indiscretion. He's proven once before he's open to temptation and a small part of me is resentful that what he's done in the past has turned me into a watchful wife.

It annoys me that I still get the urge to scrutinize him. I don't do it often these days, not like the first year or two after he confessed, but when there are new people around—new women, more precisely—I find myself following Andre's every move.

Today, I don't know what to make of what I see. He's effusive and charming towards everyone, but standoffish with Celeste. Nothing overt, but even when she's in the same circle with others chatting, he's angling his body away from her, as if trying to exclude her. Or I could be imagining the whole thing and fatigue is making me see things that aren't there.

It's not that I expect Andre to click with everybody he meets but he's gregarious. I'm used to seeing him draw everyone around him into his sphere. Ironic, that I ended up with a husband just like my father when I once vowed to find the complete opposite.

Then again, I'd tried the opposite years ago, and that didn't turn out well either.

It took me several years of marriage to work out I'd been so desperate to escape my folks and the house I'd grown up in that I'd deluded myself into believing a lie, more enamored with the idea of being in love than loving my first husband for real.

Now's not the time to lament my mistakes though. I'm over-thinking Andre's behavior, and as I see him laugh at something Celeste says, it confirms I'm seeing things that aren't there. Rehashing a time when we both screwed up—even in my head—isn't productive and is making me oversensitive.

Besides, from my brief interactions with Celeste and Saylor, I like them. I have no reason to think they're interested in my husband. Celeste is circumspect, Saylor is outgoing. Celeste has that hint of weary motherhood about her whereas Saylor is all wide-eyed wonder and excitement. A week of sleepless nights when the baby is born will knock that shine right off. It might sound harsh, but it's realistic. I adore Luna but those early days when I struggled to breastfeed and she was colicky... they were nightmarish.

That's the time I would've expected a husband prone to straying to be tempted, but after Luna's birth Andre had been the model father. He'd taken on as many freelance jobs as possible so he could work from home. He changed diapers and rocked Luna and paced the floor with her for hours at a time so I could grab some sleep. He'd been my rock and I need to remember that. He adores Luna as much as I do. He dotes on her and she's a daddy's girl. It vindicates the choice I made all those years ago.

Lloyd slaps Andre on the back, a gesture that's the epitome of male bonding behavior, before moving to a group of neighbors who live across the park from us. Andre's alone with Saylor now and I notice she becomes more animated, her hands moving as she talks, punctuating her words. Thankfully, Andre's behavior doesn't change.

Until Celeste leans closer to tell him something.

His shoulders stiffen, like someone has stuck a poker down the back of his shirt. He's still smiling but it's more forced and his gaze is wary.

Something about Celeste is definitely putting him off. Have they already met? He went out on a job late last night. Maybe he bumped into her while she was moving in? But why didn't either of them mention it when I introduced them earlier?

My mind immediately takes off on a tangent, giving them some torrid past they've hidden from me. Is she the one? He never told me who he'd slept with and I didn't want to know. I was dealing with my own issues at the time. Is his standoffish behavior a sign?

I don't like being this woman, the suspicious wife leaping to irrational conclusions. I need to subdue my insecurities and focus on the positives: that my marriage came through the worst of an ordeal that tested us, and Andre and I are stronger for it. We're in a good place now and Luna completes us.

Dwelling on the past and mistrusting my husband isn't good for any of us.

CHAPTER SIX

CELESTE

I see Frankie watching us, her stare boring holes into Andre's back. Her intense scrutiny makes me uncomfortable, which is silly, as I'm not doing anything wrong. Her husband is clearly an extrovert—he commands attention—so maybe she's insecure? Or one of those possessive women who don't like their man interacting with the opposite sex? Whatever her rationale, she doesn't have to worry about me. I'm not a husband stealer. In fact, I would almost say he dislikes me.

Then again, not many people like me. Even Roland, Vi's dad, didn't like me enough to build a life with me, to provide a stable future for our daughter. More recently, he acted like he hated me.

That's what moving to Hambridge Heights is about. Escaping the disappointments of my past. Escaping from him.

I'm a tolerant person. I've put up with a lot in my thirty-eight years. But what he'd said to me during our last screaming match…

I had to get away.

He left me no choice.

Violette runs up to me, Luna hot on her heels. I'm glad they've bonded so quickly and I greet them with a big smile. "Mom, can Luna come over for a play date? Pleeeeease?"

I glance at Andre and he's smiling indulgently at his daughter too, and in that moment I like him.

"Yeah, Dad, can we have a play date?" Luna slips her hand into Andre's and I swear I see him melt on the spot: he looks at her with open adoration, his smile goofy.

"Sure, sweetheart, but I reckon everyone's going to be tired after this party, so how about I chat with your mom and Celeste and we organize a play date for another day?"

Luna frowns and Vi visibly deflates, but after a few moments Luna's sulky expression clears and she nods. "How about tomorrow?"

Andre's gaze meets mine and we laugh in unison. "If it's okay with Celeste?"

"Fine by me," I say, the words barely out of my mouth before both girls start jumping up and down on the spot, yelling "Yay."

"I guess that's settled," he says, with a chuckle.

I'm grateful to the girls for breaking the ice between us and I smile at him. We share a moment most parents do when we know we've given in too easily to our darling cherubs and we don't give a damn.

"I've heard girls are more difficult than boys and I'm beginning to understand why," Saylor says, pressing her fingers to her ears as the girls continue to whoop and dance around.

Andre laughs, a genuine belly laugh, and I can see why Frankie is attracted to him. He has a naturalness about him, like he's hiding nothing.

Pity the same can't be said about me.

Saylor notices it too. She's staring at him with something akin to adulation and I wonder if it's the pregnancy hormones. I remember the fifth month of my pregnancy. I was mad for Roland, couldn't get enough of him. Every evening when he came home we'd be going at it and when he left the next morning I'd be teary and resentful. It saddened me because our relationship had been smooth once. Until everything changed, and we never recovered. I thought having a baby might bond us. Sure, he loved Vi, but as for me... if anything, the resentment grew.

Moving here is the opportunity I've been looking for. A fresh start, far from the sins of the past.

Frankie joins our little group. She's grinning, but there's a brittleness behind her stiff smile as she studies her husband's face intently, as if searching for reassurance. Is Frankie's perfect life not so perfect?

"Hey, girls, what's all the excitement about?" Frankie asks, reaching out to pluck a leaf from Luna's hair.

Rather than answering, Luna and Vi run back toward the cupcake table and Andre replies for them. "The girls were trying to coerce us into a play date today, but Celeste and I stood firm." He grins. "We managed to convince them tomorrow was better."

Frankie laughs at his sheepish expression and the tension dissipates.

"Is that okay with you?" I ask, and she nods.

"Absolutely fine. I'll grab your cell number later and we'll tee up a time. I'm working in the morning so maybe the afternoon? Out here in the park?"

"Perfect," I say, and it is. Today couldn't have gone better if I'd planned it.

"On that note, I think it's time I popped the balloon," Saylor says, pointing to the table where the great reveal is going to take place.

"Go ahead," Andre says, while I share a conspiratorial smile with Frankie about our mutual antipathy for gender reveal parties.

Oh yes, today has gone splendidly, better than I could've anticipated.

CHAPTER SEVEN

SAYLOR

Lloyd is buzzing with excitement. I know because he's humming a song from our wedding, one he loves. Despite my religious upbringing I've never been a fan of hymns but this one reminds me of the day I pledged to love this man and put my past behind me. A past that's turned up here when I thought I'd bid it farewell forever.

As we stand hand in hand beside the giant helium balloon I'm unaware I'm squeezing Lloyd's hand too tight until he gives a little jiggle and I relax my grip. Everyone's looking at us and I smile, pretending to share my joy with my new friends.

But I'm only interested in one person's reaction.

"Why are you so excited? You already know the sex," I murmur under my breath as he continues to hum that song about eternal love and devotion.

"Because everyone's been so welcoming and I like that we get to share this with our new neighbors."

He's right. I'm impressed by how many of our neighbors have turned up today. It shows good community spirit. I want to be a part of it but I'm scared. If they find out the real reason I'm here, I'll be ostracized. I have a thick skin, but it's my unborn child I worry about. I don't want any stigma attached to him. He's innocent in all this. I'm the idiot who created this mess.

"Just tell us already," some wise guy I haven't met yet in a funky tie-dyed T-shirt yells out and the rest of the crowd whistle and clap.

Lloyd's eyes glow with pride as he raises our joined hands clasping a giant BBQ fork. "Ready?"

"As I'll ever be."

I'm not just referring to the gender reveal and as we stab at the big balloon together and it makes a resounding pop, showering us with sparkly blue confetti, I know what I'm doing is risky. Hell, it's the riskiest thing I've ever done but if I can pull this off, my son and my family will be protected and that's all that matters.

People cheer and rush forward, crowding around us, gushing over the fact we're having a boy. I accept their congratulations for what feels like the hundredth time today, suddenly wishing this was all over. It's draining having to pretend all the time. I love Lloyd, but if he learns the truth, he'll disown me. His Christian values are one of the things that drew me to him, but they'll also be my downfall. He'll judge me. Everyone will. I know I'm a bad person; I don't need it pointed out.

I've been tempted to tell him the truth so many times over the last few months. The church is all about forgiveness so surely he'd absolve his wife of sin?

But I chicken out, terrified to take a risk and unravel the life I've built for my son. I'm here to ensure my secret never gets out; for the sake of my baby, my marriage and my entire pious family, whose reputations will be ruined if what I've done is revealed.

I'm tired, and sensing my distress, Lloyd hands me a glass of sparkling water. "Here. Looks like you could use this."

"Thanks." I gulp it down gratefully but it does little to ease the tightness in my throat.

Ruston is looking at me again and I feel the intensity of his gaze like a physical caress.

As if my situation isn't complicated enough, what is he doing here?

He's not with a woman, I've checked, and he doesn't seem to be particularly close to anyone here, so that means he's not the partner of someone or visiting a friend... hell, does he live here?

I should approach him, act casual, pretend like my pulse isn't racing at the sight of him. It shouldn't. I should be immune. I steeled my heart against him before I married Lloyd. He's my husband's opposite in every way.

For years, Ruston reeled me in, only to cast me away in favor of "keeping things casual". I knew at the time any self-respecting woman wouldn't put up with that kind of relationship, but I did because he was like a drug for me. I craved the high.

First loves are intense like that. I kept going back for more, despite my parents warning me against him and doing everything they could to steer me in the right direction. Ironic, that when I'd finally given in and opened my heart to the possibility of having something solid with Lloyd, I'd let Ruston get under my skin again and here I am.

Lying to everyone, including my dedicated husband.

As Ruston continues to stare at me, a hint of a smirk playing around his mouth, like he knows how much he still affects me, I know one thing. I can't allow him to distract me from my goal.

I moved to Hambridge Heights for one reason only.

I'll do anything to make sure everything goes to plan.

CHAPTER EIGHT

FRANKIE

THEN

I have to admit, the backyard looks amazing. My parents have gone all out for my party. Filmy chiffon in daffodil yellow and ochre drapes from tree to tree along with fairy lights and vivid fuchsia lanterns, lending the backyard a magical quality. Tealight candles atop faux lily pads float in the pool, rimmed with more of the lanterns. And a twenty-foot grazing table is covered in cheeses, antipasto, deli meats, dried fruit, nuts and crackers, like a giant charcuterie board. A small table resides behind it, with a fancy three-tiered cake draped in daisies, surrounded by tiny lemon tartlets, apple pies and chocolate mousse. It's stunning, yet I can't help but wonder if Mom went online after I left her office today and ordered extra decorations to make up for what happened.

Even now, hours after Mom told me the truth, I'm struggling, torn between disappointment and anger. I want to forget what I've learned, but I can't. Maybe moving out will give me time and perspective, because I sure as hell can't imagine sticking around and feeling like this.

I've never been good at pretending and now I know the truth about their antics I need to escape. The problem is, I didn't apply to any colleges. My folks come from old money, like many families in this enclave of Long Island, and hadn't attended college either, so they'd been supportive when I wanted to take a gap year. I love living in Gledhill and I'd envisaged getting a job until I figured out what I want to do with my life, take my time finding something to inspire passion, but now that option has been snatched away along with my respect for them.

Ideally, I'd like to head to Manhattan. Every rebellious, independent bone in my body is screaming at me to leave all this behind and make my own way in the world. But rent is exorbitant in the city and I'll need my parents' financial support to do it. Considering how our relationship has fractured today, I'm hoping they'll back my decision.

Mom joins me on the verandah overlooking the backyard. "What do you think, honey?"

She slides her arm around my waist and I struggle not to flinch. I used to love our closeness, more like friends than mother–daughter, but now I feel uncomfortable.

"It looks great, Mom, thanks."

I inject enthusiasm into my voice because I know it must've taken her ages to decorate.

"I'm glad you like it." She squeezes my waist. "The caterers will serve the finger food when everyone arrives and drinks will be self-serve."

She spins me to face her and I swallow, trying to ease the lump of emotion in my throat. My mom looks the same—wide hazel eyes rimmed in kohl, the lids dusted in gold to match her dress, high cheekbones highlighted with rosy blush, lips glossed in coral—but she's different. I wish she'd never told me about her and Dad…

"I understand your friends will be sneaking alcohol and while I don't approve, you only turn eighteen once so I'll let it slide. Just make sure no one drives home if they've been drinking, okay?"

I should be glad my parents are so liberal and will allow under-age drinking at my party. My friends have always viewed them as cool parents, but now I know just how liberal they are, I see them differently.

"You ready to have fun?" She taps me on the nose like she used to when I was little, and I fake a smile and nod. She clasps her hands as she spots the first guests arrive. "Then let's get this party started."

When my folks first told me they wanted to throw me an eighteenth party I hadn't thought to question why they wanted to invite their friends too. Old family friends who'd watched me grow up, they said. A nice addition to the celebration along with my school friends ready to party as we'd all graduated a month ago.

But as the night progresses, and I'm annoyingly sober because I got drunk once last year and hated the hangover, I understand why they invited their friends. I'm glad I haven't sampled any of the vodka, gin or whiskey on offer because if I had I definitely wouldn't be able to hide my reaction as I watch my parents getting close to their "friends". A touch here. A look there. It's all done on the sly, combined with covert glances and deliberate pressing of bodies against each other, but now I know what it means.

This has been going on for years at every barbecue, every party, and I didn't have a clue.

Bile rises in my throat and I force it down with several gulps of soda. As I watch my parents play the gracious hosts, I'm appalled all over again and I'm overcome by an urge to bolt. I need to get out of here but if the birthday girl disappears before the cake is cut it won't look good. Instead, I skirt around the crowd, past the pool, and head for the back of the garden where I know I'll have peace and a few moments to collect my thoughts. My dad has an old shed back here he rarely uses and I like the old wrought-iron bench tucked behind it. Wisteria drapes it and I know hiding out for a while will calm me down before I embarrass myself, my parents, or all of us by screaming exactly what I think of them.

However, my plans for some much-needed alone time are thwarted when I spot a guy sitting on the bench. I don't recognize him. He's about my age, maybe a few years older, with short back and sides brown hair, a white button-down shirt and dark denim that looks suspiciously like it's been ironed, whereas most guys wear distressed denim these days.

He looks up as I near and his eyes are light brown, almost golden, rather startling in his otherwise plain face. "Is it time to cut the cake?"

I shake my head. "No, I just needed to get away for a while."

His eyebrows rise. "But you're the birthday girl, and extremely popular by the looks of it. Why would you want to leave your own party?"

"None of your business," I snap, not in the mood to exchange small talk with a stranger after what I'd just witnessed with my parents and their friends, surprised when he chuckles at my rudeness.

His laughter isn't loud. It's soft and well-modulated, like the rest of him. "Am I in your go-to spot?"

"Yes, and I've had a rough day, so I'd like you to leave."

"Why can't we share?"

He pats the empty space next to him and I roll my eyes before taking a seat. I know I'm acting like a brat but I don't want to see or speak to anyone right now. I need some alone time to calm down, so I'm not tempted to march back to the party and expose my folks and their friends as a bunch of sleazy phonies.

"Want to talk about it?"

I glare at him and press my lips tighter.

He laughs again. "I'm not much of a party person myself, as you can tell." He sweeps his arm wide to take in the garden. "This is more my style."

"Lurking in the shadows?"

"There's nothing wrong with staying in the background." He shrugs. "Not everyone is born to be in the limelight."

He's intriguing. All the young guys I know are full of themselves. They talk a lot, boasting about the size of their car, their college education fund and their dick, not necessarily in that order. They want to be noticed so this guy saying the opposite... yet another weird thing in my all-round bizarre day.

"Who are you?" I ask.

"Walter."

"I'm Francesca."

"I know." He stares at me, the amber color of his eyes bordering on peculiar and a strange calmness infuses me. I like it.

"How did you end up at my party?"

"I'm your neighbor's godson from out of town and got dragged along."

Of course; the more the merrier according to my social butterfly parents. "Dragged, huh?"

"Already told you, parties aren't my thing."

"I've never seen you stay with the Schubermanns before?" They're the only neighbors at my party, because the house on our left is a summer rental. We don't socialize with them usually so I assume my folks invited the sixty-something couple so they wouldn't complain about the noise.

"They usually come visit me." He screws up his nose and it's endearingly cute. "I'm a homebody. And I have this thing about strange beds, which means if I travel, I rarely get more than a few hours' sleep a night."

I admire his honesty, even if it makes him sound a tad dorky. "Are you in college?"

"No."

An awkward silence stretches between us and I feel compelled to fill it. "You're not much of a conversationalist."

"What do you want me to say?" He shrugs. "I'm not a fan of making meaningless small talk."

I'm not deterred by his bluntness. "So what do you do? How old are you?"

"I'm an accountant. Did a part-time course at a community college while working as a clerk in a bank. I'm twenty-two. My favorite color is navy, I drive my grandfather's pick-up truck, I don't waste money, I like watching documentaries and I'm loyal. Is that enough information for you?"

He rests his elbows on the back of the bench, his expression serene, and I've never met a guy so confident in his own skin. In that moment, it hits me.

Walter is the opposite of my parents in every way. If what he's saying about himself is true, he's staid, dependable and the antithesis of everything I learned to loathe today.

I'm not sure if this realization makes him more appealing, but I find myself wanting to learn more about him. I'm drawn to him.

I haven't dated much in high school. Not many of the boys made my heart pound like it is now. Sitting here with Walter, infused by an unexpected calmness just from being in his presence, I feel like I've met someone important. Someone who can change my life.

I don't believe in the crazy notion of instantaneous lust, but there's something about him that makes my skin prickle with awareness, and I like it.

"You're not like other guys I know."

"Is that a good thing?"

"Yeah." I scoot toward him on the bench and, rather than meet me halfway as I hope, he slides away. So I spell it out for him. "I like you, Walter."

His eyes widen slightly. "You hardly know me."

"I know enough."

Our gazes lock and I swear I feel a zap, an indefinable buzz that warms me from the inside out, making me want to do crazy things, like kiss a guy I hardly know.

Maybe it's the stress of the day and learning the truth about my folks, maybe it's the overwhelming fatigue of having to pretend all evening I'm having the best night ever, or maybe it's the excitement of an unexpected attraction when I least expect it, but I do something completely out of character and lay my hand on his thigh. It clenches beneath my palm. "How long are you in town for?"

"A week."

Good. Seven days will give me time to get to know Walter, to see if I'm imagining this spark between us. A few minutes ago, I'd been hell-bent on leaving Gledhill and now, I have something to stay for, at least for a week.

"I'm glad—"

"I have to go."

He stands so abruptly my hand falls and hits the bench. As I surreptitiously rub my fingers he's looking over my shoulder, before giving a little shake of his head.

"Enjoy your party," he says, striding away as if he can't escape fast enough.

"Walter, wait."

But by the time I stand to follow him, he's disappeared.

CHAPTER NINE

FRANKIE

NOW

I love this little nook in our kitchen where we share our family meals. With a small table and three benches covered in comfy cushions surrounding it, tucked into a bay window, it's cozy. Like many families, we may not have the time to always have sit-down dinners, but I try to make the most of the ones we do. Though tonight, Luna is hyped up on sugar from the three cupcakes she scoffed at the party earlier and barely touches her dinner. It's her favorite, meatballs and spaghetti, but I let her half-eaten plate slide. I want her in bed and asleep before I chat with Andre.

I'm sure there was nothing between him and Celeste at the party but it's all I've thought about since we left. I need to be careful not to be confrontational because I'm not convinced I saw anything worth asking about. But I can't subdue my doubts. I'm hoping if I ask Andre a few subtle questions and get confirmation that they don't know one another, I'll feel better.

I'm not this person anymore. I shouldn't be. I know what's brought it on. It's my anniversary tomorrow. Not mine and Andre. My anniversary with Walter. I still feel guilty about how I used that man: that good, upstanding, stable man. If Andre has secrets, I have secrets too.

He doesn't know I call Walter on our anniversary every year.

He doesn't know we chat like old friends.

He doesn't know I consider Walter the only man I can truly depend on.

The irony isn't lost on me. I'm married to a man I love but can never fully trust, while I was once married to a man I didn't love but trusted completely.

"Mom, will you read to me?"

"Ask your father," I say, pressing a kiss to the top of Luna's head, inhaling the fruity fragrance of her strawberry shampoo.

"Okay." She gives me a quick hug and I squeeze her tight, thankful every day for this beautiful bundle of energy that is my reason for existing.

"I'll be up later to say goodnight."

She wriggles out of my arms and bounds upstairs, where I hear Andre watching basketball on cable. He'd been edgy all through dinner and as eager as Luna to escape the table once we'd finished. Because I didn't want to have our discussion in front of our daughter, I'd let it slide, but his evasive behavior makes me worry more.

I shouldn't. Luna is growing up. She'll be starting school soon. And I make more money than my husband. What's the worst that can happen if I discover he's cheated on me again? I boot him out the door, give him visitation rights and my life continues.

But it's not that simple and I know it. I'm not sure what kind of questions are raised during divorce proceedings and I don't want to tempt fate.

With Walter, there hadn't been kids involved so dissolving our marriage had been easy. With Andre… I don't want to think about the secrets that may come to light if my past is delved into…

On impulse, I grab my cell from the counter and slip out the front door. Why wait until tomorrow to call Walter? I need his steadying influence right now.

His number is under Floral Arrangements, a contact that would never raise Andre's suspicion considering I often discuss flowers and their use in prettying up a room on my channel.

I know what I'm doing is wrong. How would I feel if I discovered Andre kept in touch with an old girlfriend? Or worse, the woman he'd cheated on me with? I'd be livid. But there's a difference. I have no romantic feelings for Walter whatsoever. He's my friend, a sounding board, a voice of reason, nothing more.

I stab at his number with my thumb and press the cell to my ear. Walter is a man of routine in all aspects of his life and he always picks up on the fourth ring. Not tonight. His phone rings ten times before I get his voice asking to leave a message.

"Hey, Walt, it's me. Call me when you get a chance. Bye."

Disappointed, I hang up and glance at my watch. Walter is so predictable I know he's in front of the TV at eight every night, watching his favorite quiz show. I grew to depend on his routines, until it drove me nuts in the end. Not picking up is so out of character I'm worried for a moment, before realizing there could be any number of reasons why he's not answering and I let myself back into the house.

I've got more important things to worry about than my ex-husband, like subduing my suspicions and stop imagining things that aren't there.

CHAPTER TEN

CELESTE

I'm taking out the trash when I see Frankie slip outside her front door and close it softly behind her. I'm at the bottom of my steps and tucked around the corner, so she can't see me. I'm about to step forward so it doesn't look like I'm hiding, when I notice she's behaving oddly. She checks the knob to ensure the door is closed, then casts a furtive glance over her shoulder toward her window, as if making sure she's not being watched. Only then does she call someone named Walt, who doesn't pick up, and she asks him to call her back.

Is she hiding something from her husband? Is she having an affair? I'm disappointed, as although we've only just met I expected more from her. She presents such a perfect image online, the accomplished wife and mother every woman aspires to be. Everyone's friend. Sweet, nice, Frankie Forbes.

I wait until she's finished and gone back inside before I do the same. I don't want her discovering I overheard her. I want our daughters to be friends. It's imperative Vi starts bonding with Luna. My darling girl needs the distraction. She's been badgering me about her father since we arrived last night and the gender reveal party was a temporary reprieve, because the minute we got home she started peppering me with questions again.

When am I going to see Daddy again?

Why can't I talk to him?

Why did we move here?

I try to answer as best I can, but how do I explain to a five-year-old she probably won't see her father ever again?

Roland is my past. I can't go back.

At the start of our relationship, I thought I'd found the man of my dreams. He'd been so attentive, so loving. Then he changed and my life imploded. He wasn't the man I thought he was. He lied to me. He hurt me. Then I discovered I was expecting Violette...

Roland took his responsibilities seriously, so parenting Violette gave me hope we could recapture the magic, that he'd revert to the man I knew he could be. Sadly, in the end it wasn't enough. He didn't change, our relationship became untenable and I had to remove myself from the toxicity to give Violette the life she deserves.

As if dealing with the disintegration of my relationship with Roland isn't hard enough, Vi occasionally asks me for a sibling. I change the subject, but she won't be distracted forever. I have a bit of time to meet someone else and have another baby. Late-thirties is cutting it fine but more women are having babies in their forties these days. But what are the odds of me meeting a good guy who wants to have a baby ASAP? Increasingly slim...

I have a feeling our lives will be brighter here in Hambridge Heights. A fresh start.

Something I desperately need after escaping Roland and my past.

CHAPTER ELEVEN
SAYLOR

"That went well, don't you think?"

Lloyd is clearing the dinner table, upbeat when I can barely stand I'm so tired.

"Yeah, it was nice to meet the neighbors," I say, standing near the living room window, looking out.

The park is in darkness, barely illuminated by the old-fashioned lamplights ringing the periphery. It makes it easier to see the house on the other side of the park, directly opposite to ours, which is lit up like they don't care about the cost of electricity.

I can't believe Ruston lives there.

Even now, hours after the gender reveal party finished, I can't comprehend the coincidence. We didn't get to speak at the party because I avoided him, clinging to Lloyd whenever it looked like he might approach. Thankfully, Ruston got the message. But one of my neighbors had kindly informed me of "the hottie that lives at number 56" and how every mom in Vintage Circle has a crush on Ruston.

I don't blame them. That had been me once, when I'd been foolish, believing every line he fed me despite being let down time and time again. I should be wiser, but I fear I'm not. I can't deny the irrational surge of attraction that made me buzz when I first laid eyes on Ruston in the park.

I shouldn't focus on his house but I can't help it, my gaze unwittingly drawn, like wanting to avoid staring at a car wreck but unable to look away. He's moving around the front room, flicking through a stack of DVDs. Unusual, considering most of us stream movies these days.

He's wearing gray cotton sweatpants slung low on his hips, and a plain white T-shirt molding to a strong chest, highlighting broad shoulders, accentuating his height... I step back from the window, annoyed at myself for noticing.

"What are you looking at?"

I jump at Lloyd's nearness and force my body to relax when he hugs me from behind, his palms splayed possessively across my belly.

"I like looking at the park at night. I find it peaceful."

The lie slides from my lips, increasing my guilt. But how can I tell my husband the ex I tried so hard to get over by marrying him now resides opposite us?

"That's because there are no screaming kids running around like there usually is during the day." He chuckles.

"Hey, you're about to have a screaming kid in the near future and that comment doesn't sound too paternal."

He laughs at my teasing and I'm happy to be distracted for a moment. "I'll be a great dad and you know it."

He nuzzles my neck and tightens his hold. It should make me feel safe. Instead, I'm claustrophobic, smothered, and it takes every ounce of willpower not to shrug off his embrace. I'm edgy because of the guilt and for a moment I contemplate telling him about my past. But I'm too exhausted to get into a big discussion now, let alone fend off the inevitable probing if I reveal how Ruston used to be a major part of my life.

"Do you mind making me a cup of ginger tea?"

He releases me and spins me around to study my face. "Are you feeling nauseous again?"

"A little."

"You're probably overtired after all the excitement. Put your feet up, sweetheart, and I'll bring it in."

"Thanks."

I press a kiss to his lips, hoping he knows how much he means to me. He's right, I am overtired, and as he heads into the kitchen, I find myself looking out the window again. Ruston's sitting on the sofa now, with his feet up on the coffee table. Big feet. Big everything. I hate myself for remembering. And I hate how I found myself watching him at the party earlier. He's a popular guy, mingling with everyone. A real man's man. One of the boys. Good with the kids too, making them laugh. It shouldn't affect me but it did.

Because I'm not stupid. I may have succeeded in avoiding him today but a confrontation is inevitable. If I don't want him revealing our connection to Lloyd, I'm going to have to preempt it. Who knows, maybe if I do that we can co-exist as neighbors and the new life I've carefully built won't come tumbling down?

I can't allow Ruston's presence to distract me from my goal.

As I wrap my arms around my middle and continue to watch him, I know I need to focus on my baby.

And preserving my secrets.

CHAPTER TWELVE

FRANKIE

THEN

I didn't see Walter for the rest of my party. I didn't see him the next day either. But I only have five days left to discover if I imagined the spark between us. The last forty-eight hours have given me time to think beyond my instant infatuation. If there's something real between us, maybe Walter is my one-way ticket off Long Island?

It seems like fate when I glimpse him watering our neighbor's front yard. I don't know the Schubermanns well and they've never had Walter stay with them before. I would've noticed. It makes me smile to remember his bluntness when he'd told me why he's never visited his godparents before, because he can't sleep in strange beds. No guy would ever admit that for fear of appearing geeky, but it hadn't fazed Walter. I like that honesty about him, especially with my parents' lies fresh in my mind from a few days ago.

He's deep in thought, a slight frown creasing his brow, and I even find that cute. There's something about him that makes me want to fling my arms around him and kiss him silly, even though I've kissed a grand total of two boys before. I've never been forward with guys and, for a moment, I second-guess myself. He hadn't really flirted with me at the party, so maybe I'm imagining we shared a connection? Only one way to find out.

Wearing a skimpy red bikini one of my friends had given me for my birthday, I run down the stairs and out the front door before I chicken out. It's only as I near him and he glances up, shock parting his lips, that I realize I don't have an excuse to talk to him. I should've at least used the old "can I borrow a cup of sugar" routine from one of those ancient movies my folks watch.

I slow my steps as I reach him, unsure whether to be impressed or disappointed when he keeps his gaze on my face and not drifting south once. "Hey. You're a good houseguest. Do you have to water the garden for your supper?"

"It beats singing." He shrugs, like making a corny joke is nothing.

I swear he belongs in my parents' era. He talks like someone decades older and today he's wearing ironed khaki shorts and a beige polo top with the buttons done up. But I like that about him. His maturity is appealing after the guys in my senior class who don't care about anything but football, college girls and keg parties.

"It's hot out." I fan my face. "Fancy a swim?"

At last, some sign he notices me as a woman when he glances at my breasts briefly before refocusing on my face. He's going to refuse, I can see it in his reluctant stare, so I sweeten the deal.

"There's a stack of leftover food and you'd be doing me a favor, otherwise my folks are going to make me bring it over to the Schubermanns and force feed them."

He appears horrified by the thought, just as I intended. Either he comes over for a swim or I come over for goodness knows how long and make small talk with his godparents.

When he still doesn't respond, I say, "When we chatted the other night, you mentioned the Schubermanns visit you. Where is that?"

"Hartford, Connecticut."

"Nice."

"You've been?"

"No, but I'd like to." I'd like to live there given half a chance. Anywhere but here. "Are you coming for a swim?"

It takes him an eternity to nod and when he does, his expression says he'd prefer having a root canal than spending time with me.

So much for my plan to entice him.

"Meet you out the back," I say, making sure I put an extra sway into my hips as I walk away, hoping he's staring at my butt.

When I glance over my shoulder he is and when I catch him, a faint crimson stains his cheeks.

"I have a girlfriend," he blurts, and I merely smile.

By the end of this week, his girlfriend will be me.

CHAPTER THIRTEEN

FRANKIE

NOW

Andre is avoiding me.

Luna falls asleep about a minute after he closes the book he'd been reading to her, the exhaustion after today's festivities outweighing the amount of sugar she's consumed. I'm peeking through the door and when her eyelids flutter shut, Andre glances at me and we share a smile. The tired but happy smile of most parents at the end of a day, a "she's so darn adorable but boy am I glad she's asleep" smile.

I head downstairs and pour us both a glass of Shiraz and curl up on the couch to wait for him. But after fifteen minutes, he hasn't appeared. Too comfortable to move from my position, I text him.

WHERE R U? I HAVE WINE.

I hear him padding on the floorboards overhead so I sip my Shiraz and wait. But he doesn't appear. Instead, I hear the shower running. Annoyed my plans for a relaxing evening have been thwarted, I down the rest of the wine in a few gulps and leave his on the coffee table before marching upstairs.

I sit cross-legged in the middle of our bed, waiting. I'd hoped the wine would take the edge off my frustration at allowing insecurities to surface after watching Andre with Celeste at the party earlier, but it hasn't and I'm edgier than ever. I don't want to be the harpy housewife spoiling for an argument with my husband but having him ignore my text hasn't helped my mood. When the shower finally shuts off and he strolls into our room with a towel wrapped around his waist, I'm primed for a fight.

"Didn't you get my text?"

He shrugs like he doesn't have a care in the world. "Yeah, but I thought I'd have a shower first."

"You couldn't tell me that?"

He sighs. "Babe, I'm tired. I needed a shower. What's with the attitude?"

"Pardon me for wanting to unwind with a wine and my husband at the end of a day."

He grins. "You know you're irresistible when you're snarky."

I hold up my hand when he sits on the bed. "I want to ask you something."

"Now?" He glances at the towel, where I see hard evidence he's not put-off by my bad mood. "Come on, babe, surely it can wait?"

I ignore what's going on behind that towel and cross my arms. "Do you know Celeste?"

I wanted to be subtle, to casually ask an offhand question, but I've blurted it and he's taken aback. I watch for any telltale signs he's lying.

"Yeah, I know her." His jaw juts as he grits his teeth. "I know her because I met her earlier today."

"For the first time?"

"For fuck's sake, Frankie." He leaps off the bed and marches to the wardrobe, flinging it open so hard the door bangs the wall. He winces and I listen to make sure Luna hasn't stirred. He snatches pajama bottoms from a clean pile and drags them on, only dropping the towel when he's done.

"You didn't answer my question."

When he turns back to face me, anger stains his cheeks. "What is it with you? We've had a nice day with our neighbors, our daughter is out like a light at a reasonable hour for the first time all week and you want to waste time picking a fight?"

"I'm not picking a fight. I want to know why you were acting so weird around Celeste today."

His eyes narrow in disbelief. "What were you doing, watching my every move?"

"Something like that," I fling at him, my slow simmering temper starting to boil. "What's the big deal? I like to watch my husband. Is that a crime?"

"It is if you're doing it out of doubt rather than love," he mutters, shaking his head. "Shit, Frankie, when are you going to cut me a break? I thought we were past all this years ago."

"We are…" I'm surprised to find tears stinging the backs of my eyes. "I've forgiven you, but at times it's hard to forget…" I whisper.

His shoulders slump like I've dumped an invisible weight on them. "What have I done to make you doubt me?"

Images of him interacting with Celeste from earlier today play through my mind and I have to admit there's nothing suspicious he did, it's just a feeling… but how can I tell him that without sounding crazy?

"Nothing," I say, confusion making me doubt what I saw. Maybe I imagined the whole thing? "Sorry. It's been a long week and I shouldn't take it out on you."

"You're forgiven."

He opens his arms to me and as I snuggle into them, I hope I'm not being naïve.

CHAPTER FOURTEEN
CELESTE

Frankie's not half as friendly toward me as she was yesterday and I'm wondering if her persona at the gender reveal party was an act, like how she fakes it online every day. She must pretend, because I refuse to believe anyone is that damn perky all the time. It would be exhausting being her. I also pity Luna, who craves her mother's attention. If it's obvious to me, why can't Frankie see it? Or is she so self-centered all she cares about is her precious image?

We've been in the park less than fifteen minutes and she's hardly said a word, and I wonder why she agreed to this play date when I texted her first thing this morning.

"Are you okay?" I ask her. We're watching the girls play with their dolls in a shaded patch of grass not far from us and she takes a while to respond.

"I've been better."

"Want to talk about it?"

"Not really."

I'm not surprised she doesn't want to confide in me as we only met yesterday, but I'm hoping we can be friends for our daughters' sakes. Luna was all Vi could talk about last night and I'm thrilled the girls have bonded so quickly.

We lapse into a strained silence again, punctuated by the girls' chatter as they mimic some grand fairy tale with their dolls. I've never seen Vi so happy. She's practically glowing every time Luna smiles at her and I'm glad. While I'd like to be friends with Frankie, if I have to put up with Frankie's sullen mood for my daughter's happiness, so be it. I almost wish Andre had brought Luna out to play instead but he'd been behaving oddly around me yesterday and with Frankie watching us, what would she think of her husband and me alone at a play date?

Silly, really, because dads bring their kids to play dates all the time. It doesn't mean anything and it's not like I'm the flirty type. Most men don't know how to deal with me. My sarcasm is off-putting. Roland hadn't minded. Until he did.

"I'm glad the girls are getting on well," I say, making an effort to chat because I can't stand the silence. "It's important to me for Violette to make friends here."

I glimpse a softening in her face and some of the tension in her shoulders relaxes. "Yeah, it's great. I worry that Luna suffers sometimes because I work so much, and she doesn't get to socialize with kids her own age at play dates like this often enough."

"You've got typical working mom guilt. Don't let it bother you. You're a great mom." I gesture at the girls. "Luna's well-adjusted and happy, so you're doing okay."

She smiles in gratitude and I'm glad she appears more engaged. "Do you work, Celeste?"

"Yeah. I'm a freelance accountant. I do the books remotely for a few companies in Manhattan, long-standing clients."

"Do you enjoy it?"

"It pays the bills." And allows me to be home with Vi, something I'm eternally grateful for. "Do you like lifestyle vlogging?"

"I used to love it." She sighs.

"Used to?"

"We all have bad days, right?" She's fiddling with the hem of her top, plucking absentmindedly at a loose string, lost in her thoughts. "Imagine how you feel on your crappiest day, then imagine having to put on make-up and the perfect outfit and smile until your face aches because that's what people expect of you."

I'm not sure if she'll like my first thought but I say it anyway. "Why don't you stop?"

"Because it pays too well and I'm afraid if I do…" She trails off, gnawing at her bottom lip.

"What?"

"That I'll go back to being a nobody…"

She speaks so softly I wonder if I've heard correctly. I don't know her well enough to ask why she sounds forlorn. Ironic, how she portrays perfection online but seems so sad about her job when the camera turns off. It makes me like her a little more, normalizes her in a way.

I'm glad she's opening up to me. "Is that so bad?"

"I suppose not." She shrugs. "I'm just exhausted." She takes a breath and blows it out, and it's as if a weight has lifted off her. Either that, or she's a great actress, as her smile appears genuine. "Don't mind me. I didn't sleep well and I've been in this weird funk all morning because I've got a lot of subscriber comments to respond to." She waves a hand between us as if she's shooing away her problems. "I'll be fine."

"If it makes it easier on you, I'm happy to take Luna off your hands. Have her over for a few hours at my place later this afternoon?" I point to the girls. "Vi loves having a new friend and the girls get on well. So if you want a break, I'm not far."

She smiles. "Thanks, Celeste, I appreciate the offer." She's staring at me like she's seeing me for the first time.

"Is Andre home today?"

She stiffens and her eyes narrow almost imperceptibly. "Why?"

"I need some muscle to help me move an old trunk in my bedroom. It was there when I arrived and it's taking up too much room." I flex my arm and poke at my bicep. "And as you can see from this pathetic excuse for a muscle, I need all the help I can get."

"He's out at the moment but I'll send him over when he gets home." Her tone is friendly, but rather than continue the conversation she returns to staring at the girls and I wonder if I upset her. Perhaps I shouldn't have brought up Andre. But I don't get it. Surely she can't be jealous of me? She's gorgeous, whereas I'm... washed out, as Roland had told me before things ended, one of his least nasty insults.

"Frankie?"

"Yeah?" she replies, her eyes fixed on her daughter.

"Friends don't betray each other and I'm hoping that's what we can be, friends."

It's my roundabout way of saying she has nothing to worry about with Andre and me, and after a long pause, she gives a nod.

"Sure, I'd like that."

I'm not sure how sincere her response is, but for now, it's enough.

CHAPTER FIFTEEN

SAYLOR

Lloyd is grocery shopping and I'm sitting by the living room window when I see Celeste and Frankie in the park. Their girls are playing but the women's postures are off. They're not facing each other. Instead, they're sitting side by side and only talking occasionally. It's weird. If I sat next to someone on a park bench I'd half turn to face them, not look straight ahead, avoiding eye contact.

I didn't sleep well last night and it had nothing to do with the heartburn that's becoming increasingly persistent. Learning that Ruston lives opposite us has rattled me more than I care to admit. It's silly, because even if Lloyd learns we used to date, I'll dismiss it as a past crush, insignificant and irrelevant. But he'll wonder why I didn't mention it and I don't want my husband to start doubting me. It may lead to other questions I have no intention of answering.

As for Ruston being an inconsequential crush from the past, nothing is further from the truth.

Ruston is the love of my life. Was. And I hate that I need to make the clarification from present to past tense in my own head. Marrying Lloyd is the smartest thing I've ever done. But deep down, my emotional connection to Ruston simmers, making a mockery of my logical choice of husband.

I've been spying this morning in the hope I'll catch a glimpse of him walking or jogging and I can instigate an "accidental" meeting where I can grill him about how he ended up here and warn him not to say anything about our shared past to Lloyd. But he's nowhere in sight and the street is quiet.

While Celeste only recently moved in, like me, maybe Frankie has the lowdown on Ruston so I make an impulsive decision to join them.

They look up as I approach. "Hey, girls, mind if I join you?"

"Sure," Frankie says, almost too eagerly, pointing to the empty bench opposite. "We're making the most of this sunshine while the girls play."

"You'll get to do this soon." Celeste glances at my small bump. "Another four months and you'll be indoctrinated into the joys of mothers' group."

I pretend to shudder as I sit, when I'm actually looking forward to absorbing the wisdom of fellow moms. "I've heard about those. A bunch of new moms comparing their babies' sleep patterns and feeding habits and who has the biggest bassinet."

Frankie laughs. "They can be daunting, but it's good to hang out with women going through the same thing."

Celeste nods in agreement, but she's studying me, as if she can't quite figure me out.

What would these women think if they knew the truth?

They'll never understand. Nobody will.

Eventually I'll tell Lloyd. I'll have to, because he deserves to know the type of woman he married. I know there's a chance he'll leave me, but with his immersion in the church and one of his major mantras being forgiveness, I'm hoping he won't; that he'll be so smitten by our baby boy by then he could never leave us.

"So what's it like, Frankie, having two new neighbors?"

I watch for her reaction carefully because I get the feeling there's already tension between her and Celeste. When I walked up a few minutes ago they both wore harried expressions that had nothing to do with their kids, as the girls are happily engaged in role-playing with their dolls.

"Great, actually, considering both houses have been empty for a while." She flashes me a genuine smile. "It's a fantastic neighborhood. Everyone's friendly, no late night loud music to contend with, no barking dogs, and a general lack of any scandal."

I laugh, intending to keep it that way despite Ruston re-entering my life when I least expect it.

"We love it so far," I say, my gaze automatically drifting to the house opposite where he lives. "The way everyone came to the gender reveal party yesterday blew me away. I felt so welcomed."

"We're a friendly bunch," Frankie says, and Celeste's eyebrows raise a fraction, making me wonder if she feels the same about her own welcome. I know she only moved in two nights ago and from what I saw at the party, the street is full of happy families and couples planning the next stage of their lives. Does she feel out of place as a single mom?

I'd seen her SUV pull up and watched her unload her stuff. Not much for a woman and child—two suitcases, a duffel and a backpack—so she probably took the place fully furnished like we did. Cheaper that way and makes for an easier get-away. I understand, as depending how my plan plays out, I may need to leave quickly too.

I'm not sure what to make of Celeste. We didn't interact much yesterday. She kept to herself. She seems reserved, wary almost, like she's afraid of something.

I know the feeling.

"If you need anything in particular for the baby, let me know," Frankie says. "I get sent free stuff all the time, even though Luna is five now."

"That must be so cool. I love your vlog."

The realtor had mentioned our house being next door to Frankie Forbes and I hadn't known who that was until I looked her up.

I'm beyond impressed with her massive following and she appears like a natural in front of the camera, at odds with the woman in front of me, who seems more introverted.

"Thanks. It's a fun job," Frankie says, but her brow furrows slightly. "But our house is stuffed to overflowing so I donate a lot to charity and give away the rest once I've promoted online, as more keeps coming."

"I'm happy to take stuff off your hands," Celeste says, waving. "Any time."

We laugh and I'm glad I ventured out to join them. However, I had a reason for approaching them and I need to discover more about Ruston.

"Everyone was so lovely at the party yesterday, but are you close with any of the neighbors in particular?" I ask Frankie.

Frankie holds up her hand and wavers it. "Yes and no. I mean, we're all friendly, and we do gatherings in the park for some of the big holidays like Fourth of July, but I'm pretty busy most of the time so I don't catch up regularly with anyone."

I snap my fingers. "Damn, so you don't know the hot guy who lives across the park?"

I'm fishing for information, to see how much Frankie knows.

She screws up her nose like she's thinking and I laugh. "If you have to think that long, you don't know him."

"There's a hot guy?" Celeste rubs her hands together and we laugh in unison again.

"Yeah, and he lives alone."

Celeste sends a pointed glance at my belly. "And you're asking because?"

"No harm in looking." I hold up my hands in surrender and Celeste smiles, but she's eyeing me again, like I'm a puzzle to solve.

"Oh, you mean Ruston," Frankie says, and I stiffen, wondering what she'll say next.

But before Frankie can elaborate, the girls abandon their play and run up to us. The cute blonde tugs at Frankie's hand. "Mom, did you bring snacks?"

"Yeah, beetroot juice and spinach cupcakes," Frankie deadpans, winking at Celeste, whose daughter has paled at the mention of the food.

"Mom!" Luna hops from foot to foot, obviously used to her mother's sense of humor. "What did you really bring?"

"Apple juice and oatmeal cookies." Frankie looks at Celeste. "Sorry, I should've asked if Violette has any food allergies."

"She doesn't," Celeste says. "All good."

"Great."

As Frankie unzips a cooler bag and sets out snacks for the girls, offering us cookies too, I experience a pang of regret. Hambridge Heights is a good neighborhood and Frankie would make a great neighbor.

I hope I can stay when the truth comes out.

CHAPTER SIXTEEN

FRANKIE

THEN

I'm floating on my back in the pool and Walter is sitting on the side, his feet dangling in the deep end. He's wearing plain black board shorts that show off surprisingly muscular legs. His chest is bare, with a smattering of dark hair in stark contrast to the pallor of his skin. I've been eyeing him off for the last hour, my pulse racing and my heart pounding in the throes of my first full-blown crush.

He's nothing like the guys at school, who can only converse about football and college and parties. It must be an age thing, because Walter exudes a quiet confidence I find extremely attractive. He's not verbose yet he's easy to talk to, and we've covered a range of topics over the last sixty minutes, from how much he loves his job at the bank and being on a fast-track to manager, to my passion for books across genres.

But he hasn't mentioned one salient fact and I've finally worked up the courage to ask him about it.

"Where's your girlfriend?"

"She left yesterday morning." He sounds relieved rather than unhappy about it.

"Was she at my party?"

"No, she had a migraine."

"Too bad." I would've liked to suss out the competition. Then again, the way Walter has been checking me out since he arrived for a swim, I'm quietly confident he returns my interest.

I can't explain my attraction to him. But from the moment we met I felt a bewildering mix of excitement and calm around him, two conflicting emotions that make me want to do crazy things, like beg him to take me with him when he leaves.

I don't want to talk about his girlfriend but I don't want to encroach on her territory either if they're serious. "How long have you been going out?"

"A year."

Yikes. That's bad. Twelve months is a committed relationship and I experience a flicker of remorse. Maybe I should back off?

But then I catch him staring at my breasts from behind his sunglasses and I know I have to make a move or I'll regret it forever. My priorities have changed. I'd been looking forward to my gap year at home, to figure out what I want to do with my life before heading off to college. But meeting Walter, the first guy I've ever been interested in, hot on the heels of discovering my parents' secret, has made me re-evaluate. Maybe I need a fresh start away from here to work out where my life is heading?

"Do you love her?"

"What kind of question is that?"

He's bemused rather than angry so I persist. "Because if you love her I won't pursue this and today is about two new friends hanging out and getting to know each other."

"And if I don't?"

"Then you better get your ass in here and find out."

He laughs, a loud bellow that startles some nearby starlings into taking flight.

"Just so you know, I don't usually talk to guys like that. In fact, I've never said anything so forward to a male in all my life, but I like you, you're leaving at the end of the week and I don't want to waste any time."

In response, he swings his legs out of the water and stands. Great, I've screwed this up monumentally with my uncharacteristic bluntness. I swim to the shallow end so I can stand too. When I do, he's still staring at me like he can't quite figure me out.

"Where are you going?"

"Home," he says.

"Will I see you tomorrow?"

"No. I'm not going 'home' as in next door, I'm heading home to Hartford."

"Oh."

Not only have I failed in my quest to get him to like me, I'm so damn unlikeable I've driven him all the way to his hometown.

"Aren't you going to ask me why?"

I shake my head and water droplets fly in a pretty arc, glinting in the sunlight. "I think I've said enough."

He shrugs and turns away, and my heart sinks, before he pauses and glances over his shoulder.

"I'm going home to break up with my girlfriend because I'd never cheat."

I think I fell a little in love with him right then.

He grins and gives me a funny half salute. "And in case you don't understand, I'll be back."

CHAPTER SEVENTEEN

FRANKIE

NOW

After the play date, I don't feel like working. I have a slight headache, the kind that always comes on when I'm stressed. Silly, really, because Celeste made an effort to be friendly and having Saylor pop over to join us was nice. Both women are lovely and I hate that I'm letting my insecurities taint what could possibly be great friendships.

I feel like I'm unraveling. I can't believe I told Celeste my innermost fear about being a nobody if I quit my job… I overshared, something I never do. But she's a good listener and asked the right questions without coming across as probing or inquisitive. And she offered to take Luna if I ever need a break. That was thoughtful. It's been a long time since I've had a friend close by I could rely on.

While there are many perks with my job, a major downside is the isolation. Sure, I have many "friends" and followers on social media, but I drifted away from my school friends when I left Gledhill and didn't form any real attachments to Andre's crowd when we lived in Manhattan. I guess I've always been a bit of a loner and it's suited me. I didn't need anyone apart from Walt in my first marriage. He'd saved me in a way, taking me far from Gledhill, and I'll always love him for that. With Andre, our relationship had been so intense, so insular from the start, I didn't need anyone else. These days, I wonder if that's a good thing.

Luna and Vi are besties already and I'm glad, considering I'm too busy to take her to play dates with other children she's met at dance class and most of our neighbors have boys. Luna having a friend the same age next door is handy so it looks like we'll be spending a lot of time with Celeste. I need to get over my suspicions and she's presented me with the perfect opportunity to do just that, asking for Andre's help to move stuff for her. My husband has a hero complex so he'll love to help, and I'll tag along with Luna on the pretext of the girls spending a bit more time together. Underhand, maybe, but I need to get over this funk once and for all and if I see them interacting together up close and personal I'll know whether this is all in my head.

Ironically, my session online today is on hiding vegetables in popular foods for kids. I'd joked around with Luna in the park today but my daughter has no idea on the number of times she eats vegetables she hates. Violette's horrified expression had been priceless and I'll make sure to ask Celeste about her daughter's eating habits later and if she's as sneaky as me. It's something we can bond over, our commonalities as mothers, and I'm determined to make an effort.

As I do my make-up in the mirror, I hate how tired I look. I didn't sleep well after confronting Andre last night and the dark shadows under my eyes prove it. While I'd tossed and turned he'd snored softly beside me, oblivious to my turmoil. He played the wounded husband well, like he couldn't fathom me doubting him. But I can't help but remember he played that role once before, that even after his confession he couldn't figure why I couldn't trust him.

I squeeze a dot of primer onto my fingertip and use it to smooth away the frown line between my brows, a line that's becoming increasingly prominent the more I obsess about things I shouldn't. With a final slick of a nude gloss with peach undertones over my lips, I'm ready. The outfit I've chosen today is a simple white long-sleeved cotton top with cutesy pineapples all over it to go along with my food theme.

I try to mix up my content: food, fashion, decorating, skincare, whatever I feel like. It seems to work better than the set days I started with, like Food on Friday and Skincare Saturday. At the beginning I was lucky to make it online once a week but as my hits and my followers grew, I upped my game. Today, I'm guaranteed to have over a million views at least and so many comments I can't respond to them all. Andre says I should hire someone to help me, but I'm a control freak and like reading through all the comments, even if it is becoming onerous.

Luna is great with my live streams. She knows not to interrupt, probably because she gets more screen time to play games than I'd usually allow. I peek into her room, my heart swelling with love as I hear her giggle at her favorite show.

"Honey, I'll be online for about half an hour, then you can help me prepare dinner, okay?"

"Sure, Mom," she says, without looking up from the screen.

Like most parents, I'm anti-screens, but I'm honest enough to admit they're a godsend at times.

I have everything set up in the kitchen. It's a perfect space for filming, with a massive island bench covered in a white marble top, and five trendy chrome lights resembling peppershakers hanging over it from above. Behind me is a row of white cabinets over an induction stovetop, with subtle hints of lighter wood throughout. It's modern, bright and airy, and many have commented on the decor. It's professional yet homey and I love this kitchen as much as the rest of the house.

What I'm about to do—fake it in front of a camera—pays for this house. Growing up, I always dreamed of living in a brownstone one day. I'm lucky, because this is no ordinary brownstone. Converted about a year before we bought it, the street level is a giant rumpus room that we admittedly rarely use, the first story is our lounge, dining room and kitchen, while the upper story has a generous master bedroom, along with Luna's room and a spare. Andre and I don't mention the spare room. I'm terrified he'll want another child; he's probably scared of my answer.

In all honesty, I don't know if I want another child. Luna is enough for me. And if my fanciful imagination over the last twenty-four hours is any indication, maybe a part of me doesn't want another child because I still don't fully trust my husband. I don't know if I'll ever be able to forget what he did.

He's made the occasional flyaway comment about using the room as a nursery, but I don't respond or make light of it, and I assume he's got the message. I half expected him to bring it up again yesterday after the gender reveal party—would've been the perfect opening—but he hadn't and I'd been relieved.

I check the bench top to make sure my ingredients are lined up. I've got flour, sugar, grated carrot, zucchini, beaten eggs and butter arranged in white bowls, with spoonfuls of cinnamon and nutmeg on a white saucer. After switching my ring light on, I take a deep breath and blow it out.

I'm prepared for this charade I perpetuate, that I have the perfect life, if only for thirty minutes.

When in reality I'm doing my best day-to-day, trying to gloss over the cracks.

CHAPTER EIGHTEEN
CELESTE

It doesn't surprise me when Frankie and Luna follow Andre into my house. She texted me earlier saying Andre would be over after dinner around seven to help move my furniture, and though she didn't mention she'd be coming too I'd expected it.

I sensed an undercurrent when I'd asked for Andre's help in the park earlier today... like she's okay being my friend but doesn't trust me completely.

It saddens me, because I admired her for opening up to me, for sharing how she's feeling about her job, about her imperfections. It had been a real bonding moment, until Saylor had interrupted. Not that she'd been unwelcome, but it's Frankie I have more in common with, and with our daughters' friendship fast developing I envisage us spending more time together.

"Where do you want me?" Andre asks, pointing upstairs. "Frankie mentioned something about moving a trunk in your bedroom?"

I see Frankie stiffen at his flyaway question, which could be interpreted as flirtatious if I was prone to that kind of thing. I'm not. I have no interest in her husband. He's not my type and even if he was, I meant what I said to her earlier today. I don't betray my friends. And I want us to be friends, more than anything.

"Yeah, it's upstairs, second door on the right," I say, because no way in hell I'm following him up there after Frankie's odd behavior in the park when I asked for his help.

Andre's halfway up the staircase before he notices I'm not following. "Uh, do you want to show me where you want it moved to?"

"Sure," I say, turning to Frankie, determined to include her. "Do you mind coming up too so I can ask your advice about an outfit I want to wear to an interview?"

It's BS but I know I've done the right thing when I see relief flicker in her eyes. She is angsty about her husband helping me and I have no idea why. We barely spoke at the party in the park.

"Okay," Frankie says, and I wait until she follows Andre before moving behind her up the stairs.

When we enter the bedroom Andre is eyeing the trunk with a raised eyebrow. "Uh, how strong do you think I am?"

Frankie says, "Don't be a wuss."

I laugh and point to the walk-in closet. "I want it in there, out of the way, so I can put my desk near the window and work in natural light. I hate staring at a computer screen all day."

"Makes sense," he says, bending his legs and giving the trunk a tentative push, surprise lighting his features when it moves.

"Easy for you to push. Me, not so much," I say, feeling like I have to justify inviting him over to help when I see Frankie's eyebrows quirk in surprise.

"Where's this outfit?" she asks, an overt challenge to my earlier excuse, and I really want to tell her not to worry about me, but it's awkward with Andre around. I enter the closet and grab the first suit I see. It's my favorite, a deep plum slim-leg pants and matching jacket combo that I wear with an ivory silk blouse.

I barely glance at Andre pushing the trunk into the farthest corner of the closet and try not to flinch as our shoulders brush. I quickly leave the closet, brandishing the suit. If Frankie's eyebrows rose a few moments ago, they hit the stratosphere as she looks at the suit.

"That's beautiful. The perfect interview suit."

I pretend to dither, holding it up to the light. "You think? I've worn it a few times and while I liked it initially I'm not sure it gives off the right vibe. This new client I'm trying to woo will give me enough work to last a year so I really want to dress to impress."

"Well, if you're trying to give off a professional, stylish, confident woman vibe, I'd stick with it." She gives a self-deprecating chuckle. "Then again, what do I know? My uniform of choice is whatever freebie has landed on my doorstep the week before."

"You always look amazing."

She zeroes in on my slip-up, looking confused, and I inwardly curse. "You watch my show? Because when we met you didn't know who I was?"

"I mean since I've met you," I say, covering quickly and hoping she believes me. "But I will definitely watch your show now I know I'm living next door to someone famous."

"About that, please don't post where I live anywhere online. Social media is great for business but I'm very protective of my privacy, especially with Luna."

"Of course. I can empathize about needing to ensure complete privacy." All she has to deal with is the potential overzealous fan or odd stalker, whereas I need to hide my whereabouts at all costs.

She hesitates, as if she wants to ask more, but before she can Andre barges out of the closet, announcing, "All done. Anything else you need a hand with, Celeste?"

I shake my head. "No, thanks, all good. I appreciate you moving that for me."

"Any time."

I see Frankie's frown as she glares at her husband and I stifle a sigh. There's no way I'll be asking for his help even if the roof caves in and I need to fix it myself.

"See you at home, sweetheart." As if sensing Frankie's disapproval of our relationship—even though it's nonexistent—he kisses her on the lips before clomping down the stairs.

"Roland used to be like that, sounding like stampeding elephants…" I have no idea why I let that slip, but her frown disappears.

"Is he the reason you need to maintain privacy?"

I nod and bite down on my bottom lip to stop from blurting too much.

Her eyes glimmer with understanding and, thankfully, she doesn't probe. "We've got each other's backs, right?"

"Absolutely," I say and mime zipping my lips. "You can trust me."

CHAPTER NINETEEN

SAYLOR

Lloyd is in Manhattan, having drinks with some fellow youth workers from various churches tonight, and I'm back to my favorite pastime, spying on Ruston across the park. He must be in the kitchen or somewhere because the front room is in darkness. Before I let the curtain slip back into place, I see Frankie, Andre and Luna on Celeste's doorstep. I experience a moment of jealousy. I'm new too. Why didn't Celeste invite me over for their meet-the-neighbors session?

Then again, I'll never be part of their friendship. I'm not a mother yet and moms tend to stick together. I felt it this afternoon in the park, like I was on the outer no matter how hard I try to fit in. I hated that feeling growing up and it's no different now. Back then, I didn't buy into my parents' fervent beliefs and they never fully understood me. When I preferred meeting friends at the skate park on a Sunday after service rather than having morning tea with the holier-than-thou kids of their friends, they'd disapprove. When I shortened my school uniform to mid-thigh like the other girls in school, they frowned. When I fell in love with Ruston and would've followed him anywhere, they made sure they found the perfect candidate to help me settle down.

The funny thing is, I'd liked Lloyd instantly. I'd been determined to dislike him, because he'd been my parents' choice. But he'd been so funny and warm and charming I couldn't help but fall for him.

It helped that Ruston had broken my heart for the umpteenth time just before I met Lloyd and it had seemed like the perfect time to move on.

So why the hell does Ruston have to turn up here now when my life is already in disarray, even if nobody knows it? Has he done this on purpose? Then again, why would he seek me out considering how things ended between us?

Whatever his rationale, I can't allow him to distract me from my goal. To get my life back on track, I need to become a part of this community. I need to be trusted and that means I need to befriend Frankie and Celeste. There's one sure-fire way to ingratiate myself with these women. I already know Frankie's a lifestyle vlogger. I've watched her show religiously over the last few months. But it's Celeste I'm more interested in. Of the two, she's the one I can't get a read on and I like to be prepared.

I sit on the sofa, rest my laptop on a cushion and type CELESTE REAGAN into the search engine. A host of hits pop up, referring to some politician in England, a small-time television producer in Australia and an indie author, but nothing on my neighbor. I click on the "images" icon and scan the photos but don't see her. So I open several social media sites, one by one, and search them all.

Nada.

It's like Celeste is the invisible woman. She doesn't exist.

It's strange, because most women in their thirties have some kind of online presence, if only to snoop on their exes or check out what their old classmates are up to. Of course, there could be any number of reasons why she's offline—a cyberbullying incident when she was younger, an obsession with privacy, an introvert who doesn't care what the rest of the world is sharing online—but the most obvious reason is she's hiding from an ex. Turning up here with only a carload of possessions supports that theory. Then again, maybe I'm being overly suspicious because I've had to cover my tracks well out of necessity.

I type FRANKIE FORBES into the search engine and there are countless hits, pages and pages of them. Not surprising, considering her online fame. ANDRE FORBES elicits fewer hits. His graphic design website showcasing his work, several mentions in newspapers, nothing out of the ordinary.

I'm so tempted to type RUSTON REYNOLDS into the search engine but I don't. It's not conducive to relegating him to the past, no matter how shocked I am he's barged into my present.

Besides, why do I care what he's been up to since we broke up for the final time? I know too much about him already: the scattering of tiny freckles on the bridge of his nose, the small scar from a skateboarding accident at the base of his right collarbone, the intensity of his gaze that made me feel like I was the only woman in the world.

I close the laptop and squeeze my eyes shut, wishing I could block out my memories, despising myself for wasting time thinking about him at all.

I have a baby to focus on and a plan to execute.

CHAPTER TWENTY

FRANKIE

THEN

True to his word, Walter comes back a week later.

He's broken up with his girlfriend and doesn't seem all that cut up about it. I ask if she's okay because I feel bad for ruining some other woman's relationship and he reassures me they'd been headed for a split anyway. She'd become too clingy, too possessive, but he won't say more than that. He's too nice a guy to bad-mouth anyone and he looks plain uncomfortable when I try to probe for more info on his ex, so I drop it.

Besides, I can't believe this is happening. Walter came back for me, to explore the spark I'd hoped wasn't one-sided. Heady stuff for a girl who may have just fallen in love for the first time.

"What do you want from me, Francesca?"

We're sitting by the pool again, side by side at the shallow end, our legs dangling in. His are pale like mine, but he has big feet that seem at odds with his average height. I wonder if it's true what I read in a book once, that big feet equate with a big... uh, appendage. Considering I'm a virgin, I'm not sure whether to be scared or thrilled. That's the thing about having parents who are open about sex, and have been since I hit puberty; it makes me want to cherish it, to make my first time special, and not treat it like a party trick to be shared freely among friends.

"I want you." It's the boldest thing I've ever said and my heart pounds so hard I can hear an echo of the beat in my ears. "From the moment we met I felt a connection and I want to explore that."

I don't tell him the whole truth; that while I like him, the reason I'm also drawn to him is because he's the opposite of my parents and he'll take me far away from this place.

If he's taken aback by my brazen declaration of wanting him, he doesn't show it. I like that about him, the calmness he exudes, like he's unshockable. "I'd like to get to know you too, but I can't stay in town for long. I have to get back to work."

"Then take me with you," I blurt, impulsive and rash and totally out of character for me. But I don't want him to leave so soon before I have a chance to know him, not when leaving with him will accomplish my goal to escape my parents and Gledhill too.

"Francesca, look at me."

I do and his brown eyes are wide with wonder, like he can't believe I'd leave my home to be with him.

"You've just turned eighteen. You haven't been to college. Why on earth would you want to give up your home to be with me when we hardly know each other?"

Doubts replace amazement as his steady gaze clouds over and I know I have to give the performance of my life in order to convince him.

"Haven't you ever done something so spontaneous, so wild, it makes your head spin?" I fling my arm wide to encompass the garden. "That makes you want to run around and do a happy dance for the hell of it?"

"No. I'm not that kind of guy."

"Do you want to be?"

His brow creases in confusion as if he can't fathom the question.

"I've done the right thing my entire life. Been the good student, the good daughter, always toeing the line. But I want more out of life and I don't want to spend the next twelve months of my gap year stuck here figuring out what I want, when the moment I laid eyes on you I knew."

I reach out and snag his hand. "I've never been in love and I certainly don't believe in love at first sight, but the way we connected in the garden the night of my party… I can't put it into words. I wish I could. Because I really want to make you understand how much I'm drawn to you and how it feels right, in here."

I press my other hand to my heart and his stunned gaze follows it. I take advantage by thrusting my chest out a little, using my assets to reel him in. Maybe I have a little of my mother in me after all?

"I don't know what to say." He drags his gaze away and shakes his head.

"Say yes." I squeeze his hand in encouragement. "Say you'll take me with you so we can have a real relationship."

The flicker of excitement in his eyes makes me want to punch the air in victory. "What about your folks? Do you seriously think they'll agree to letting their only child leave with a virtual stranger?"

"They won't be a problem, trust me."

I'll make sure of it. I'm not averse to a little blackmail. Either they let me go or I'll let their precious pastor know what really happens at their parties. It makes me sick to my stomach to think of how pious they are at church yet so debauched in private. Not that I'd actually reveal the embarrassing truth to anyone but I'm hoping the threat of what I'll say will ensure they won't stop me leaving.

"This is crazy." He slides his hand out of mine to press fingertips to his temples. "I don't do impulsive things."

Good. Because once I'm far away from here and living with Walter, I want dependable. I crave it, with every cell in my body. I want stability and peace, not this riotous out of control feeling since I discovered the truth about my parents.

"What if we leave together and discover we're not compatible? What then?"

I knew this wouldn't be an easy sell. His steadiness is one of the qualities I admire but also a quality that will make him second-guess everything I say.

"What if you leave here and always wonder 'what if'? Isn't it better to take a chance on us than never know?"

After what seems like an eternity, he gives a rueful chuckle. "I can't believe I'm even contemplating this."

I clamp down on a triumphant whoop. "We're going to be happy, Walter. I know it."

"This is nuts."

"This is fate."

As if to prove it, I clasp his face in my hands and draw him toward me. I press my lips to his, tentative, exploring, my first kiss. He surprises me by taking over, his hands stroking the skin along my torso, his thumbs toying with the undersides of my breasts as he deepens the kiss. His tongue slides between my lips, tangling with mine, and I like it. As he moans I feel an answering throb deep within.

I'm not sure how long we make out for and I don't care because when he releases me his dazed expression matches mine.

"Let's do it," he says, his smile goofy.

I fling myself at him and we tumble onto the grass edging the pool in a flurry of limbs and laughter.

I've made the right decision.

I know it.

CHAPTER TWENTY-ONE

FRANKIE

NOW

I'm not in the mood for another party but Luna heard Violette talking about it with Celeste last night and has been bugging me about it ever since. I'm not a pushover when it comes to Luna but to see her so happy with her new friend makes me capitulate, when I'd rather be home enjoying some rare time off binge watching the latest romcom on TV.

Celeste is the other reason I'm attending. I'd glimpsed genuine fear in her eyes last night.

I'm worried about her. Is she hiding from an abusive ex? It's looking increasingly likely and, if so, I want to reassure her she's not so vulnerable here, that she does have people who care. That's one of the great things about this neighborhood: we may not live in each other's pockets but in times of need, like after Mrs. Obermeier's hip replacement or Mr. Mac's wife dying unexpectedly from a heart attack, we pull together.

I'm surprised Saylor is throwing this party, where everyone in the neighborhood who wants to attend brings a plate to share, only a few days after her gender reveal. When I'd been five months pregnant I wanted to sloth around with my feet up as much as possible.

Not as many neighbors have come tonight but there are enough of us, about twenty, that with a little music and the share plates—mostly cheese and fruit platters—we're having a good time.

Celeste is sitting with the girls on a patch of grass, playing charades with Luna and Violette. Andre and Lloyd are chatting, while Saylor is deep in conversation with some guy. She's animated, he appears less interested, and when he turns I realize it's Ruston, who she thinks is hot.

He is handsome, in that polished way some guys favor these days, with the slicked back hair, clean-shaven jaw and manicured hands. I like my guys a little rougher around the edges and as my gaze is drawn toward Andre again I wonder if he knows how much I'm still attracted to him, despite how close we came to splitting up years ago.

"Daddy, come look at this," Luna shrieks, and Andre joins the girls and Celeste on the grass.

At a casual glance they look like the perfect family and I'm struck by how that could be me if I had another child, a sweet family of four.

As if sensing my gaze, Celeste looks my way and for a moment I'm unsure whether a shift in the light makes her look smug. But then she waves me over and her smile is genuine when I join their cozy circle on the grass.

"Mom, Dad's hopeless at charades," Luna says, collapsing into giggles when Andre starts tickling her until she's rolling next to him, squealing "Stop, Dad, please." He does and Luna clambers onto his lap, before he moves a few feet away and starts telling the girls an elaborate fairy tale about a dragon. He wraps his arms around Luna and beckons Violette to come closer, and I swear I hear Celeste sigh in unison with me.

"He's a good father," she says softly. "You're lucky to have him."

"I am," remembering a time I didn't feel so lucky.

"Roland would never sit on the grass with Vi or be so openly affectionate."

She's given me the perfect opening to ask more about her ex, to mention how supportive this community can be if she needs it, without appearing too curious.

"Will he be visiting you here?"

"No."

Short, sharp, ominous, and like last night, I glimpse fear in her eyes. She doesn't want to talk about Violette's father but I hate her obvious vulnerability—the look away glance, the fiddling fingers, the slumped shoulders—and I feel obliged to ask more. "Are you divorced?"

"We never married. I think life's all about timing and it never aligned for us." She gives a self-deprecating laugh. "A good thing, as it turned out."

Sadness mingles with regret in her voice and I feel sorry for her. "You can tell me to shut up if you like, but did he do something?"

She's clasping her hands so tight in her lap the knuckles stand out. "What didn't he do? It's only now I'm away from him, I realize how toxic he is. He's never going to change and I can't keep hoping for a miracle." She shakes her head. "Holding onto false hope is the worst. It eats away at you until you question everything."

She sounds so forlorn I want to hug her. I like that we're bonding and she's revealing snippets of her life, but I feel sorry for her too.

I don't know what to say about the situation, so I settle for, "Violette seems well-adjusted."

I mean it as a compliment but her eyes narrow with displeasure. "She's shy, anxious and jumps at her own shadow. I want her to discover her inner confidence before…"

She trails off and I know, by her shuttered expression, I'm not going to get anything more out of her. Then again, do I want to? I may be reaching out on the pretext of friendship but I know we all have secrets that can never be shared.

"Do you girls want some fruit?" Celeste leaps nimbly to her feet and the girls abandon Andre's storytelling and follow her, leaving Andre and me alone.

He's watching them walk away and a frown appears between his eyebrows.

"What's wrong?" I reach out to touch his hand.

"You'll think I'm nuts, but I don't get a good vibe from that woman."

"What do you mean?"

He shakes his head, the frown deepening. "I can't explain it but I'm not sure you should befriend her."

It doesn't make sense he wants me to avoid her, especially when I feel like we're growing closer, and having Celeste open up about her ex has further cemented our friendship. Andre's warning could be from a good old-fashioned gut reaction, or is it because he doesn't want me getting too close for what I'll discover?

"Luna already loves Violette and she doesn't have any girls her age to play with around here, so we might be hanging around Celeste more than we'd like regardless."

I'm surprised by my instinct to protect the fragile friendship I've built with this woman despite my earlier suspicions. But with every interaction, I realize the misgivings are all on me and my insecurities regarding Andre; Celeste has been nothing but friendly toward me since she moved in and I value that.

"I guess…" He shrugs. "Just be careful, okay?"

"What do you mean?"

"I'm not sure…" He smiles but I see it's forced as he reaches for my hand. "Maybe I should stop streaming those psychological thrillers every night?"

I chuckle as he intends, but I can't shake the feeling something isn't right. My extroverted husband always sees the good in people and loves expanding our social circle; he's never warned me off anyone before.

What is it about Celeste that has him worried?

CHAPTER TWENTY-TWO

CELESTE

I'm standing at the buffet table where all the shared plates are lined up, supervising Luna and Violette as they serve themselves. They're endearingly cute, dithering over what to have first.

"Luna, what's your favorite fruit?" I point at the platter. "Watermelon, grapes, cantaloupe or strawberries?"

She's adorable, with her tongue poking out between her lips as she concentrates. "My favorite isn't here."

"What is it?"

"Apple," she says, with a shrug. "But I guess I can have strawberries."

"Apple is my favorite too," I say, using the tongs to place a few strawberries on a paper plate and handing it to her.

"And grapes are mine," Violette adds, her cheeks already puffed from sneaking grapes while I've been serving Luna.

"You look like a squirrel," Luna says, with a giggle, pointing at Violette's cheeks, and puffing out her own with air.

This sets the girls off and they laugh so hard they almost double over. I smile at them, enjoying how they've bonded so quickly. Children rarely have the hang-ups of their parents and it's refreshing. No bickering, no slyness, no jealousy, just a genuine enjoyment of each other's company.

When their laughter dies down and they resume eating I serve myself a piece of watermelon and beckon them to the bench near the table. That's when I see Frankie and Andre are watching me. It's unnerving, being the subject of their scrutiny. They're probably talking about me. I guess it's natural, considering what I just divulged to Frankie about Roland. Also, I'm new to the neighborhood and they're curious about the mother of their daughter's new best friend, but there's something in their body language—crossed arms, rigid shoulders—that's off-putting.

I don't have the time or the inclination to figure out why they are staring at me, so I say, "Luna, tell me what you like to do."

She screws up her face, thinking. "I like playing in the park and gymnastics and Mom's started taking me to this ballet school near the waterfront because I love dancing so much."

"That sounds like fun. What else?"

Children are so trusting they'll open up to anyone who asks the right questions and engages with them. Especially if their own parents are distracted by work and too busy to interact on a level beyond telling them to eat their veggies and clean their room.

"I like drawing and coloring and jigsaw puzzles and watching TV."

"Me too," Vi says, and they're soon lost in conversation again, discussing their favorite colors and what's better to draw, unicorns, monster trucks or fairies. I let their conversation wash over me, making a mental to-do list for tomorrow.

Starting with enrolling Vi at the same ballet school on the waterfront that Luna attends.

CHAPTER TWENTY-THREE
SAYLOR

I can't believe I had to throw another party in order to speak to Ruston but I'm tired of watching and waiting. He has no intention of visiting me and I can't exactly stroll across the park and knock on his door without people talking. In the last half hour alone I've heard several women gossiping about the dubious male visitors the married woman who lives at number fourteen gets during the daytime and I have no intention of being the next target.

I don't want to talk to him, but I'm obsessing, thinking about him day and night when I shouldn't be, scared he'll let slip we know each other to Lloyd, and I need to make sure he doesn't. Our paths rarely cross so this social situation is the only way I can think of to confront him.

I bide my time, mingling with everyone, answering solicitous questions like "How's the morning sickness?" to "Have you made a birth plan yet?" I'm bored but my time will come and when the opportunity presents itself—he's near the buffet table nibbling on cheese, I'm there on the pretext of filling a plate for Lloyd—I pounce.

"Hey," I say in a soft voice, not wanting our conversation to be overheard.

Ruston glances up from the cheese platter and smiles, appearing genuinely happy to see me. I can't work him out because any other guy would feel bad about how he treated me—many times—over the years, but he seems oblivious to the tension.

"Hey, new neighbor, fancy seeing you here." He leans in closer and I hold my breath against the rush of pheromones his signature citrus body wash never fails to elicit. "Are you stalking me?"

"You wish," I mutter, hating how he slips into flirtation mode without trying. "What are you doing here?"

"House-sitting for a friend. She's a campaign manager for a senator and is on the road for six months."

I zero in on one word, "she", annoyed at myself for caring. I flounder for something to say, other than "I hate you for breaking my heart, I hate myself more for still caring."

He smirks as the silence grows between us and points at my belly. "I guess congratulations are in order. I would've said something at the gender reveal but you seemed to have your hands full meeting everyone."

"I wanted to talk to you too."

His eyebrows rise. "About?"

Everything. Anything. But I can't, not anymore. I'm married and expecting a baby. Unfortunately, confronting Ruston, getting the first awkward meeting out of the way, hasn't helped. He still has a ridiculous hold over me, like we're bound by invisible strings and all he has to do is jerk on them and I'll dance for the puppet-master.

I know Ruston. If he suspects how anxious I am about revealing our past to Lloyd, he'll do it to spite me. I need to lead into it, so I settle for a lame, "Just wanted to say hi," and he nods, his stare too intense, as if he sees right through me.

"How are you settling in?"

"Fine," I say, when talking to him like this is anything but.

"Good. This park is great for get-togethers like this."

"Yeah, that's why I moved here, for the *family* community."

If he notices my emphasis on family, he doesn't acknowledge it. He nods in agreement, content to stuff his face with wedges of Brie on crackers, and I wonder if I'm doing the right thing, trying to establish some kind of truce with my new neighbor, when I know deep down he's always been so much more.

He points at my ring finger, where the shiny gold band feels a tad tight; probably from a retention of fluid and not an imaginary constriction I feel being someone's wife. "How long have you been married?"

"Nine months."

"Your hubby's a fast worker," he says, glancing at my belly again. "He seems like a nice guy."

"He is."

He hesitates, before saying, "Does he know about us?"

"No."

He winks. "Don't worry, your secret's safe with me."

I don't want to buy into his buddy-buddy act, like we're co-conspirators in some elaborate ruse. He's my past. I need to remember it.

Besides, I'm harboring a secret far worse than the two of us being ex-lovers.

"Thanks, I appreciate that." I flash him a serene smile when I'm feeling anything but inside. "I hope we can be friends."

"Friends, sure."

Before I can react he clasps my hand between his, infusing me with warmth, making me remember when I shouldn't.

I clamp down on the urge to yank my hand away and ease it out of his grip, turning and walking away before I say something I'll regret.

CHAPTER TWENTY-FOUR

FRANKIE

THEN

Turns out my parents don't take kindly to their only child having a mind of her own and leaving them without a backward glance, because when I marry Walter six months later in a tiny ceremony at City Hall, they don't turn up. Considering I'd tried my blackmail spiel on them so I could leave Gledhill with Walt and they'd blown up, followed by a massive argument to end all arguments when we'd hurled awful accusations at one another, it's no surprise. We've had zero contact since but a small part of me hoped they might still show up for my wedding after Walt insisted I invite them. Their no-show hurts and Walter, intuitive, as ever, does his best to make me laugh.

"Hey, I've got a surprise for you."

"I bet you have." I bat my eyelashes, more to blink away the sting of tears rather than an attempt to flirt.

"Not that." He rolls his eyes but I know he loves my teasing. It's our thing ever since he brought me to Connecticut. He's the responsible one, I try to make him laugh, and it works surprisingly well.

While I fell for him at the start, I didn't know what to expect. I'd been so hell-bent on escaping home and getting out of Gledhill and off Long Island I'd tried not to think too far ahead. I'd almost expected Walter to realize he'd made a mistake and ditch me after a month or two, but that hadn't happened because he was easy to like, and easy to be around with, and we gelled. He had his own house, a modest Californian style bungalow, worked regular hours at the bank and liked nothing better than being with me in his free time. That was a heady feeling for a loner like me, having a man love me so much.

We fell into a routine when I moved in with him. I assumed the role of a fifties housewife—grocery shopping, cooking, cleaning—and he was the provider. He paid the bills and when I suggested getting a job he said to make the most of my gap year and figure out what I wanted to learn. I liked that about him, that I was enough for him. He didn't place expectations on me, he didn't give me grief when I exhausted my limited cooking repertoire of mac'n'cheese, potato salad and steak, and chili con carne, and he didn't mind when I let the house go occasionally in favor of getting lost in a latest streaming release.

Our life was good and when he asked me to marry him I didn't hesitate. But the moment he slipped a modest half-carat square-cut diamond on my ring finger, the incidents started. Small things at first—the rose bush I planted uprooted, the veggie patch doused in weedkiller, a dead squirrel on the back step—but escalating to finding only my clothes slashed to pieces on the washing line, a pair of my shoes at the front door smeared in dog poo, and "bitch" scratched into the driver's door of the compact Walter had bought me.

I assumed it was some psycho ex of his but he denied it, saying the breakup with Julia—the girlfriend he'd dumped for me—had been amicable. But he couldn't meet my eyes when he said it and I knew he was trying to placate me.

"Should I be scared of her?" I'd asked at the time and he'd distracted me with a brochure for our honeymoon, a long weekend in Manhattan at a trendy new hotel.

But now, as he leads me down the steps of City Hall, I wonder if Julia, or whoever is responsible for those incidents, will back off because we're married.

"So what's this great surprise?"

"You'll see."

He raises my hand to his lips and presses a kiss on the back of it. Genuine love radiates from his eyes and in that moment I feel a flicker of remorse. Because, while this man has become my everything, I'm beginning to wonder if deep down I don't love him in the same way he loves me. It's only after living together for six months I realize how much I wanted to escape my parents, and maybe I convinced myself of our attraction to latch onto him as a way out. I do love him but I'm not sure it's enough; not that I'd ever let him know.

I hope I can be the wife he deserves.

He leads me toward the realtor's office and when we stop in front of the glass, he says, "Close your eyes."

I do and feel him stepping in front of me, before brushing a soft kiss across my mouth. "Okay. Open them."

As I do he steps away and I see a wedding bell with gold and cream streamers hanging from it pinned to a photo of a tiny cottage in New Haven.

"Surprise." He smiles, throwing his arms wide, before pointing to the photo. "I bought us a vacation cottage."

My mouth drops open. I know he has investments. His parents died in a ski accident four years ago and left him the house and some money, but we live frugally and his wage at the bank isn't huge. At twenty-two he's doing better than most who are struggling with student loans, but I brought nothing to our relationship beyond the five grand I'd saved working part-time at the local grocer when I was in high school.

But to buy a second house… I'm gobsmacked and he laughs at my obvious shock.

"I know I'm all about security and hanging onto investments but being with you has taught me it's okay to take a chance when you know something's right, and we're right." He hauls me into his arms and hugs tight, before releasing me as I battle tears again. "I know you miss the ocean. You get this look on your face when ads come on TV… anyway, I bought this for us, a seaside getaway whenever we feel like it."

"I don't know what to say…"

This man has given me everything over the last six months and now this. His generosity makes me want to burrow into his arms and never let go.

"Say you'll make me the happiest man alive." He snaps his fingers, his smile lop-sided. "Wait, you already did that about ten minutes ago when you said 'I do'."

This time, when he embraces me, I cling to him, hoping I can continue living up to his expectations of making him happy.

Because that's the thing about making dreams come true.

Sometimes, they turn into nightmares.

CHAPTER TWENTY-FIVE

FRANKIE

NOW

I had two left feet growing up and never had an interest in dance, but Luna has been bugging me for the last year to do ballet and I gave in a month ago. I can't see myself being a stage mom, doing hair buns and make-up, and I sure as hell can't sew beyond a button fix or darning holes, but she's so excited and watching a class of five-year-olds trying to do twirls and pliés is beyond cute.

This is her fourth class at the Madame L'Viste School of Dance. Many of the parents don't hang around. They drop off and return to pick up but I like the enforced downtime, when I'm not planning my next live stream or doing stuff around the house. For these blissful sixty minutes I can relax and watch my daughter having fun. Her wide smiles, her laughter and the genuine joy on her face as she dances makes me happy in a way I haven't been for a long time. That's the thing about presenting a perfect front to the world. Soon it becomes a habit and when the camera turns off, I'm still pretending.

The class of about fifteen girls has just started. They're warming up at the barre, lifting their little legs as high as they can while arching their arms, their pink tutus translucent in the sunlight filtering through the floor-to-ceiling windows offering stunning views of the waterfront. I'm the only parent here, along with a dad who's engrossed in his cell, tapping away like his life depends upon it, which is perfect for me. It means I won't have to make small talk for the next hour.

But before I can relax, the door behind me opens and a late-comer walks in. A little girl rushes past me and into the studio, followed by the mother who's apologizing profusely for their tardiness. Surprised, I peer through the glass separating the waiting area from the studio.

Violette rushes over to Luna while Celeste chats to Daphne, the instructor for the junior class. I cast a glance at the door, wondering if Celeste has seen me and if it's not too late to make a quick getaway. Not that I want to appear unsociable but having sixty minutes to myself is so rare I treasure it, and I'd been looking forward to reading a new romance I'd been saving.

However, she turns before I can move and looks straight at me, like she's known I'm there all along. I wave and fix a smile, despite having my escape plans thwarted. She returns my wave and I know I should be happy she's chosen this dance studio for Violette because Luna will love having her new friend here, but slightly miffed I'll have to share my limited downtime.

It's a coincidence, Celeste enrolling Violette here. Hambridge Heights is filled with young families so there are several dance studios for kids. I'd checked out five before choosing this one. More than likely, Luna mentioned it, and with Celeste so keen to foster a friendship between the girls, she'd done this without telling me. Not that she owes me any explanation but I thought we'd started to establish a real friendship and it's nice to know stuff.

When she comes back into the waiting room, I say, "Hey. Fancy seeing you here."

"Small world." She pulls up a chair next to me and sits. "Vi's been wanting to do ballet for ages but this is her first time. Hope she's not going to be too far behind."

"Luna only started a month ago and honestly? At this age it's all about the tutus and leotards than any real skill."

She shoots me a grateful smile, one mother to another. "Thanks. It's just that Vi is so shy most of the time and hasn't wanted to do any classes, so when she expressed an interest in ballet I'm all for it."

"She doesn't do any other classes where you're from?"

I realize I don't know where Celeste grew up despite her revealing snippets about her relationship.

"No, though Southampton had a lot of choice for kids who wanted to join in."

"You're from Long Island? I grew up in Gledhill."

"No kidding? It's a lovely part of the world."

"Yeah. Even if I couldn't wait to escape."

She arches a brow in curiosity but I have no intention of telling her about my past when I'm far more interested in hers. "Why did you leave?"

"I don't have family there any more. My parents died a long time ago, I'm an only child, and when things with Roland escalated I left and moved here."

I wonder if she has money. Living in Southampton isn't cheap and rent around Hambridge Heights is escalating. I'm lucky Andre had the money to buy our brownstone so we own it outright and my wage pays for the upkeep. There's a lot to be said for security, especially when you don't have any. After I left Gledhill my folks sold the family home, bought a motorhome and drove around the country, as I'd learned from their forwarding address when I asked them to my wedding to Walt. Though I hadn't heard from them since, Andre convinced me to invite them to visit after I had Luna so I'd reached out again but they'd declined, citing their current location as somewhere between Santa Barbara and Los Angeles. They haven't been back to the east coast since.

"What about you? Have you lived in Hambridge Heights long?"

"About five years. We moved here after I had Luna."

"And where were you before that?"

"Manhattan."

She has the strangest expression on her face, like she doesn't believe me, so I rush on, "I loved the city vibe but I think it's nicer to raise kids in a place like this."

"True," she says, her gaze drawn away from me when she hears the girls in the studio squeal with excitement. I see her expression soften as she focuses on Vi, who's one of the excited girls surrounding Daphne. "What do you think that's about?"

"When I was researching dance studios, I learned this place puts on a show at the end of each term. That could be it?"

"That's wonderful, a way to recognize the children's achievements."

"I think it's more an inclusive thing, giving them all a chance to shine regardless of their skill level."

"Of course, that's what I meant. I don't care who's the best."

She sounds like she does. "I'm not competitive at all," I say, testing her, and when she looks at me, the ferocity in her eyes is disconcerting.

"I like to win." She eyeballs me, as if daring me to disagree, and when I don't respond she laughs. "Don't mind me. I was hopeless at sports growing up, so I know I'm going to be one of those terribly obsessed moms who tries to live vicariously through her child."

I join in her laughter but it's uneasy rather than genuine. I saw a hint of something a moment ago, a woman driven to get what she wants. Perhaps that's what Andre's warning had been about?

Regardless, we're friends now, something I don't have many of, and I'm willing to give her the benefit of the doubt. From the snippets of her past she's shared with me, she hasn't had the easiest life. She deserves to feel welcomed here and that's what I can do to make her transition easier. We all deserve a fresh start.

CHAPTER TWENTY-SIX

CELESTE

No matter how hard I try, I get the feeling Frankie's still a tad guarded with me.

So I have to try harder.

As the girls come running out of class, chattering about the end of term show eight weeks away and the costumes they might wear, I ask, "On my way here I saw a great café that's dance themed. Shall we take the girls for a snack?"

I'm underhanded because I know once the girls latch onto "dance-themed" they'll bug us until we capitulate and by Frankie's weary expression as Luna starts to badger her, she'll give in.

"Okay, okay, but just a quick snack so you don't spoil dinner." Frankie holds up her hands in surrender and Luna and Vi start cheering.

"Let's go, girls." I take hold of Vi's hand, something she doesn't allow these days most of the time. My little girl is growing up and before she gets too much older I'd love her to have a sibling.

One of the reasons I'd ended it with Roland. Every time I brought it up over the last few years, he'd fob me off with an excuse.

"Our lives are settled. Our family is perfect the way it is. We can't afford it."

Lies, all of it. Because during our last confrontation he revealed the real reason why he didn't want to father another child with me.

The ensuing rage hadn't been pretty.

"How did you like your first dance class, Violette?" Frankie asks.

My daughter looks up at Frankie. "It's okay. Though I'm not sure I'd like it as much if Luna wasn't there. She's my best friend."

"That's sweet," Frankie says, but as her gaze meets mine I can see she has questions.

I would never prompt Vi to give specific answers to questions when asked because kids can't be trusted not to slip up. And I can see Frankie's puzzled by Vi's wishy-washy response after I said earlier she's been wanting to do ballet for ages. I'm not worried. I can explain away Vi's less than stellar enthusiasm.

"We're lucky to have moved next door to Luna and Frankie, huh?" I swing Vi's arm high as she yells, "Yeah," with Luna joining in, and Frankie's indulgent smile eases my niggle of worry.

That's what this invitation to hang out after dance class is about, another way for the girls to grow closer, to bond. I need that so badly for my daughter.

The café is a block away from the studio and it's more rock-and-roll themed than dance, but the girls are instantly captivated by the waitresses on roller skates and the jukebox with flashing lights in the corner. As we settle at a table with red vinyl booths, the girls grab the menus. Vi's reading is coming along slowly and I know she'll choose something according to the pictures.

"Mom, can I have a strawberry milkshake?" True enough, Vi points to a frothy pink concoction in a sundae glass topped with whipped cream and sprinkles.

"I wish they had apple milkshakes." Luna pouts. "Remember when you were asking me about my favorite stuff, Celeste, and I said I liked dancing and apples best?"

I quickly school my face into a mask of indifference but it's too late. Frankie is looking at me in the same way as when I asked for Andre's help to move the trunk. Suspicious. She thinks I only enrolled Vi at Madame L'Viste's because Luna attended classes there.

And she's right. It took me all day to scour the dance schools to discover which one Luna attended. Not that any of the schools wanted to give out privileged information, but when I showed them a snapshot I took of the girls on my cell, and gave a spiel about just moving here and wanting to surprise our best friends, two schools had been forthcoming. Thankfully, one of them had been Madame L'Viste.

"Yes, it's lucky Vi gets to be in your class. I'd actually enrolled her at a different school but they called this morning and said they'd overbooked and recommended we try Madame L'Viste."

By her frown I can tell she's not buying it.

"Which school?" she asks.

"Mayberry's, at the other end of the waterfront," I say, glad I'd spent time checking out all the schools so my lie sounds convincing.

She appears mollified and nods. "Yeah, their classes are always packed. I almost enrolled Luna there before I saw the numbers." She smiles at Vi. "If your mom says it's okay, would you like to share a plate of churros with Luna?"

I'm annoyed at her presumptuousness. She should've asked me first, not Vi, but I smile when Vi turns to me, practically jumping up and down in her seat.

"Can I, Mom?"

I nod and the girls let out a whoop. But I don't like being undermined and wonder if it's Frankie's warped way of paying me back for grilling her daughter on her likes and dislikes.

When our orders arrive—iced teas for Frankie and me, strawberry milkshakes and churros for the girls—I'm starting to relax.

Until Frankie says, "Did you like living near the beach, Violette?"

I immediately tense. Maybe this post-dance play date isn't such a good idea? I want the girls to bond but I don't want Frankie asking Vi questions.

"Uh-huh. I liked building sandcastles with my dad." Her bottom lip wobbles a little and I hold my breath. "When he was around."

Frankie appears remorseful that she's upset my daughter, and quickly says, "Dads can be like that sometimes."

Solemn, Vi nods. "Yeah, he only visited when he came to town for work, which wasn't very often." Her face screws up as she looks at me. "What was his job again, Mom? A free... something..."

"A freelancer, honey."

Frankie's eyes widen slightly. "Luna's dad is a freelancer too. He designs stuff for companies so he travels sometimes." She slides an arm around Luna's shoulders. "You miss him too when he does that, don't you, sweetie?"

"I hate it." Luna pulls a face, before asking Vi, "Where's your dad now? How come he doesn't live with you?"

Vi's face crumples like she's about to cry and I see Frankie's expression is sympathetic now rather than suspicious. I'm relieved and slide an arm around Vi's shoulders before replying to Luna. "Vi's father didn't want to move so we won't be seeing him anymore."

I'll make sure of it. Protecting my daughter is my number one priority.

CHAPTER TWENTY-SEVEN

SAYLOR

I stroll into the kitchen, where Lloyd's fixing an early dinner of fajitas. "Something smells good."

He doesn't turn away from the sizzling beef strips giving off a tantalizing aroma. "Who's that guy you were talking to last night?"

I freeze. Lloyd's question comes from left field. He isn't the possessive type and he doesn't care who I talk to usually...

"I talked to a lot of guys last night," I say, carefully blanking my expression when he switches off the stove and turns to face me. "Which one?"

"The one who looked like he stepped off a stage after modeling men's underwear."

I laugh at his dry response and the very accurate description. Ruston has an excellent body.

"That's Ruston. He lives across the park, almost directly opposite us. He's house-sitting for a friend who's on the road for six months, a campaign manager for a senator. How's that for a high stress job? It'd be way too much pressure for me." I'm babbling and feel an incriminating heat creep into my cheeks.

"Why are you nervous? I'm only asking because you two appeared to be chatting like old friends."

Now's my chance to tell him everything. How Ruston was my first love, how he took my virginity, how I would've done anything he asked to be with him, how he broke my heart time and time again, how Ruston was the reason my parents introduced us, how we crossed paths on a marketing job about five months ago.

But I've never heard Lloyd sound like this and telling him the truth now will look like I'm deliberately hiding something. Which I am, and that secret is far worse. I need him to believe in me, because when I tell him the truth I like to think we'll have a hope of staying together, despite common sense telling me otherwise.

"I'm not nervous. What's with you? You sound jealous."

"I am." Lloyd's nose crinkles adorably when he's insecure. "He's much more your type."

My husband is absolutely right but he can't ever know that.

"You're my type." I tap his butt. "Want me to show you?"

He pushes his glasses up the bridge of his nose with his finger, his bashful grin warming my heart. Just not as much as Ruston once did. "Later. I'm starving."

"So am I."

I give a little shimmy and he laughs. I know he likes my larger breasts courtesy of this pregnancy.

"What kind of ridiculous name is Ruston anyway?"

I chuckle and waggle my finger at him. "Jealousy is beneath you."

"As long as he's not beneath you," he mutters, almost as if he knows something.

But he can't. My parents certainly wouldn't have told Lloyd how they'd carefully handpicked him like the juiciest, ripest peach and presented him to me knowing I wouldn't resist. The timing of our meeting had been too coincidental for them to be doing anything other than matchmaking. I'd mentioned moving to Manhattan with Ruston, they'd introduced me to Lloyd a week later. Seven long days during which I discovered Ruston had slept with a woman he'd picked up at a bar and it hadn't been the first time.

Lloyd may have been my rebound guy but he's the right guy for me. He'd never hurt me the way Ruston did. I made the right choice. So why does seeing Ruston again make me question that?

Lloyd will make a good father. I want a man who'll love my child more than himself, who'll be around all the time, who'll put my child first.

Lloyd is that man.

No matter how fast my heart beats or my pulse races when Ruston looks at me, I need to forget about him and move forward with my plan. To do that, I need to up the ante.

I never imagined I could stoop this low—to blackmail someone—and every day I regret it. But I have no choice. I've been pushed to this. And I need to put the needs of my son above the guilt consuming me.

Besides, they don't need the money as much as I do. They'll be okay. I just need them to understand they have no choice but to give in. They've been reticent. Ignoring my calls. Avoiding me when we see each other. That's why I need to confront them in a general setting, to ramp up the pressure so they capitulate to my demands.

Mustering every ounce of nonchalance I can, I say, "I think we should host a dinner party. Invite some of the neighbors. Maybe Frankie and Andre? Celeste?"

"What about your pretty boy Ruston?"

My heart skips a beat. The last thing I want is to sit across the dinner table from the guy I've shared countless meals with. "Why would I invite him?"

"So I can see for myself you don't prefer him over me."

Maybe I've underestimated Lloyd and he has better intuition than I think?

He's inadvertently backed me into a corner. If I make a fuss and refuse to invite Ruston, he'll wonder why, so now I'll have to ask him. "You're crazy, but I love you. Okay, I'll ask him."

He laughs. "Actually, it might be nice getting to know him. Andre mentioned he's a photographer and the church is on the lookout for someone new to update our promotional material.

Though is a dinner party too cozy? Too much too soon when we hardly know these people?"

"Do we intend to move any time soon?"

He shakes his head. "No."

"Then doesn't it pay to become friendly with our closest neighbors, especially Frankie and Celeste who both have kids and could be a big help to me after our baby arrives?"

"I suppose you want me to cook for this dinner party too," he says, with a rueful grin.

I nod. "Thanks, honey. We'll keep it simple. Maybe grill some steaks and serve a few salads, with a store-bought cheesecake for dessert?"

"Sounds doable."

"You're the best." I wrap my arms around him, grateful to have him in my life.

Once I get through this charade I'm perpetuating and he knows the truth, I'm hoping our lives will be easier. But it's a foolish, futile wish. This dinner party will be awkward and hiding the truth from my husband difficult.

Who am I trying to kid? Our lives won't be easier once the truth comes out and in the interim, it's more than likely to get a lot more complicated.

CHAPTER TWENTY-EIGHT

FRANKIE

THEN

Walter's decision to surprise me with the vacation cottage in the small seaside town of Ziebellville, near New Haven, on our wedding day proves to be a godsend during the first few years of our marriage.

It saves me, because I soon learn that what had initially drawn me to Walter—his stability, his calmness, his quiet inner strength—turned to boredom once we married.

At his prompting I joined a local community college and did a marketing degree. The classes were okay but what I really loved was the social interaction with people my own age. Most of them couldn't believe I was married at nineteen; not without a kid, that is, pregnancy being the reason many youngsters in Hartford married apparently. I hung out with them during lunch and sometimes after classes, but I never quite fitted in.

Not that Walter minded me attending keg parties and staying out until all hours. He trusted me and while I did have a small crush on a long-haired guy who played in a rock band part-time, I never acted on it. I may have escaped Long Island but my parents' morality—or lack of—ensured I would never cheat.

It surprised me that Walter waited until my twenty-second birthday to bring up the subject of kids. We'd talk about it occasionally, but in that laughing way couples do when they see an ad for diapers or formula on TV. I guess I should've expected it, with him now twenty-six and my course finished. It was like he'd given me permission to spread my wings, to get a feel for college life, but was rescinding the offer and wanted me back as a full-time wife with the mom moniker tacked on for good measure. I'd seen him with some of his friends from the bank, older couples who doted on their kids, and had known he'd want a family of his own sooner rather than later.

"How do you feel about having a baby?" he asks me.

We're sitting on the back verandah at our beachside cottage, our wooden chairs perched on the end of the deck so I can dig my toes in the sand. A brisk breeze is blowing off the ocean, the tang of brine strong in my nostrils. I inhale, letting the familiar smell quell the rising panic. I don't want to be a mother. And I'm increasingly terrified I don't want to be married.

"I'm not ready," I say, when I should tell him the truth: *"I'm not sure if I'll ever be ready."*

Because nothing eases my claustrophobia when I'm around him these days, not even regular weekend jaunts to this place. I'm suffocating beneath the weight of his expectations—he wants me to be someone I'm not.

It's not his fault. I fell for him—and the idea of what he represented for me at the time, freedom—too quickly, and now I'm older I know I want more. Walter is far from controlling but that's how I feel. I'm tired of being married, though I have no idea what to do.

He's too good a man and doesn't deserve to be with someone who's second-guessing her decisions now. I hoped this weekend at my favorite spot would help clarify things but now he's asked me this…

I'd loved our escapes here in the beginning, when we'd pack the car with enough groceries for two days and drive the forty minutes to another world away. Walter had been right about that too. I had been missing the ocean and hadn't known it, so being here revived me. It kept me happy. It distracted me from my doubts.

I'd been foolish, saying yes when Walter popped the question. I should've expressed happiness in our relationship and asked for more time. Instead, I'd tied myself to a man who wants more from me than I can give.

And the thought of hurting him now kills me.

"We've been married three and a half years, Francesca. Our finances are stable, your course is completed. I think now would be a good time to start trying for a family—"

"I'm sorry, Walt, I'm not ready." Sadness laces my response, a deep-seated sorrow that I can't give him what he wants.

He swipes his hand over his face to mask his disappointment, but I see it nonetheless. "This is a good time for us—"

"Please don't push me on this."

I'm scared if he does I'll tell him how I'm feeling and that will devastate him more than my reluctance to have a baby.

"I'm not pushing, but I want us to have this conversation. We need to be open about what we want and I think having a child now is perfect timing—"

"I said no!"

I leap to my feet and run down the path toward the ocean, thankful the roar of the waves crashing against the sand will drown out the rest of what he has to say.

He won't come after me. He'll give me time to calm down. This is what we do. How we argue. Me growing increasingly impatient and snapping at the slightest provocation, him annoyingly patient, giving me time to work through my angst before apologizing and him forgiving me.

How much longer can we do this?

It's not a healthy relationship, me deliberately pushing him away in the hope he'll end things so I won't be the bad guy. I'm delusional. That won't happen. Walter has the patience of a saint and nothing I do will drive him away.

Which means I'm going to have to tell him the truth.

And break his heart.

I stand at the water's edge for an eternity, letting the waves wash over my ankles. I stare out to sea, scanning the horizon, wishing I'd made smarter choices. Wishing I loved a good man like Walter more.

"You've been out here a long time."

I jump as he lays a hand on my shoulder, surprised he's followed me down here. Usually, he waits at the house for my funk to dissipate.

"I've been thinking," I say, my throat tightening with the hurtful words I have to say but can't get out.

Slowly, gently, he spins me to face him and as I drag my gaze from his chest to meet his, my lungs seize.

He knows.

His eyes are filled with tears and the ache in my chest spreads.

"You want a divorce."

A statement, not a question, and I can't believe that even now, at a time like this when I'm cleaving us in two, he's so calm.

I'm unhappy, but I haven't thought that far ahead. Divorce is so final, so complete. I thought maybe some time apart will help clarify my feelings, but as he looks at me with more understanding than I deserve, I realize he's right. There's no other outcome for us. If I stay, I'll continue to feel stifled and take it out on him, and this kind man doesn't deserve that.

I nod, biting down on my bottom lip to stop the sobs from spilling out.

"I don't make you happy?"

He almost whispers the question and something inside me cracks. I've hurt this man so much and he's done nothing wrong. I'm a bad person. The worst.

I know nothing I say will help him understand but I have to try. I owe him that much.

I place my palms flat against his chest and feel his heart pounding erratically. "You're an amazing man and I've loved being married to you—"

"But you don't love me."

His tone is flat, broken, and I hate myself for hurting him.

"I do love you," I say, and refrain from adding *"but I'm not in love with you."* "To be honest, I fell for you so quickly when we first met and allowed myself to be swept away into a fantasy that I secretly craved. I wanted to escape and you gave me that. You were everything to me at the time. But eighteen isn't a great age to be making decisions that impact a lifelong commitment and—"

"We've been happy," he mutters, sounding hurt and a tad resentful.

"For the most part, yes. But lately…" I shake my head. "I'm starting to take my discontent out on you and you don't deserve it." I clutch at his shirt, almost shaking him, trying to make him understand. "You haven't done anything wrong. This is all on me. And I wish I didn't have to hurt you this way."

"Your mind is made up."

Once again a statement rather than a question from this man who knows me better than I know myself.

"Yes," I whisper, a second before he hauls me into his arms, our sobs mingling, our hearts breaking.

CHAPTER TWENTY-NINE

FRANKIE

NOW

I'm setting up for a live stream when Andre wanders into the kitchen and tries to snaffle a scone from a batch I made earlier.

"Hey, wait until I'm done." I slap his wrist playfully, and he sends me his doleful puppy look, the one that never fails to make me laugh.

"Jeez you're bossy, but I love you." He pecks me on the lips because he knows I've got my "game face" on for the camera and won't want my make-up messed up. "Even if you are a crackpot for obsessing over a coincidence."

I poke my tongue out at him. Before Luna had called him upstairs a few minutes ago, I'd told him about Celeste and Violette showing up at Luna's dance class. Not that I suspect Celeste of enrolling Violette in Luna's class deliberately—and even if she did, what's the harm? She wants to facilitate their friendship—but I've been ruminating over our conversations and the distressing snippets she keeps dropping about Roland.

If Celeste has fled an abusive relationship—and it's sounding increasingly likely that she has—is it wise for me to foster Luna's friendship with Violette? What if her ex locates Celeste and is hell-bent on taking back Violette? I don't want my daughter exposed to any potential danger and it's something I haven't been able to stop thinking about since our outing at the café.

Articulating my fears to Andre will reinforce that I'm overthinking this, so I say, "I'm not obsessing but come on, out of all the studios, what are the odds?"

"Did you ask her about it?"

I nod. "She said she enrolled at Mayberry's first but they called her back saying they'd overbooked, so she chose Madame's instead."

"Sounds plausible."

"Yeah, it's just… she's everywhere, you know? She's barely moved in and she's pushing the girls together every chance she gets."

"She's probably lonely."

I jab him in the chest with a flour-covered finger. "You were the one who told me to be careful, now you're defending her?"

His mouth eases into a bashful smile. "I may have bumped into her while taking out the trash earlier."

"And?"

"She's actually really nice and I feel bad for getting my hackles up at the party."

"She is nice…" I place the last of the scones in the tray and slide them into the oven before dusting off my hands. "You made me wary of her, mister." I poke him again and this time he snags my hand and pulls me flush against him. "I'm blaming you."

"You're a lunatic, you know that, right? First you were jealous of her, thinking she was coming on to me, then when I say be careful you agree, now I'm taking back my preconceptions and you still think there's something wrong."

"Yes to all of the above, except the lunatic part." We kiss, lipstick smudges be damned, and I snuggle into him, loving that after all these years I feel good in his arms. "Though I might've been mad for ever agreeing to marry you."

"Hey." He swats my butt and we play wrestle, until his cell rings.

"A job I'm waiting to hear on." He frowns as he glances at the screen, before picking up his phone and leaving the kitchen.

It reminds me. I never heard back from Walter. With all the parties and socializing and worrying about Celeste, I've forgotten about it. It's unusual because he's a stickler for manners and would always call back.

Andre has gone outside to take his call so I pick up my cell. Once again, Walter doesn't answer and I leave another message.

"Hey, Walt, it's me. Again. Are you okay? Please call me back. If you don't I'm going to harass you at work and you know how much you hate getting personal calls at the bank. Call me."

I hang up and on impulse I call our old beachside cottage number. He may have left his cell in Hartford and can only be contacted in Ziebellville the old-fashioned way. Unlikely, but plausible. However, the landline at the cottage rings out and he's disconnected the answering machine. I feel foolish, worrying about him. He's a grown man and we're nothing but distant friends these days that only speak once a year.

Discounting those extra few fraught calls lately I don't want to think about.

But Walter is a creature of habit. His life runs by rote and no way would he leave his cell anywhere let alone not return a call. But I'm not his keeper and I'll back off, give him a day or two. Maybe he's done with me? Is tired of our annual chat? He seems to enjoy them as much as I do otherwise I would've given up years ago.

No, it's not that, and I can't help but think he's sick or injured or lying in a hospital somewhere. Julia would know but the last thing his partner wants is his ex-wife calling and explaining we still catch up yearly in some warped attempt at sentimentality.

My work threat will do the trick. When we were married he forbade me from calling the bank. He loathed mixing business with pleasure and when he made manager he banned his staff from accepting personal calls too. He'd hate for me to contemplate it, let alone do it, so he'll definitely return my call.

After checking on the scones I arrange the raspberry jelly, whipped cream and fresh strawberries on white serving dishes and clean the counter. I'm doing an English theme for my stream today after a local company sent me an exquisite hand-painted teapot covered in tiny poppies. By the way Andre had been drooling over my handiwork earlier, he'll have no problem demolishing the rest of the scones after I finish filming.

My cell rings and I grab it in relief. But it's not Walter calling me. It's Celeste.

I contemplate hitting the decline button but she'll leave a voice message I'll have to respond to regardless.

I stab at the answer button. "Hey, Celeste."

"Hi, Frankie. Does Luna like jigsaw puzzles?"

Luna loves them. I remember doing her first with her a few years ago when she'd just turned two, a zoo theme comprising sixteen giant pieces that covered the floor of our living room. She delighted in making the pieces fit with my help and loved breaking it up and doing it all over again. Since then, we give her a puzzle for her birthday and Christmas every year and it's a family thing we do, sit with her to complete it.

"She does."

"Vi does too and she's just opened a new one. Would Luna like to come over and do it with her?"

My first instinct is to say no. Despite Andre's reassurances earlier I still can't shake my fear that Celeste's ex is dangerous and by letting her close to my family, particularly Luna, I'm exposing us all.

But Celeste is new to the neighborhood and a single parent trying to do the best for her daughter. And while I don't know enough about her past to allay my fears, I've already let her into our lives and it would be cruel to renege now.

"How about you bring it over here? I've got a few things to do but our living room is quiet." This way, I feel better about not putting Luna in a potentially dangerous situation.

There's the barest hesitation before she says, "That sounds great. We'll be there in five minutes."

She hangs up before I can respond and I wonder anew whether she's lonely too and it's not just Vi who needs friends. I'm not comfortable with sending Luna alone next door but having Celeste and Violette here means I can keep an eye on them. I have a direct line of sight from the kitchen where I'm filming, to the living room, even with the sliding glass doors closed.

Yeah, I've done the right thing.

Then why can't I shake the feeling I may be inadvertently putting my family at risk?

CHAPTER THIRTY
CELESTE

One of the things I always loved about Roland was his manners. My most precious memories of our time together were family lunches and dinners, when we'd sit around the table chatting about anything and everything, and he'd make appreciative sounds every time he forked my food into his mouth. I'd loved preparing him meals: lasagna and lemon cake had been his favorites.

I'd harbored dreams of us marrying one day. He loved Vi instantly and that made me love him all the more. Watching him build sandcastles with her in the early days or patiently posing as she drew him in stick-figure version or their mingled laughter at some whacky cartoon used to make me feel complete.

Until it didn't.

The possibility of having another child, a sibling for Vi, drove an irreversible wedge between us. It resulted in me moving to Hambridge Heights to get away and Vi not having a father anymore. He left me no other option.

"Hurry up, Mom, ring the doorbell." Vi's impatient, practically juggling the puzzle box in her hands, as she bumps my hip with her shoulder.

I do as I'm told and Frankie opens the door looking like she's stepped off the pages of a magazine. She's wearing a red sundress covered in white daisies, her hair snagged in a high, glossy ponytail and her make-up flawless.

"Are you going out?"

"No, I'm about to start filming, but come on in. You'll be doing me a favor keeping Luna occupied with that puzzle." She smiles at Vi. "That looks like fun."

"It's an octopus." Vi brandishes the box toward Frankie. "I saw one at the beach once with my dad. Mom's made his favorite cake. It's really yum."

Frankie's eyes meet mine and she's awkward, unsure how to respond to my daughter's mention of a father who's no longer around. She has no idea what I've been through. She leads the perfect life and for a brief moment I wonder how she'd feel if Luna didn't have her dad around anymore? Would she be resilient, like me, or fall apart?

"I'm looking forward to trying it," Frankie finally says, opening the door wider. "Come in."

"Thanks for having us over," I say, trying not to let my envy show as I step inside. If Frankie looks like she belongs in a magazine so does her house, with its gleaming honey-colored floorboards, trendy prints in vibrant crimson, orange and peacock-blue arranged artfully on the walls and understated modern furniture that appears comfortable but is probably worth my quarterly wage.

"Head into the living room, make yourself at home," she says, taking the cake from my hands when I hold it out to her. "And thanks for this. We can have it after I finish."

It's a statement, not a question, and I bristle at her take-charge attitude. Why did she invite us over if she had to work? When she'd mentioned on the phone she had a few things to do, I'd envisaged her tidying up, not filming.

As Luna bounds into the room, waving hi to me and making a beeline for Vi, who's already sitting on the floor in front of a coffee table with the puzzle box open, I see Frankie's doting gaze follow her daughter and I know why she invited us over.

She didn't want to send Luna to my house alone.

I'm disappointed. I thought we were becoming friends. What does she think, that I'm a crap mother and I won't look after her daughter as well as mine? That I don't have boundaries and rules for a child to follow? It's undermining and I don't like feeling like a bad mother when I'm not. I'll do anything for Violette.

I hide my frustration and smile. "You go ahead and do your stream. The girls and me will be fine in here." I sit on a suede sofa not far from the girls and she hesitates, as if she can't bear to leave me alone with them.

Gritting my teeth, I make a shooing motion with my hands. "Go. The sooner you finish the sooner I can have a coffee with that cake."

Her smile is tight and I belatedly realize I've insulted her by implying she hasn't offered me a drink. When I'm nervous I'm not good around people and this is one of those times, saying the wrong thing.

"Truly, Frankie, we'll be fine. Do your work and we can relax later."

"It should take about fifteen minutes, twenty max."

"No worries."

She hesitates for a second longer before heading into the kitchen, where she places my cake on a side counter, then closes the glass doors to the living room. She can still see us, probably her intention, though considering her picture-perfect kitchen I'm not surprised she always films there.

I re-watched a few of her videos last night after Vi had gone to bed. They exhausted me. How someone could appear so confident in front of a camera, so competent as a mother, I'll never know. I'd watched her make raspberry jelly and cucumber pickles, whizzing around the kitchen and smiling at the camera like a natural. She's pretty in a wholesome way, with all that thick shiny blonde hair and big blue eyes. I'd been beyond envious.

Now I get to watch her perform again, though I can't hear what she's saying, like a mute film, all glossy perfection without the distracting chatter. She's demonstrating how to make scones, with a pre-prepared batch off to one side to bring in at her grand ta-da moment. Even from a distance they look light and fluffy.

I'd made Roland scones once. They'd had the texture of rocks. He hadn't approved.

Does Andre appreciate his wife? He has a great body, which means he must do a hell of a lot of working out if he consumes everything she prepares. He's handsome, in a boyish way, with that underlying hint of spontaneity many women find appealing, like they don't know what to expect from him. He unnerves me a little.

"What happened to your dad?"

I tear my gaze away from Frankie and focus on the girls, curious to hear Vi's response to Luna's innocent question. She'd been at a birthday party during my last argument with Roland, the day I'd finally realized I had to escape. It had been ugly and despite doing my utmost to protect Vi from the worst of it I fear she still blames me for taking her away from her father.

"He's not going to visit us anymore," Vi says, handing Luna a corner piece from the jigsaw.

"How come?" Luna takes the piece and lays it on the table.

"Mom said sometimes parents don't get along and it's better to have a fresh start." Vi glances at me somewhat fearfully. "Isn't that right, Mom?"

"It is, sweetheart."

A fresh start far from the pain of the past.

"You can share my dad if you want," Luna says, oblivious to the way my heart seizes. "Not all the time, but just if you need to do dad stuff like open jars and reach into the top cupboards."

Vi frowns, as if she's never heard of sharing fathers, before shaking her head. "Don't be silly. He's your dad. He can't be mine too."

I release the breath I've inadvertently been holding and silently wish Frankie would hurry up. I need a coffee, pronto. Not that caffeine will soothe my jangling nerves. I need to get out of this house, away from its cloying perfection.

Perfect home, perfect couple, perfect family.

But if anyone knows there's no such thing as perfection, I do.

CHAPTER THIRTY-ONE
SAYLOR

I wait until Lloyd's out for his run before heading across the park to knock on Ruston's door. I know he's home because I've been watching out the window like some bored housewife from the sixties, spying on the neighbors. I don't like the woman I'm becoming since moving here but I need to be on the lookout.

Being blackmailed does that to a person.

I remember the day I received the first phone call. I'd just announced my pregnancy at thirteen weeks and had been high on hormones and congratulations. Once my folks absorbed the news, they threw us a celebratory dinner and invited all the church elders, who bestowed copious blessings on us. While their religious fervor made me uncomfortable, it had nothing on my reaction when my cell rang the next morning and I heard that sinister, distorted voice extorting me for money.

Pay up or my secret will be revealed.

I could've dismissed it as a crank, but the blackmailer knew details and I realized then what I had to do.

Move to Hambridge Heights and set my own blackmail plan into action.

I don't worry about the neighborhood gossips this time because I have a legitimate excuse to visit Ruston: issuing my dinner party invitation. I have no idea if he'll accept. I'm half-hoping he won't. But it had been Lloyd's idea to invite him and it'll look weird if I don't.

While I felt relieved after talking to Ruston at the share-plate supper—having our first confrontation after the last time I'd seen him five months ago hadn't been as bad as I'd imagined—it didn't last, and in some perverse method of self-torture, I looked him up online. Since we broke up, his photography and modeling careers have escalated and he's done several big shoots. I'm happy for him. I'm less happy with the photos of him draped over that campaign manager, the one whose house he's living in, his "friend."

It's silly, as I have no right to be jealous, and I felt petty when critically appraising her shoulder-length mousy brown hair, snub nose, murky gray eyes and tiny teeth that vaguely resembled a rat. I'm not this person, bitchy and judgmental, so I'd been grateful when Lloyd had come home and I'd quickly closed the browser, ashamed of my online reconnaissance.

I'm about to knock again when the door opens and he's there, sexy as hell in low-slung denim and a fitted white T-shirt that clearly delineates every muscle I've had the pleasure of running my hands and lips over. Damn memories.

"Hey, Say. Can't keep away from me, huh?"

He's a conceited ass and I wish he didn't have the power to still make my heart beat faster. But I need to relax, to issue my invitation in the name of fostering neighborly harmony and proving to my husband Ruston means nothing to me anymore.

"We're having a dinner party and you're invited." My tone is friendly but I'm faking it hard.

"Really?"

His grin is smug, like he knows exactly how uncomfortable I am around him.

"I thought it might be nice, getting to know some of the neighbors in a more intimate setting."

"Intimate, huh?"

I scrub a hand over my face, wishing I could eradicate his smug image. Was he always this much of a jerk?

"Look, Ruston, can we leave the past in the past and just hang out as friends?"

"That depends."

"On?"

"Whether you still have a thing for me."

Damn him. He hasn't changed a bit. Too cocky for his own good. The problem with Ruston—that my parents had seen way before I had—is his complete self-absorption that means he can never commit to any woman because he's too in love with himself. He gets off on attention and that makes him bad partner material. Inherently selfish, he'd been late for our dates more times than I can count and preferred partying with equally beautiful model types than a quiet dinner with me.

I need to focus on his bad qualities and forget he can also be sweet and attentive and generous. "I know this is your *thing*, flirting with any woman over the legal age. But I'm over it."

He quirks an eyebrow, as if he knows that's BS. "I'm just messing with you. Sure, I'll come. When's this dinner party?"

"Friday night."

He flashes me a smile and damn if I don't feel it in the one place I don't want to: my heart. "I'll be there. Want me to bring anything?"

"No, all good."

I stand there way longer than I should, wanting to say so much to this man—why did you hurt me, why wasn't I enough for you, why are you here, now, disrupting my life when it's bad enough—but I don't. His answers to my questions won't change anything, and I have enough drama in my life without adding to it.

"Everything okay?" He's looking at me with concern. Too little too late.

"Yeah."

But as I turn away, tears sting my eyes, because nothing is okay—my life as I know it is in danger of imploding.

CHAPTER THIRTY-TWO

FRANKIE

THEN

When I met Walter I thought I knew what love was. That love embodied comfort and stability, and having someone kind and reliable to come home to every day. Meeting Andre made me realize I was wrong.

Ever since I first saw Andre strolling along the beach outside the cottage in Ziebellville, I felt something shift, making me off-kilter, like the first time Walt took me out in his dinghy. I'd still been living in the cottage at the time—even after we divorced Walter let me live there until I figured out where I wanted to go—and I'd just come home from work, finishing a marketing plan for the grocery chain in New Haven I freelanced for. I was sitting out back on a deck chair when he'd walked right up to me and said hi. His deep voice sent a shiver of excitement through me and when he'd asked me out, brazen and confident, I accepted.

We've been inseparable since that first momentous meeting. He's a free spirit and the opposite of Walter in every way. Andre is laid-back, carefree and funny. He makes me laugh every day with his acerbic observations on everything from our favorite bagels at the corner store to the newest boutique opening on the Upper East Side.

I thought I'd loved Walter but now I know this is love, this heady, hedonistic, crazy, overwhelming emotion that inspires me.

Maybe Walter has the same realization too. He's back with Julia, the girlfriend he dumped because of me, and I'm glad. I can't imagine what it must've been like for her to learn I'd divorced him, that I'd broken up their relationship for nothing. I suspected she'd been behind those incidents when Walt popped the question, especially as they stopped after we married and she probably realized our relationship was serious. Regardless, I'm pleased Julia and Walt are back together. He deserves to be happy, and we haven't seen each other by mutual agreement because while our divorce was amicable it'd be too awkward. I don't need a reminder of how I broke his heart.

We made a clean break, and when Andre asked me to move in with him shortly after the decadent weekend we spent in bed after we met, the timing was perfect.

Andre's job as a freelance graphic designer affords him a beautiful apartment in Manhattan, and as I sit here, stroking the wedding band he slipped on my finger months ago—a spontaneous, chaotic, wild decision that feels right—I'm madly in love for the first time in my life.

Everything is perfect.

I hear the front door open and I leap to my feet, eager to see him. I'm wearing a dress he loves, lemon dotted with tiny stars, strapless and skimming my knees. I wore it as a welcome home and because he's been away, I know I won't be wearing it for much longer.

My steps falter as he dumps his overnight bag near the door and kicks it away. He can barely meet my eyes, and I know by the expression on his face that something is seriously wrong. After being away on a work trip he usually greets me with a giant smile, before sweeping me into his arms and kissing me senseless. We rarely make it to the bedroom.

"Hey, honey," I say, crossing the room to hug him. "Everything okay?"

He doesn't answer and when our gazes meet, my heart stops. Guilt, opaque and murky, darkens his eyes to indigo when I can usually see gold flecks in the blue depths.

"I'm sorry, babe, I'm so, so sorry."

He opens his arms but as I step forward he lowers them, as if he can't bear to touch me. That's when I know the worst has happened and I can't breathe.

"What did you do?"

He stares at the floor, his hair brushing his collar, and I irrationally wonder if whoever he cheated on me with loves his hair long as much as I do.

"It was one night. She meant nothing." Seven words that hack my heart in two. "And if it makes you feel any better, I'm never going back to Hartford again. I swear it."

Hartford. Like the cosmos is having one giant laugh at my expense. I'd fled to Hartford from Long Island with Walter, only to escape Hartford and my ex-husband, yet here it is again, front and center in my life, in the worst possible way.

"Who is she?"

"Nobody. A meaningless distraction because I lost a major account and drank too much. I'm mortified..." He trails off and when he raises his face I see tears tracking down his cheeks. "I love you, babe, and I'll do whatever it takes to get us back on track."

I can't speak. I want to say so much. I want to scream and rant, "How could you do this to us after only eight months of marriage? Do I mean that little to you? Were our vows meaningless?"

"Frankie, say something."

Once he started calling me Frankie, it stuck. I didn't like it at the start but shedding good girl Francesca along with my first marriage seemed like a smart thing to do at the time.

I can't help but think of Walter. He never would've cheated on me. Hell, he'd made his views on cheating clear from the start when he wouldn't instigate something with me until he'd dumped his girlfriend. Guess there's a lot to be said for staidness over impulsivity.

"I need some time away to get my head together," I say, holding up my hand to stop him when he reaches for me. "If we're to have any kind of chance of getting past this, I need some time alone. Can you give me that?"

He doesn't want to. He probably fears I'll leave and never come back. In this moment, I'm unsure what I'll do but I know one thing. I need to get away from him. I need breathing space.

"Where will you go?"

"Anywhere but here."

I head for the bedroom to pack, because I know exactly where I need to go. The only place I've ever felt truly safe.

CHAPTER THIRTY-THREE

FRANKIE

NOW

By the viewer comments I scan after I turn the camera off, they haven't noticed I've ended my live stream earlier than usual. Only one woman, Kazz70 from Oklahoma, mentions how quick it was. I don't care. I can't stand by for another second, fake smiling for the camera, when I can see Celeste chatting to my daughter.

She's so good with the girls but I'm anxious. The worrying things she's said about her ex is giving me insomnia and I can't help but feel a little uncomfortable with her being around Luna. If Celeste fled out of necessity, her ex could turn up here. If so, is he the sort of person who might do something drastic, like take back his daughter?

My mind is whirling as I stand here looking at them play. Am I being ridiculous, like Andre said? I know some of my reticence toward Celeste can be attributed to my wariness of strangers in general. It doesn't take an Einstein to figure out when this started. My parents were always bringing strangers home and treating them like long-lost friends. Unfortunately, I discovered why on my eighteenth birthday.

I'd looked up swinging online once, after I'd married Walter. I couldn't fathom that kind of lifestyle. I would've scratched another woman's eyes out if she went near my husband, let alone had sex with him. He'd met my parents a grand total of three times in the week he came back to Gledhill and liked them, so he didn't understand why I cut all ties with them after we left Gledhill. I told him we had a severe falling-out that was irrevocable. Being a peacemaker he'd wanted me to reconcile, which is why we invited them to the wedding, but they didn't show up and I never forgave them. He didn't understand my adamant stance. Andre hadn't either, so when he insisted we invite them to visit after Luna had been born, I told him: about what happened on my eighteenth, my parents' life choices, and how I'd cut off all contact. Thankfully, Andre sided with me and he never pushed the issue again. I do feel bad at times, that my folks haven't seen their granddaughter, but Luna is my priority and I don't want them insinuating their way back into my life for her sake.

I resent them for installing this seed of mistrust I have for strangers. If I couldn't trust my own parents, who can I trust? Since I discovered the truth, I've been wary, reluctant to allow people to get close. I don't make friends easily and I blame them. They shattered my belief in them and it's hard to trust my judgment since. Maybe that's why I'm worrying so much about everything Celeste has said?

I slice the lemon cake into small wedges and place it on a tray alongside two juice boxes for the girls and a coffee pot with mugs. She sees me approach the glass doors and leaps to her feet to cross the room and slide them open.

"Thanks, got my hands full."

"Here, let me help." Before I can protest she's taken the tray from my hands and places it on a side table next to the sofa. "Girls, cake and apple juice."

Luna and Violette, who've been engrossed in the puzzle and have completed half of it, yell "Yum" in unison and I laugh as they choose the biggest wedges of cake, grab a juice box each, and return to their puzzle.

"They seem to be enjoying themselves," I say, pouring the coffee. "Cream and sugar?"

"Cream, no sugar, please. And, yes, that puzzle has kept them entertained." She points at the kitchen. "How did your live go?"

I add cream to her mug, stir the coffee, and hand it to her. "Good. One of my easier ones."

"Are they usually that quick?"

I feel heat seeping into my cheeks and hope she can't guess why I wound up my filming so quickly. "Sometimes. Scones are pretty easy to make. I like to mix it up, have longer sessions interspersed with shorter. Keeps things interesting."

Her nose crinkles. "I could never do that, get up in front of people and talk about cooking and stuff."

"You get used to it." I sip my coffee, savoring the bitterness. Walter put me onto this roasted blend many years ago and I've been hooked ever since. "I'm an introvert but talking to a camera on a computer is nothing like talking to that many people face to face."

"It sure beats accounting in the interesting stakes." She sips at her coffee and a strange expression crosses her face.

"You don't like it? I can make you another drink."

She grimaces and lowers the mug. "I rarely drink coffee." She makes circles at her temple. "The caffeine makes me go loopy. It's been months since I last had a cup and I forgot how strong it can be."

"I can make you tea or—"

"It's fine, it's always that first sip that throws me."

To prove it, she raises the mug to her lips and takes several sips, appearing more appreciative this time. "See? Fine."

"Okay, but if you want something else, let me know."

"No worries."

We sip our coffees in silence, content to listen to the girls jabber. The lemon cake has been demolished and the last of the juice slurped through the straws so they've returned to poring over the puzzle. They're cute together, Violette's dark hair a contrast against Luna's light, their heads bent close.

"Vi's an introvert too," Celeste says softly, her gaze on the girls too. "She got that from her father."

She's given me the perfect opportunity to find out more about her ex and, hopefully, provide reassurance I'm worrying for nothing. "What was he like?"

"A nice guy." Her lips compress. "Until he wasn't."

So much for allaying my fears. Her response makes me more suspicious. I have no idea what that means and want to ask more, but before I can she continues, "He cheated on me."

I hear the slightest quiver in her voice, an underlying hint of pain, and I'm catapulted back to the night Andre confessed his infidelity. I recognize that pain because I've lived it. It endears Celeste to me like nothing else can.

"What did you do?" I ask.

"I forgave him." She shrugs like it means little, when I can see the devastation darkening her eyes. "For Violette's sake."

I never over-share and I'm not about to tell her about Andre's slip-up, but she pins me with a glare that makes me want to squirm. "Have you ever been through something like that?"

I don't want to tell her but she's opened up to me and if anyone understands betrayal, I do. She's had a rough time and we have that in common. The least I can do is support her rather than allow my irrational fears, obsessing over Luna's safety from a perceived threat that may not eventuate, to ruin our friendship.

I nod. "I've been betrayed in the past." I leave it at that, not willing to reveal any more.

Thankfully, Luna interrupts. "Mom, can we have more cake?"

I look to Celeste for approval and when she nods, I say, "Sure, sweetie. But one piece each otherwise you'll spoil your dinner."

"Yes, Mom," she says, in that exasperated way only a precocious five-year-old can manage.

Before Celeste can probe for more information about my past, I ask her about the dance studio's end of term recital and what part Violette is playing. Thankfully, she accepts my change of subject and we make small talk for the next fifteen minutes until I drop a hint about having to do grocery shopping. It's a task Luna loves and I know that, otherwise I wouldn't have used it as an excuse because I know Celeste will offer to mind her and if it's any other task than grocery shopping Luna would bug me to let her.

We walk Celeste and Violette to the door and I'm oddly relieved after I close it. While I like finding common ground with Celeste beyond our daughters—albeit us both having cheating spouses—I can't shake my misgivings. Every time she shares a snippet of her life with me, like her ex being a nice guy until he wasn't, I second-guess my decision to foster a friendship with her, and between our daughters.

As Luna starts to prattle about all the stuff she talked to Violette about, I know I can't lower my guard just yet. I need to listen to my gut and, in this instance, it's telling me to be wary for the sake of my daughter.

CHAPTER THIRTY-FOUR
CELESTE

After the last time Vi asked me about her father and I snapped at her, she hasn't broached the subject. But we barely make it home and close the front door before she says, "I don't want to share Luna's daddy. I want mine. Can we call him?"

Pain stabs my heart for all we've lost but I need to put on a brave face for Vi. She's blameless in all this and I won't allow the drama of my relationship with Roland to taint her. I wish things could've been different for us but Roland had left me no choice but to flee.

I have to protect my daughter at all costs, but that doesn't stop me from sobbing into my pillow most nights when I lie awake unable to sleep because of how we ended.

I lead her into the kitchen, sit, and pull her onto my lap. "We've been through this. Your dad doesn't want to see us anymore."

"But he loves me. Even if he hates you."

I'm shocked by her vehemence as she glares at me, her bottom lip thrust out in a stubborn gesture so like Roland my chest aches with remembrance.

"Why do you think he hates me?"

"Because I heard you yelling at him that last time we saw him, before I went to that birthday party and he didn't visit anymore. Daddy hates loud voices. I know that. So he must hate you."

"He doesn't hate me."

But what I hate is that Vi overheard us fighting, I hate that Roland did this to us too, and I need to make her understand.

"Sweetheart, sometimes parents don't always agree. And rather than using calm voices like we tell children, we argue and it can get loud. It doesn't mean anything."

"Yes it does." She folds her arms and her usually soft, pliant body is rigid on my lap. "It means you hate each other."

I sigh, knowing all too well how hard it is to rationalize anything when Vi is in this mood.

"But we love you."

"Daddy likes to talk to me. He told me many times. He says he likes hearing my voice, so why can't we call him?"

My obstinate daughter isn't going to give in so despite every self-preservation mechanism telling me not to call, I do it for Vi. I pull up his number, relegated to contacts and out of my favorites on my cell, and hit the call button. Vi starts jiggling excitedly on my lap and I set her on her feet. I know what will happen. Roland won't answer. My name flashing on his screen will ensure it.

When his voicemail kicks in, I hold the phone out to Vi so she can leave a message. She's disappointed but this is better than her pestering me to call him again.

"Hi, Daddy, it's me, Violette. I miss you. I wish I could see you. I want to talk to you. I have a new friend. And I'm doing ballet now. We have a park outside our house. It's fun to play there. Bye."

Tears prickle my eyes as I hit the call end button. I may despise Roland for what he did to us but he's still Vi's father and I have to remember that.

"When will I see him again?"

I stare at my daughter, filled with self-loathing that I have to lie to the only person in this world I love. "I don't know, sweetie. But you've left a message. Let's wait and see, huh?"

Vi appears mollified and scoots out of the kitchen without a backward glance. I hear her running upstairs and I sag against the back of the chair.

Not having Roland in our lives any longer will get easier with time but as an acute ache spreads through my chest, I realize I miss him as much as Vi.

I shouldn't. He's no good for us.

I ran away to Hambridge Heights for a fresh start and that's what I need to focus on. Building a new life for Violette and me. Our family.

CHAPTER THIRTY-FIVE
SAYLOR

By the time Friday night comes around, I'm a wreck. I haven't been sleeping well, envisaging all sorts of scenarios where this dinner party ends in disaster. Maybe I haven't thought this through? Trying to extort someone over the phone is one thing, but faking it to their face while upping the ante? I never thought I'd be capable of something like this but whoever is blackmailing me has left me no choice. I need to protect what's mine.

As for Ruston, he's a complication I don't need but I'm counting on his discretion. He won't deliberately hurt me, though that's exactly what he's done countless times before. But this is different. We're not involved and he knows I'm happily married so he won't reveal our past. But I know sitting across the dinner table from him and pretending like we're nothing more than acquaintances is going to be difficult. Am I that good an actress?

I know the answer when Lloyd catches sight of me and his eyes light up, like I'm a goddess. If this good man remotely suspects what I've become embroiled in he'll be devastated. I hope when I tell him the truth he'll forgive me but is he that much of a saint? Sadly, I fear that once he discovers my treachery, I'll be left a poor single parent in debt to a monster that has the potential to ruin my life: more precisely, the lives of those closest to me.

If my secret gets out, it won't affect me much. People who know me would glance at me sideways, gossip, maybe avoid me, but

ultimately my life would go on. My parents on the other hand…
having a well-known pastor who runs a church with branches
in Syracuse, Buffalo, Poughkeepsie and Saratoga Springs, and
broadcasts his sermons to hundreds of thousands more, mired in
disgrace because of me… my family will be ruined.

Growing up, my parents had insisted I know the responsibilities
that came with being a pastor's daughter, one of them being to
avoid scandal at all costs. I'd rolled my eyes at the time and snuck
around behind their backs every chance I got in our hometown
of Syracuse, until I witnessed firsthand the kind of damage a kid
can wreak on their parents. A pastor in a nearby town had a son
who got caught selling weed and the entire congregation turned
on the pastor, abandoning his church, leaving him with nothing
but a tarnished reputation.

After that I'd been more circumspect in the forbidden stuff
I got up to—sex, drugs, drinking, the usual—until I finished
school and left Syracuse as fast as humanly possible. Though
even at college I'd been more careful than most, determined to
do my folks proud. I saw how hard they worked, how much they
supported the community and those less fortunate, how utterly
selfless they were and no way in hell did I want to be responsible
for ruining all that.

Since then my father's popularity as a pastor has only grown.
I never imagined his weekly services would be broadcast let alone
watched by so many. Not that I'm terribly religious now but I do
occasionally tune in because he's a good dad and I love him for
not forcing his beliefs down my throat. He's a dynamic speaker
and can hold a congregation spellbound, and together with my
mom they do a lot of good for many people.

If my secret ever gets out, it will destroy them. I can't be
responsible for that. I won't.

"You look amazing." Lloyd plants a soft kiss on my neck. "Tell
me again why we have to entertain these virtual strangers?"

"They're not strangers, they're our neighbors and we may need their help when this baby comes, that's why I'm doing this."

"You think that pretty boy from across the park is going to help us with our son?" He studies my face and I manage a smile, wondering if Lloyd has a sixth sense. He never teases me about other men but there's something about Ruston that's making him edgy. It convinces me I've done the right thing in not telling him about my past. My husband's a calm man but I have a feeling he'll be shattered by my deception if he discovers how big a role Ruston had in my life.

"He might." I playfully slap his chest, desperately trying to blot out the appealing image of Ruston bouncing my baby on his knee. "Already told you, those pregnancy books terrify me so I'll need all the help I can get when this one puts in an appearance. I want to make friends with the women at least."

I take his hand and press it low against my belly, knowing he melts every time I do this. His goofy grin has me biting back a relieved sigh. He's been suitably distracted.

"Just don't sit him next to me, okay? I don't need you making comparisons between the two of us."

"Don't be silly." I force a light laugh and place my hand over his, and as his moves in a slow caress I really hope I'm doing the right thing.

Two hours later, I'm not so sure.

The steaks have been grilled and consumed, the salads demolished and I'm slicing the cheesecake to serve as dessert when Lloyd comes into the kitchen.

"Need a hand?" My husband's handsome in a navy polo and jeans, his hair uncombed, appealing in a rumpled kind of way, but nothing on the perfection of Ruston, who's incredibly sexy in black slacks and silk shirt, and I hate myself for making the comparison.

"Thanks, but I've got it covered." I slide the server under a slice and place it carefully on a plate before adding a swirl of whipped cream on the side. "Though you can help me take these plates in once I'm done."

"Anything for you, sweetheart." He presses a kiss to my lips. "And before you say 'I told you so' later, I take back what I said about Ruston making a play for you." He points to the dining room. "He seems very enamored with Frankie."

I'm relieved my acting skills are better than I thought, and Lloyd has dropped the idea I have some kind of connection with Ruston. It will make things easier when the truth comes out.

"They're sitting next to each other at a dinner party making small talk, big deal. Stop being such a gossip."

Lloyd shrugs, his grin bashful. "Maybe moving into a close-knit community is making me a gossip, but I don't think Andre likes Ruston chatting up his wife."

I brandish the server toward the dining room, waving away his concern. "Frankie's being polite. What do you expect her to do, ignore him?"

"No, but she's hanging on his every word and I can sense the tension." He grimaces and swipes a hand over his face. "I've actually been enjoying myself but now, I think we should wind it up."

"Good idea," I say, sliding the last piece of cheesecake onto a plate. I agree with my husband. Nothing has gone to plan this evening and rather than put more pressure on the person I'm blackmailing, I've ended up feeling on edge. "Let's have dessert, then gently nudge them out the door."

"Sounds good to me," he says, and chuckles as I hand him a few dessert plates. "I'm just glad the lovely Frankie is melting in a puddle when Ruston talks to her and not you."

"The lovely Frankie?" I pretend to pout. "Are you trying to make me jealous?"

He grins. "Is it working?"

"You're a one woman man and don't you forget it." I waggle my finger at him before picking up the remaining plates, balancing two on my opposite forearm and holding one in my hand, mimicking his expertise.

"Duly noted," he says, amusement glinting in his eyes at the thought of making me jealous. "For what it's worth, I think you did a good thing here tonight, inviting the neighbors over."

"Thanks." I melt under his admiration. "Your support means the world to me. You know that, right?"

"Yeah, I know." He squares his shoulders, striking a pose. "I also know you find me irresistible."

I smile, wishing our relationship could always be this good. But I know it's futile, because when I tell him the truth, it will change everything.

CHAPTER THIRTY-SIX

FRANKIE

THEN

When I let myself into the beach cottage using the spare key hidden in a conch shell tucked under the back step, I'm surprised to find the living room blinds up and a tempting aroma of garlic bread and simmering tomatoes wafting from the kitchen.

I'd called Walter to ask him if it was okay if I spent a few days here and he'd agreed, saying the cottage had been vacant for months since the last tenants left and he hadn't been near the place. Either he has squatters who cook divine Italian food or he's forgotten he's rented the place out to someone else.

"Hello?" I call out, placing my suitcase near the door before making my way to the kitchen.

"In here."

I'm surprised to hear Walter's deep voice. The last thing I want is my ex-husband hanging around while I contemplate strangling my current one.

I enter the kitchen to find the small dining table set for two, with the mismatched crockery we'd once joked about, a bottle of uncorked Merlot next to a bowl of salad in the middle. "What are you doing here?"

"You sounded pretty bad on the phone so I thought you could do with a meal." He lifts the lid on a pot and my memory receptors leap for joy. About the only good meal he cooked while we were married was spaghetti bolognaise and I realize I haven't eaten since last night. When Andre had arrived home this morning I'd had an orange juice, foolishly thinking we could grab brunch at our favorite deli.

"You didn't have to do all this." I point at the table. "But I'm glad you did."

He dishes the spaghetti onto two plates and covers the pasta with bolognaise sauce. It gives me a chance to look at him. He hasn't changed at all since I last saw him two and half years ago, in this very house when we parted and he wished me well. He didn't come near me during our year-long separation and when I informed him why I'd be leaving the cottage, to move to Manhattan with Andre, he'd been upset yet stoic.

There's comfort in familiarity and when he turns and catches me watching him, the corners of his mouth kick into a smile of understanding. "Long time no see, huh?"

I nod. "I was just thinking that."

Rather than badger me for information, he places the plates on the table and gestures at the seat opposite. "Let's eat."

After not being able to swallow a sip of water past the lump in my throat since Andre delivered his bombshell this morning, I find myself ravenous and I eat two helpings of pasta, salad and garlic bread before I speak a word.

True to form, Walter leaves me to eat, his gaze watchful but content, like he's pleased with me for eating. When I drain my second glass of Merlot and he lays down his cutlery in the middle of his empty plate, I'm ready to talk.

I could hedge around why I'm here, even lie about it and make up a story, but in the end I blurt, "Andre cheated on me."

He recoils, his mouth twisted in distaste. "Stupid bastard."

Walter isn't one for swearing and my eyebrows rise in surprise. "Cursing? I see you've picked up some bad habits since I've been gone?"

"Fuck, yeah."

We laugh and I marvel at how easily we've slipped into our old camaraderie. Being with Walter has always been comfortable and while I may have resented his presence initially I'm glad he's here. Admitting out loud what Andre did has dissipated its hold on me, like maybe I have a chance of eventually moving past it. Or maybe that's Walt's calming effect on me, the way he truly listens to anything I have to say.

"You said on the phone you needed a few days out here to think?"

"Something like that." I shrug. "We've been happy, so when he confessed this morning it threw me. He had a drunken one-night stand with a woman in Hartford while on a work trip."

"The man's an idiot to cheat on you."

He sounds so outraged on my behalf I want to hug him. He's always supported me and despite our divorce he's still on my side. It means a lot, especially when I'm still reeling.

"Honestly? I don't want to be twenty-five and have two divorces under my belt so I'll probably go back and make a go of it once I calm down." Sadness wells in my chest. "Though I'm still so damn mad at him I could hit something."

He pretends to duck. "Do you want me to go mess him up?"

The thought of sedate Walt getting physical with anyone makes me smile. "You'd do that for me?"

"You know I'd do anything for you."

I know he's joking but his serious expression makes me realize how much I used to depend on this man, how I knew without a shadow of a doubt he was always in my corner. I miss that reliability, especially now Andre has shattered my trust in him.

"You're a good guy, Walt, but I need to deal with this on my own. Besides, I love him and I'm not willing to throw that away."

He flinches and I'm stricken as I realize what I've implied. That I didn't love him so I willingly threw him away.

"I'm sorry. I didn't mean it like that—"

"It's okay."

But it isn't. I see pain lingering in his gaze before it dips to his plate and I'm gutted that I've caused him heartache again.

So I do what I've always done when uncomfortable. I deflect. "How's Julia?"

"Away at a conference."

Which explains his presence here.

"You two are solid?"

He takes an eternity to answer and when he finally raises his gaze to meet mine, he's resigned.

"She's not you."

His declaration makes my breath hitch and then I'm crying, the tears I've been suppressing all day spurting out of my eyes in a torrent.

"Hell, Francesca, I'm sorry."

His use of my full name makes me cry harder and he pushes back his chair and comes around the table to drag me into his arms. I bury my head into his chest, the fragrance of his laundry detergent and citrus soap mingling in a familiarity that makes me want to cling to him forever.

He strokes my back as I cry, his head nestled next to mine, his soothing words like "It's okay" not helping as much as the familiar lulling cadence of his voice.

When my tears finally stop, I'm still clutching at his shirt and it reminds me of the last time he comforted me on the beach when I told him we were over.

I can't believe this man is as dependable now as when I first met him, how he's still willing to be here for me despite the way I treated him.

I ease back but he doesn't let me go, his arms wrapped tightly around my waist, and when I look into his eyes I know he's offering me more than a hug.

"You're not a cheater and neither am I," I murmur, hating how tempted I am to prove the opposite.

"It's up to you," he says, rubbing the small of my back in slow, concentric circles. "You'll always be the one I love, Francesca, and I hate to see you hurting. If all I can do is offer you comfort for a night, I'm okay with that."

"You'd let me use you?" I leave off *"again?"*

"I'm here if you need me."

He releases me, giving me a chance to decide.

This is wrong on so many levels.

But as I look into Walter's eyes and the peace I'm seeking washes over me, I know what I want.

CHAPTER THIRTY-SEVEN
FRANKIE
NOW

For someone who acts like the hostess with the mostess online I'm not good in social situations and I don't hold dinner parties. I've never had to. With Walter, he was more of a homebody than me and only socialized with bank colleagues occasionally, usually at a bar for farewell drinks or to welcome a new worker. Living with Andre in Manhattan, his graphic design crowd wasn't the type to host dinner parties. They preferred lurking in dingy underground jazz bars or attending gallery openings. After tagging along to the first few I deferred and he never minded.

So I have no idea what the seating etiquette is and am surprised to find my name tag at the end of the table next to Ruston, with Saylor on his other side, which places Andre opposite me, Celeste to his right and Lloyd at the end. I'm relieved to see Celeste at ease with Andre and my husband showing no hint of his once-wariness toward our new neighbor.

But I'm also awkward sitting next to a good-looking guy like Ruston and because I'm hopeless at small talk our limited interaction is clumsy. To make matters worse, he seems to be as reserved as me so our conversation, what little there is of it, is stilted at best. Saylor tries to engage him several times but he almost turns his back on her and angles toward me.

Increasingly gauche, I start drinking, consuming three glasses of Chardonnay in quick succession, and my reservations loosen.

"What do you do, Ruston?" I ask, trying to make more of an effort.

"I'm a photographer, but I do a lot of modeling too."

As he looks at me, I notice his incredible eyes, a unique pale green, like jade mixed with aquamarine, a color I've never seen before. They're fringed with long dark lashes the same color as his dark brown hair, an attractive contrast. I'm oddly flustered and it doesn't help when I note his sharp cheekbones and strong jaw remind me of the gorgeous heroes in the romance novels I devoured by the truckload when married to Walter.

"You definitely should be in front of the camera, not behind it."

The corners of his mouth quirk in amusement and I realize I've spoken aloud, articulating my thoughts. Heat flushes my cheeks and I'm beyond embarrassed.

"Thanks for the compliment." He smiles, looking more relaxed.

"It's the wine," I say, picking up my glass and bringing it to my lips. "I rarely drink."

"You should, if it makes you that honest." He leans closer, like he's about to impart some great secret. "I like it."

I have no idea how to respond. I didn't date in high school and Walter was my first boyfriend. Before bumping into Andre at the beach house I hadn't entertained the idea of being with another man so soon. Only having two relationships with men means I have no idea if Ruston is flirting with me. By Andre's glare when I glance up after Lloyd places a dessert plate in front of me, he is and my husband doesn't like it.

I flash Andre a "you're my one and only" smile but it must get lost in translation because he ignores me and resumes his conversation with Celeste. She's not flirting with him. There's no coyness or giggling, just a genuine interest in what he's saying. It makes me like her more. I can't stand women who deliberately flirt with every man in the room.

Is that what Ruston thinks I'm doing, flirting with him? I'm mortified at the thought.

"You've gone quiet again, Frankie. Maybe you should have some more wine?" He's teasing me, being friendly, so I nod and hold out my glass to Ruston for him to top up.

I'm not sure if the three wines I've already consumed make my hand shake but before I know it he's steadying the glass by wrapping his fingers around mine while pouring with the other.

I know that infuriating blush is back. My cheeks are burning, a beacon to my inexperience with an attractive man. With any kind of man, come to think of it.

Once the glass is half full he releases my hand and I hope my flustered reaction has gone unnoticed.

I look up, half expecting to find Andre glowering at me from across the table.

Instead, I see Celeste watching me.

CHAPTER THIRTY-EIGHT

CELESTE

I'm on the way back from the bathroom when I see Frankie and Andre almost toe to toe on the small patch of grass in what passes for a backyard with these brownstones. It's obvious they're arguing, and I wonder what it's about. It hadn't been the flirtation between Ruston and Frankie at the dinner table earlier, because Andre had been amused rather than annoyed and had made a comment to me about how Frankie rarely drinks and when she does he finds it cute.

Personally, I found her flirting uncomfortable, especially with her husband sitting across from her. Andre's a nice guy and doesn't deserve to be treated that way. I enjoyed chatting with him. It makes me wonder if their argument is about Andre and me. Knowing Frankie's paranoia, she probably thinks I was flirting with him and maybe that's why she behaved the way she did? Some kind of silly payback?

I'm trying my best to befriend her. I know I'm prickly with almost everyone and don't make friends easily and I get the feeling she's the same. We're dancing around each other, afraid of revealing too much. But I'm willing to take a chance because of my daughter, why can't she?

I can't hear what they're saying through the closed glass door but I see Frankie jab Andre in the chest with a finger. She's gesticulating wildly with her other hand and he takes a step back, shaking his head.

That's when I spy Luna. She's tucked in a corner of the kitchen, her face and palms pressed against the glass, watching her parents argue. I hear a muffled sob and my heart constricts. No child likes seeing their parents fight and at her age it's even scarier. Young kids don't have the insight to understand arguments are as natural a part of marriage as divvying up duties like taking out the trash and toilet cleaning.

She should've been upstairs with Vi, watching a movie. The last time I'd checked on them they'd been on the verge of falling asleep but something has drawn Luna downstairs. A window is probably open upstairs and the sound of her parents' angry voices might've drifted up.

Whatever it is, I need to distract her. I approach carefully, not wanting to startle her, especially when she's upset.

"Luna, I have a surprise for you."

She turns and her tear-stained cheeks break my heart. "Mommy and Daddy are angry."

I squat to her level so we're eye to eye. "That happens sometimes. It doesn't mean they don't love each other and love you."

She doesn't look convinced so I continue. "Have you ever been mad at a friend in ballet class?"

She nods, her eyes wide and solemn.

"Yet you're still friends, right?"

"Yeah."

"Well, that's what an argument with grown-ups is like. We may say angry stuff but we still like each other."

Not always. I'd said some angry stuff to Roland I can never retract. I've taken Vi away from her father, ensuring he'll never come near us again, and that's a guilty secret I'll have to live with every single day.

"I guess that makes sense." Her shoulders lift in a little shrug. "I know I'm not supposed to be down here but Violette fell asleep and I'm hungry."

"Well, that's part of the surprise I mentioned. I know you like strawberries, but do you like cream?"

"Yeah, they taste good together."

"They do. How would you like a bowl now?"

An adorable frown crinkles her brow. "But Mom says I shouldn't have snacks after nine o'clock."

It's not my place to be mad at Frankie but I am. For putting Andre through that ridiculous display at the dinner table earlier and for making her daughter cry inadvertently now.

"Just this once, okay? It'll be our secret."

Finally, her eyes light with mischief rather than sadness. "Okay."

"How about you sit on one of those stools at the island bench and I'll get it for you?"

She does as she's told and I place some of the strawberries Saylor used to decorate the cheesecake into a bowl, and swirl whipped cream over the top. When I stick a spoon in the bowl and place it in front of Luna, she looks more like the young girl I've seen on previous occasions, her face alight with excitement.

"This looks so good," she says, a moment before ignoring the spoon in favor of using her fingers to swipe a strawberry through the cream and popping it into her mouth. "Mmm… yum…"

I laugh at her ecstatic expression. Vi eats well but it requires a lot of coaxing and bribing on my part. I've never seen my daughter enjoy food the way Luna is.

"What are the grown-ups doing?" Luna asks, picking up another strawberry.

"Talking at the dining table."

"Have they finished eating?"

"Yes."

We finished dessert ten minutes ago and I can't wait to leave. I'm not sure why Saylor hosted this intimate dinner party. She seemed on edge and I caught her casting Frankie several malevolent glares when Ruston had been flirting with her, almost like she'd been jealous.

I can't figure this group out. Saylor should be mad for Lloyd, the father of her child. She should be focused on her pregnancy, not coveting another man. Instead, I get the feeling she has a thing for Ruston, who talked at length about his career as a model and I found him quite boring and self-absorbed. Lloyd is the quintessential nice guy; a man easily duped if his partner is so inclined and I definitely have my suspicions about Saylor. As for Frankie and Andre, I think they're happy but tonight casts doubt on that.

I enjoyed talking to him and for a scandalous second, while we discovered our mutual love for sitcom reruns, I allowed myself to wonder what it would be like to have him in my life, a man to be a full-time father to Vi, a man to depend on.

It had been a fleeting thought and one I can't encourage but the warmth of sitting next to a man like him, of having him pay me attention, still lingers and a small part of me is happy he's fighting with his wife.

The whole evening has been fraught with an underlying tension I can't define and don't want to. I'll make nice with these people for Vi's sake but it's best I don't get too close to any of them. I never know when I'll have to leave in a hurry again.

I've drifted off with my thoughts so when I refocus, Luna is licking the bowl clean. I stifle a smile. "Does your mom allow you to do that?"

She puts the bowl down, guilty yet gleeful. "No. She says it's bad manners."

"It is." I see her stiffen in fear so I add, "But I won't tell."

She smiles and slides off the stool. "You're nice."

"You're nice too," I say, surprised when she comes around the counter and opens her arms for a hug.

As I envelop her in my arms, I'm struck by how perfect this is. I want Vi and Luna to be close and now this sweet girl trusts me.

CHAPTER THIRTY-NINE
SAYLOR

Despite his initial reluctance to host the dinner party, Lloyd is the only person who actually had a good time tonight. Celeste appeared bored, except when chatting with Andre. Frankie drank too much and ended up making a fool of herself with Ruston, and he'd played up to her like an idiot. And I'd hated having to watch the whole thing unfold.

I wanted one guest in particular to feel hassled, that I can reveal their secret at any moment if they don't pay up, and I'm not going anywhere until they do. I'd watched for signs during the evening, to see if they appeared uncomfortable. But their acting ability is on par with mine and I saw nothing. Though I sensed a general tension in the group, so I've done the right thing getting us all together. The more pressured that person feels, the better.

I've set this in motion. It will escalate. And I'll either get everything I want or the entire thing will blow up in my face and I'll be left with nothing.

If this stupid plan of mine goes pear-shaped, I'll lose my family. My parents will never speak to me again. We may not be close these days but I respect them. They're good people and don't deserve to have their world come crashing down courtesy of a daughter who lost her mind for a few hours and made a monumental mistake.

"Everything okay?" Andre comes up beside me as I watch Ruston stalk across the park toward his place, a small part of me wishing I could run after him and demand he listen.

"Yeah, just tired."

"I'm waiting for Luna. She's in the bathroom."

"Sure."

Our conversation is stilted. We barely know each other. And no amount of dinner parties is going to change that. We have nothing in common.

"You and Celeste seem to get on well."

"She's nice," he says, with a noncommittal shrug. "Good conversationalist. Easy to talk to."

"Not sure if your wife approves."

His expression hardens. "Frankie's drunk. She's probably passed out on our bed right now."

From what I'd seen, it looked like Frankie had a good time. Considering we haven't lived in Vintage Circle long I don't know her that well. But every time I've seen her she seems tightly wound, like she's doing her utmost to pretend everything is fine when it's not.

If anyone knows the pressure that comes with perfection, I do. Growing up, I had to ensure my skirts were never too far above my knees and my V-necks didn't dip too low in the front. I couldn't wear too much make-up and my jewelry remained modest, tiny silver stud earrings and a delicate cross necklace.

I'd flown under the radar at school too, trying my best to get good grades, pleasant to everyone so I didn't get singled out by the cliques, never smoking or drinking in public where I could get caught.

Ironic, that the one night I cut loose all these years later is the one night that can unravel it all.

"I don't know Frankie well, but is she usually that flirtatious when she drinks?"

"No, because she rarely drinks, and if she does she's funny," he mutters, thrusting his hands into his pockets. "I've never seen her like that before."

"You weren't impressed."

"I was fine with it." His reply is aggressive, snappy.

I hold up my hands. "Hey, no need to bite my head off."

He grimaces. "Sorry…"

"Maybe give your wife a break? She's drunk. We've all been there."

He scowls, and I have no intention of delving into his marriage, so I try to deflect. "Are you sure you're not jealous?"

"Ruston is an asshole."

There's no heat in his response and he's just grouchy after an argument with his wife. What annoys me is my instantaneous reaction to defend Ruston, when in reality Andre's right. If anyone knows I do.

"Does Frankie know the three of us worked together on that advertising campaign?"

He glares at me, his brow furrowed. "No, and I'd like to keep it that way."

If anyone knows about keeping secrets, I do. I have no intention of divulging to anyone how Ruston, Andre and I know each other. Besides, I understand his reticence. I know too much about the last time we all worked together.

"You should go," I say, my tone devoid of emotion, but my accusatory gaze pinning him until he practically squirms.

"I will, once Luna's done." He takes his hands out of his pockets, only to fold his arms, stiff and defensive. "I don't know what you're playing at, Saylor, but I'm over the whole neighborly-buddy act, okay?"

I can say so much. I can ruin him. Instead, I force a sincere smile and shrug. "Okay."

He glowers at me a moment longer before heading back inside to get his daughter. He's rattled. I glimpsed a flicker of fear in his eyes before he stormed off.

But he's not the only one floundering and I need to double my efforts to get what I want.

CHAPTER FORTY

FRANKIE

THEN

I feel so guilty for sleeping with Walter I have to forgive Andre. Waking next to Walter, the sheet draped across his torso, hiding the scratch marks I made in desperation to lose myself for a few hours, rams home my guilt. I'm not this person. I shouldn't have used Walter no matter how furious I am with Andre. And now that I've cheated, I'm no better than him.

Shame makes me ease out of bed, careful not to wake him. I dress in record time and take a walk on the beach to clear my head, my regret overwhelming. I can't believe I had sex with another man while married. I hate it. Self-loathing fills me and I break into a jog, trying to outrun my mistakes and failing.

I never should've sought comfort with Walt. It's wrong on so many levels. I'm mortified that I'm my parents' daughter after all, that I use morality for my own whims.

Walter and I part ways a few hours later. He isn't angry or resentful. Instead, he wishes me well in true Walter fashion and says to stay in touch.

With him gone, I stay on at the cottage for another two days before heading home to Manhattan. Andre welcomes me with open arms and I contemplate telling him about my indiscretion for all of two seconds before deciding to keep it a secret. Because I know my husband. He's inherently selfish and will make our problems all about me rather than him. He'll pass the buck, expecting me to shoulder the blame…

Not that I'm justifying my shoddy behavior. I never should've slept with Walter but it's one of those things, two old friends seeking solace that is a one-off and never to be repeated.

After I return home, I sleep with Andre on my second night back. I need to forget my mistake with Walt and reclaim my marriage. I expect it to be fraught, tense, but we're as compatible as ever and as the weeks proceed, we learn to be a better couple. I embrace hope and forgiveness, determined to move forward. We do couples therapy where we're both as honest as can be. He admits to growing complacent in our relationship and taking me for granted, but rather than blame me he understands he could make an effort to spend more quality time together. He doesn't take on as many freelance jobs that require travel and I spend more time with him, like we did in the first heady days when we met. In front of the therapist, I'm honest about my hurt, how I can't understand he can "grow complacent" and feel trapped after only eight months of marriage. My resentment spills out and the mature way he handles it, taking full responsibility, goes a long way to healing the rift in my heart.

We're in a better place after therapy, a more honest place, and we're determined to make a fresh start. We take long walks through Central Park, we eat at new restaurants, we spend every evening curled up on the sofa watching old movies before having the best sex of our lives. I'm happy. I think. I'm making the most of our situation because I'm right about one thing: I'm not getting divorced twice by the time I'm in my mid-twenties.

I'm curled on our couch, my legs tucked under me, trying to read. But I've skimmed the same paragraph five times, not absorbing a word, as I listen to Andre potter around the kitchen, so grateful we're in a good place again.

I hear him slide the leftover takeout sushi we had for lunch into the fridge, before he joins me in the living room.

"What are you thinking about?" Andre sits beside me, rests his arm across my shoulder, and smooths a finger between my brows. "You get this cute little crinkle when you're thinking."

"Are you saying I've got a frown line?"

"No, but if you do too much thinking I'd be looking for a cosmetic surgeon soon."

He chuckles and I whack him on his chest, which he clutches with mock outrage. "Hey, watch it, Fran, you pack a powerful punch."

"And don't you forget it."

It's a throwaway line, a funny comment, but with his infidelity lingering in the background it sounds like a threat and his laughter dies.

"We're okay, you and me?"

He asks me this periodically, usually when I least expect it, showing me he cares by checking in. I think it's sweet, but it also serves to underline we'll always have this shadow hovering over us and I'll never be able to fully trust him again.

Hypocritical, considering what I did, but for me it wasn't about sex, it was about comfort, and I know by how crap I feel whenever I think about it I'll never do it again.

"We're okay," I say, surprised when my stomach churns with a sudden wave of nausea.

The sushi from our favorite café didn't agree with me last week either and as I make a dash for the toilet, I vow to forego it for a while.

"The sushi again, huh?"

"Yeah," I manage to say, before I sink to my knees in front of the toilet and lose my dinner.

However, not eating sushi for a while is the least of my problems as my nausea escalates over the next week. I'm woozy in the mornings, the café lattes I guzzle lose their appeal, and I can't stomach the prime sirloin Andre cooks to perfection.

When I throw up one night, my sneaking suspicion coalesces into a startling truth. I'm at the pharmacy first thing the next morning and home twenty minutes later, peeing on a stick.

As I sit on the toilet seat, waiting for the result, I'm not sure what I feel. Is having a baby so soon after Andre and I worked through his infidelity a smart choice or will it put an unexpected strain on our relationship?

Will he be happy having a child or will he see it as another sign of being trapped?

For me, I'm equal parts terrified and hopeful as I wait the requisite two minutes. When I glance at the tiny box and see two blue lines, I exhale the breath I've been inadvertently holding.

I'm pregnant.

CHAPTER FORTY-ONE

FRANKIE

NOW

I'm mortified. I made a fool of myself at Saylor's dinner party last night and to make matters worse, to cover my embarrassment I'd accused Andre of flirting with Celeste when I know that's not true. We hadn't waited to get home either; we'd gone at each other in Saylor's backyard. We rarely argue. Sure, we have disagreements but nothing like the verbal bashing last night. The alcohol had made me irrational and his calmness had infuriated me. Then he'd had the audacity to laugh at my "pathetic attempts at flirting with a single guy" and I'd lost it.

So it's okay for him to smile at every woman in the room and I can't chat with a man? I know I'm useless at flirting because I never do it, which is why him calling me "pathetic" really rankled. Does that mean he's an expert because he does it often when I'm not around? Does he flirt at work every chance he gets?

I forced myself to move past this jealousy when we finished therapy because it would have ruined us and we've been happy for the most part. But it's times like this when the vast differences between our personalities are rammed home. Andre will always be the life of the party while I only come alive in front of a camera, perpetuating a giant sham.

"Look at my perfect life. Look how competent I am. Look how I have everything together." When that's far from the truth. I'm over it. Over everything at the moment and I have no idea how to extricate myself from this web of self-delusion I've spun.

I can't remember everything I said last night and after our argument I stomped through the kitchen on the way home, and saw Celeste hugging Luna. I hadn't wanted my daughter to see me in such a state so I'd given Celeste a grateful nod and kept going, barely stopping to thank Saylor and Lloyd for hosting, and bidding farewell to a bemused Ruston. Yeah, I'd made a spectacle of myself and I'm not sure whether to apologize to all involved or hope they forget it.

After a shower that makes my head pound a little less I get dressed and head downstairs. I hear Andre and Luna chatting and I can smell he's made her favorite buttermilk pancakes. I pause on the fourth step from the bottom, which gives me an angled view into the kitchen, and let the calmness of the domestic scene between daddy and daughter wash over me. Andre is dishing pancakes onto three plates and Luna is perched next to him on a stool, in charge of toppings. The tip of her tongue protrudes from her lips as she focuses on scattering choc chips on her father's, pouring maple syrup on mine, and sprinkling sugar on hers. I hate that she might have witnessed us fighting last night.

Is that why Celeste had been hugging her? Had she been comforting my daughter? If so, I should thank her. I feel like an idiot for accusing Andre of flirting with her when I'd seen no sign at all. I'd flung it at him because I'd been deflecting from my own behavior. As for the way she'd been watching me make a fool of myself with Ruston, I'm not surprised if she thinks I'm an idiot.

It's not Celeste's fault I overreacted. I haven't been happy for a while now and the pressure of faking it for my adoring audience almost daily is taking a toll. I need some time away and my mind immediately goes to the one place I always felt at peace.

It's crazy, craving the beach house that belongs to my ex-husband, but the thought of listening to the waves crashing on the beach while I lie in bed, the calming long walks and the fresh air, is infinitely appealing. Though considering Walter hasn't returned my calls, it's outlandish to consider saying out of the blue, "Hey, I need some chill time away from my family, mind if I crash at your seaside cottage?"

I traverse the remaining steps, take a deep breath and enter the kitchen. Two sets of eyes, one wary and watchful, one innocent and joyous, meet mine, and rather than feel happy I want to escape even more.

"Mom, Dad made pancakes!" Luna wriggles like an excited puppy. "And they're ready, so can we eat now?"

"Sure thing, sweetie." I place a kiss on the top of her head, and touch Andre's hand with mine. "Hey."

"Hope you're hungry," he says, handing me a plate, knowing full well I won't be able to stomach more than half a pancake.

"Funny guy." I take the plate and manage a wan smile, glad his eyes have warmed when they meet mine.

"Want a coffee?" he asks and I'm relieved he's calmed down since last night.

"Please." I sit at the dining table and Luna sits next to me, waiting patiently for Andre to join us like we've taught her. But she's practically drooling all over her pancakes so I say, "It's okay, sweetie, you can start."

"Thanks, Mom."

Her wide smile makes me want to cradle her close and never let go, but she's already licking sugar off her fork and I leave her to it.

I stare at my plate, willing myself to have a bit but my stomach is still roiling. When Andre brings me a coffee, he smirks and points to my plate. "You know you won't be allowed to go outside and play if you don't eat your breakfast."

"Yeah, Mom," Luna says, her mouth full of pancake, and I laugh at my husband's cheekiness, knowing I'd flip him the finger if Luna wasn't around.

He sits opposite me, his lopsided smile and flop of hair over his forehead and blue eyes so familiar the tightness in my chest eases. I don't want to escape my family. I love them. But it's been a long time since I've had a break and taken time for myself, so it's something I need to consider.

"Feeling okay?"

I hold up my hand and waver it side to side. "Been better."

"Maybe less of this next time and you'll feel great." He grins and mimes drinking from a bottle and this time I do flip him the finger at table level, so only he can see.

He laughs and slices his pancakes in precise quarters like he usually does while I sip my coffee. Soon, Luna's prattling about her next ballet class and what she wants to watch later and I drift off, content to let her chatter wash over me.

So when she says, "I have a secret with Celeste," I almost drop the mug in my hands.

Andre shoots me a warning glare, as if he knows I'll overreact to anything involving Celeste. "Luna, we've told you before. It's not good to keep secrets from us and especially not with another adult."

Luna's lower lip wobbles and I lay a comforting hand on her shoulder. "You know you can tell us anything, sweetie, and we won't get mad at you."

She doesn't deserve our anger; Celeste does, for putting our daughter in this position. What kind of adult would keep a secret with a child when any parent knows we want the opposite?

"Last night when you and Daddy were fighting, she gave me strawberries and cream to make me feel better because I was sad." She raises tear-filled eyes to mine and I hate I made my daughter feel this way. "It was after nine o'clock, when I know you won't let me have snacks, but Celeste said it could be our secret and I thought that was pretty cool so I said yes." She tilts her chin up in defiance. "And I ate the whole bowlful and it tasted yummy."

I'm at a loss. We shouldn't have argued in front of her. Our rare disagreements take place behind closed doors because I remember witnessing my parents having some rip-roaring arguments and they always terrified me, even in my early teens. I'd always feared they'd get divorced. In the long run, that wouldn't have been a bad thing. They could've slept with as many people as they liked, without damaging my psyche.

While I'd never paid attention to what was being said back then, deliberately distancing myself by going to my room or slipping headphones on and cranking up the music, I wonder if those arguments had been about their lovers and they'd been jealous, despite embracing that kind of lifestyle.

"Parents sometimes argue, Luna, it's what grown-ups do," Andre says, and I shoot him a grateful nod for taking the lead on this. "Doesn't mean we don't love each other."

"That's what Celeste said too."

Thankfully, Luna's tears have dried and she's back to alternating glances between us and her pancakes.

"And we're sorry you felt sad when you saw us, but it's not right to keep secrets from us about anything, okay?"

She's so solemn, her eyes wide, and I want to sweep her into my arms and squeeze her tight. "Okay, Daddy. Can I finish my pancakes now?"

"Sure thing," Andre says, but I see the deepening frown lines between his brows. He's not impressed with the whole secret thing either.

When Luna's forked another piece of pancake into her mouth, he stands on the pretext of clearing his plate and comes around to murmur in my ear. "Do you want me to go next door and talk to Celeste about not encouraging our child to keep secrets?"

I touch his leg. "Thanks, but I'll handle it."

"Okay." He straightens and winks. "Go easy on her."

"I will."

It's time I had a heart-to-heart with Celeste.

CHAPTER FORTY-TWO

CELESTE

Someone is pounding on my door rather than knocking and when I peek outside and see Frankie, my heart leaps. She's alone, which means this isn't a social call for the girls and for a terrifying moment I wonder if she's discovered my secret. But Andre isn't with her and he would be if she had.

I break into a sweat and try to get a read on her expression but can't. Dragging in a few deep breaths to calm my racing pulse, I subdue my panic and open the door.

"Hi, Frankie, what can I do for you?"

My voice is a tad high and she casts me an odd look before saying, "Can I come in?"

"Sure."

After she steps inside I close the door and gesture to the sparsely furnished living room, a far cry from her luxurious haven.

"Where's Violette?" she asks, looking around, and I breathe a sigh of relief. She's acting perfectly normal, which she wouldn't be if she'd come here to confront me about what I'm hiding.

"She's on her tablet upstairs." I roll my eyes. "It's an educational game at least. I hate screens as much as the next parent but for a single mom, they're a godsend."

"For those who aren't single too."

We share a moment and thankfully her anger drains away, replaced by weariness. She looks awful, with dark smudges under her eyes and the faintest red capillaries bracketing her nose. That's when I realize it's the first time I've seen her without make-up.

"I'd planned on barging in here and telling you off for encouraging Luna to keep a secret from us, but I think I should be thanking you for comforting her instead."

I'm floored. My shock must show because her smile is bashful as she sinks onto the sofa and I sit next to her.

"Have I been that much of a bitch since you've arrived?" She mimics my astounded expression. "Because going by how stunned you look, I think you expected me to slug you."

"You were looking angsty when I answered the door. As for being bitchy…"

I can give her a trite answer she probably wants or take a risk and tell her the truth. I settle for the latter. "Honestly? You seem kind of tense all the time. I thought we became friends at the gender reveal party but since then you've been odd around me." I briefly touch her arm. "I'm worried about you. Because I think you're a good mom and the way you were arguing with Andre last night at Saylor's, you looked like you were on the edge."

"I don't usually drink," she says, as if that explains it, but I know there's more going on. I've seen that weary look before. On me.

In those early heady days with Roland, I'd been the model girlfriend. Doing whatever he wanted. Trying to make him like me. I hadn't had a boyfriend before and he'd been my first love, my only love. When we'd broken up, I'd never lost faith we'd reunite. Couples destined to be together do it all the time. So when he'd come back to me I'd made sure he'd never leave me again. I got pregnant.

If he suspected I'd done it to trap him, he didn't say. He'd been there for me, through the birth and beyond. Until he emotionally checked out and I knew we were done. I tried to hold onto him. I tried everything. Turns out, I wasn't enough and after our last nasty confrontation I know why.

"You're exhausted," I say, settling into the cushions. "And I think it's got nothing to do with a hangover."

Her eyes widen in surprise but she still regards me with reserve. "Do I look that bad?"

"I've seen the look before." I pat my chest. "In the mirror. A few years ago, I hit breaking point with Roland until I realized I was overdoing it, trying to do too much, be everything for everybody, and it was slowly killing me."

She stared at me for an eternity before finally nodding. "That's how I feel." Her sigh is heavy. "I'm so tired of being perfect…"

Tears start trickling down her cheeks but she's silent, swallowing her sobs, striving for perfection even when crying.

I usually only hug Vi, who loves cuddles. But last night Luna had needed comforting and now Frankie needs a hug too, so I scoot closer and envelop her in my arms. She's resistant, being her usual stoic self, and I wait until she relaxes into me. That's when the sobs start, like a dam has been breached, and she's shaking and heaving to the point I'm seriously worried.

I murmur platitudes like "It'll be okay" and "You'll be fine" but I'm not so sure. If this woman who's been reticent with me at times since we met is comfortable enough to break down like this, she's in a bad way.

When she quietens I release her and she shuffles back on the cushion, putting some distance between us. Her eyes are bloodshot, her nose is like a red swollen blob and her cheeks are blotchy, but there's a calmness in her gaze that wasn't there before.

"I'm beyond embarrassed to blubber all over you like that, but I think I needed it."

"You did," I say. "Want something to drink?"

"Water will be fine."

I head to the kitchen and fill two glasses, wondering if this is the breakthrough in our friendship I've been hoping for. Either she'll retreat after this, mortified, or she'll realize I can be an ally if she gives me a chance.

I hand her the glass of water and she gulps it down.

"Dehydrated, huh?"

Sheepish, she nods. "I've never drunk four glasses of wine in my life. And considering how I feel today, and the fool I made of myself last night, I never will again."

"Want another water?"

"No, I'm good, thanks." She hesitates, as if unsure how to phrase what comes next and I wait, curious. "And thanks for more than the water. You comforted Luna last night when she needed it most and I really appreciate it."

"You're welcome. They're so precious at that age. Precocious one minute, clingy the next."

I see a shift in her eyes so I preempt her dressing-down. "And I apologize for telling her to keep a secret. I was trying to distract her because she was upset and thought I'd improvise by making eating the strawberries fun, but I'd never encourage her to keep secrets from you usually."

"Thanks, Celeste, I appreciate you saying that."

We lapse into silence and for the first time since we met it's comfortable.

"Can I ask you something?"

She nods. "Sure."

"Was Andre upset about you chatting to Ruston?"

"No, I was just being an idiot." She rolls her eyes. "But even if he was, he has no right. Like he's some kind of saint."

She eyeballs me and I get what she's implying.

"Hey, we were just talking. I would never flirt with your husband—"

"It's not you," she says, then looks away as if she's said too much. "We all have pasts, right?"

"Absolutely."

If she knew mine, she'd run a million miles in the opposite direction.

"Anyway, if you ever need to sort things out or talk with him or whatever, I'm happy to mind Luna."

"I might take you up on that," she says as she stands and taps her watch. "I better get back. I've got some planning to do."

"You're filming today?"

She grimaces. "Do I look that bad?"

"Well…"

We laugh together and it's nice. I like being friends with my neighbor. It's good that she trusts me.

I hope it stays that way.

CHAPTER FORTY-THREE
SAYLOR

After the dinner party I lay low for a week, trying to stay busy with scouring baby websites for nursery furniture, reading pregnancy books, desperate to rein in my impatience as I wait to see if gathering my neighbors in my home for a meal had the desired effect and I'm closer to getting the money I need. Lloyd has been busy with work and I've done a few marketing quotes for companies I've worked with before. I never valued working from home more than now, when my ankles tend to swell by the end of a day and my back aches if I stand too long. All perfectly normal for a pregnant woman but sometimes I forget I'm carrying a child, I'm that focused on the outcome.

I'm strolling around the park when Celeste comes out of Frankie's house with Violette and Luna in tow. They find a spot in the park where Celeste sits on a bench, the girls at her feet, and I can't pass them without saying hello. I haven't spoken to Celeste since my dinner party and I can't envisage us ever being close, but it's only polite to stop.

"What are you three up to?"

Celeste looks up as I approach and there's a flicker of unease before she quickly masks her expression. "Frankie's working so I thought the girls and me would spend some time out here in the fresh air."

I raise a brow as I see they're both glued to a tablet, watching a princess cartoon.

"Just you wait. Your life will depend on any kind of screen by the time your boy's two."

"I have to wait that long?"

We share a chuckle and I sit next to her on the bench. "How are you? Settling into the neighborhood?"

"Yeah, I love it here." She sweeps her arm wide, encompassing the park. "I've never lived anywhere as pretty as this."

"Where exactly are you from again?" I ask.

"Southampton."

There's the slightest hesitation before she answers me, almost like she has to get her story straight. It makes me wonder what she's hiding, especially as she has no online presence. As someone who's had to become secretive out of necessity since I got pregnant, I recognize the signs.

"Violette's father not in the picture?" I continue to probe.

"Nope. I painted over him a long time ago."

I laugh but notice she's not smiling anymore. She's looking at me, but her gaze slides away every now and then, like she can't quite meet my eyes.

"Do you know Ruston well?" Her question is from left field, like she's trying to deflect attention off her, and this time, she's looking at me with blatant daring, calling my bluff. I freeze and try not to let my worry show. This is what I get for digging into her past. She's trying to delve into mine.

"As a neighbor, yeah."

Her eyebrows rise. "Seemed like there was a bit of tension between the two of you at your dinner party so I wondered if you knew each other from the past."

She's fishing. She can't know anything. I've been careful. Nobody knows, and I need to keep it that way. The last thing I need is for her to tattle to Lloyd and my marriage to suffer. Time enough for that to happen when I tell my poor husband the rest.

"No. He came to the gender reveal party and I met him then." I fan my face, mimicking that he's hot. "He stood out, you know?"

She laughs. "Yeah, he's good-looking, but he knows it."

"You think?" I bite my tongue at how swiftly I've defended him and it hasn't gone unnoticed as Celeste pins me with a curious stare.

"Men like him know they can have any woman they want and he seems the type that even if he was in a committed relationship he'd sleep around."

Something I'd found out the hard way. I will the heat seeping into my cheeks to subside. By Celeste's raised brows, I've failed.

I aim for blasé. "You could be right. He was flirting outrageously with Frankie at my dinner party and she seemed to lap it up."

"I think he dazzled her, but it was a game to him. He saw how she responded to him and he played on it." She tut-tuts. "Not a nice move considering her husband had a front row seat to his games."

I want to say so much but I can't. My future depends on not revealing the truth until it's the right time and that isn't now. "You're right. Game players are the worst."

"You're lucky you have Lloyd. He seems lovely."

"He is."

"Have you been married long?" She's turned the spotlight back on me, delving into my private life, making me uncomfortable.

"Nine months. My folks introduced us." Enough information without giving away too much.

"At the risk of sounding jealous, Lloyd looks at you like you've hung the moon. You're so lucky."

Celeste is right, I am lucky, and I'm a better woman for basking in his attention. It makes what I've done all the harder because I know he'll never look at me the same way again once he finds out; if he sticks around, that is.

"Lloyd's amazing and he'll be a great dad," I say, trying not to squirm under the intensity of her stare. She's looking at me like she can see straight through me—my past with Ruston, the mess I've made of my marriage because of one stupid, impulsive night—and I'm uneasy. It's too soon for the truth to come out.

"I know this is none of my business, but take it from someone who knows, don't get too hung up over how boring you think your life will become after you have the baby or how much you'll miss out on, and just make the most of what you've got."

Her stare is spooky and I resist the urge to rub my bare arms. She's giving me some kind of warning and I wonder again if she knows more than she's letting on.

But how can she? I'm careful. At least, I hope I am.

CHAPTER FORTY-FOUR

FRANKIE

THEN

I never envisaged having kids like many girls do. I remember some of them as seniors in high school, pointing out the cute jocks and imagining what their babies would look like if they got together. Back then, I couldn't think of anything worse. Which is ironic, considering I got married at eighteen and if I hadn't been vigilant with contraception I might've been a young mom.

It saddens me to remember that Walter's keenness for a baby ultimately ended us; that the day we argued about it at the beach cottage was the day we both admitted we were done. Choosing not to have children with Walt had been a conscious decision because I'd been too young and increasingly unsettled in our marriage, craving an escape I didn't know I wanted until it crept up on me.

Now, I think I'm ready. As ready as any woman can be with an unplanned pregnancy. I'm happy about it overall, but I'm also scared, and my fear has to do with more than the trials of a natural birth.

I'm terrified my baby's paternity may be in question.

Getting pregnant doesn't make sense. I'm on the pill, and when I had sex with Walter we also used a condom. This baby has to be Andre's. But that niggle of doubt is there and my indiscretion dogs me throughout the pregnancy, my fears growing until I'm perpetually stressed; my blood pressure shoots through the stratosphere and my ob-gyn orders me to be on complete bed rest for the last few weeks of the pregnancy until it's under control, making me feel helpless and frustrated.

Sadly, all the lying down in the world can't fix my blood pressure. Only one thing will do that, and it involves a paternity test after the baby's born.

While I suffer extreme stress through the pregnancy, Andre takes to impending fatherhood like a champion. He scours countless parenting sites online and continually quotes pregnancy facts, he buys birthing books and reads them every night, he thrives in every Lamaze class. He becomes so baby focused I can't imagine what he'll be like after the birth, and I send countless prayers heavenward that this baby is his.

I can't lie to him if it isn't. The guilt will consume me and I'll be a bad mother because of it.

The birth passes by in a blur of drugs and pain, with Andre by my side the entire time. I even relent and allow him to contact my folks so they can visit their granddaughter at a later date. That might've been the drugs.

But when I see our baby girl's face for the first time and she snuggles into my neck, I know whatever happens I'll protect her with every fiber of my being.

It takes five weeks until I can get the test done, without Andre hovering over every visit to the doctor or hospital for check-ups because I'd lost a lot of blood and had an episiotomy. I ask for the results to be emailed to me and now, as I sit with a sleeping Luna in my arms—we'd called her that because she'd been born on the night of a full moon—my cell pings with an incoming email and I know.

This is it.

The email that may change my life; and the life of my precious, innocent daughter.

I hate myself for potentially putting her through this. She's blameless. Whereas me... I'm the most horrible person on the planet for what I did and what it may result in.

Not only will our lives be upended but what of Walter? He deserves to know the truth if he's Luna's father and the thought of having that conversation... my skin pebbles as ice trickles through my veins.

I cradle Luna close as I tap the email icon on my cell and the new email that just landed.

My pulse skips a beat as I scroll through the email, the breath I've been inadvertently holding whooshing out in a rush as Luna's paternity is confirmed.

Luna lets out a little whimper and in that moment, as I gaze down at my beautiful daughter's face, I know what I have to do.

We need a fresh start.

Far from the memories of the past.

CHAPTER FORTY-FIVE

FRANKIE

NOW

A lot can happen in a week.

Following my chat with Celeste the day after I'd made a fool of myself at Saylor's dinner party, I let go of my reservations and we've grown closer. I should've recognized she's an introvert like me rather than wrongly assuming her diffidence means she has something to hide. I should've known better. I'm not one to share secrets with virtual strangers or invite them into my home, but Luna and Violette have become inseparable and that means I'm spending more time with Celeste.

We've had several play dates in the park and we chatted at ballet class yesterday. She's just a mom who wants to give her child everything, like I do, and I feel bad for misjudging her. Not that I've opened up to her entirely. It will take time for our friendship to grow but the way she listened to me when I told her about my exhaustion with appearing perfect all the time... she understood and I value being heard.

Andre doesn't get it and I sometimes wonder if he'd love me if I revealed my true self, the one who'd rather lounge around in yoga pants and old T-shirts with no make-up. He's never seen me at my worst. Ever since we met I've put on a front for him to try and slide into his perfect Manhattan world, to hide my insecurities that an inexperienced girl from Gledhill could ever be good enough for a rich boy from New York City. Sometimes, in the dead of night, when he's snoring softly beside me, I can't quell the doubts.

I've just finished filming a segment on bullet journals and am keen to get some fresh air and join the girls in the park. Celeste has been watching them all morning and I spy Luna and Violette sitting at her feet playing with some spinning ball thing while she reads. It's a peaceful scene and I'm grateful to her for giving me time to work in peace. Andre has been away on an assignment in Connecticut all week, doing graphics for some big tourism company, so it's nice to have someone share the child-minding duties. Though I'm glad I can see them from the window. Celeste hasn't mentioned her ex over the last week and I've quashed my concerns, but I can't forget all that she's told me and I'm still a tad on guard.

I pull the front door closed behind me but before I join them I have to make a call.

I do a quick online search for the number of the bank Walter works at and when I find it I tap the call button from the website. He's going to hate this but my threat to call him at the bank hasn't worked and he still hasn't returned my call seven days later.

Someone picks up on the second ring. "Regional Bank, how may we help you?"

"May I speak with Walter, please?"

"I'm sorry, our manager is on vacation at the moment. Can I redirect your call to someone else?"

"No, thanks. Do you know when he's back?"

"Tomorrow." There's an impatient clacking on a keyboard in the background. "Is there anything else I can help you with today?"

"No. I'm fine."

"Have a nice day."

The dial tone hums in my ear and I feel foolish. If he's on vacation maybe he doesn't want to be bothered by his ex-wife or reminded of a past he'd rather forget. But we talk on our anniversary every year, and he always seems fine.

Maybe this is a sign I should forget this annual phone call? We don't say much beyond making small talk anyway. I know why I do it. Sentimentality. I owe Walter. He saved me at a time I needed him most and got me out of Gledhill. He was a good husband and looked after me. And when I turned to him for comfort after Andre cheated, he gave it freely without expecting anything in return. He's a good man. Besides, I wouldn't bother following up if it wasn't for those unexpected calls of his lately, calls that have broken our "once a year rule"; and I want to make sure he got my letter and the paternity test results. It's way past time that chapter in my life is closed.

I'll wait a few days and try one last time. If he doesn't respond, I've got the message loud and clear. Seeing factual proof of Luna's paternity might have shown him it's time to move on and let go.

I walk down the steps and cross the road to enter the park. Celeste spots me and waves, her smile reserved yet genuine as I approach.

"Hey, girls, having fun?"

"Yeah," Luna and Violette answer in unison, without looking up from their spinning ball device.

"How's it going?" I sit next to Celeste and point at her book. "Getting much reading done?"

"You know how it is when you're keeping half an eye on kids. I've read the same paragraph six times."

We laugh and I lean back, resting my elbows on the back of the bench and tilting my face to the sun. "It's lovely out here."

"Beats poring over accounts."

"Is work keeping you busy at the moment?" We haven't spoken much about her job before.

"Yeah, I've been looking after several small companies for a while so I always have work to do."

"Having that ongoing security must be a relief," I say and she nods.

"As a single parent, absolutely."

I hear raised voices and straighten, to see Saylor gesticulating wildly at Ruston on his doorstep.

"What do you think that's about?"

"No idea," Celeste says, watching the interaction too. "Though she's not happy about something."

Saylor yells again though at this distance we can't hear what she's saying.

"That night you chatted with him at her dinner party, did he mention them being friends or anything?"

I shake my head. "We made small talk mostly. I wonder what their story is?" I jerk my head in the direction of Saylor and Ruston.

"In a neighborhood this small we'll probably find out eventually. Besides, I've learned not to delve too deep into other people's business. You might not like what you find."

It's sound advice, but as I glance down I see Celeste has mangled the corners of her book, creasing and folding with nervous fingers, and I wonder if she's thinking of others beyond our new neighbor.

CHAPTER FORTY-SIX

CELESTE

Frankie takes the girls inside for some fruit and a drink, but I wait for Saylor. Even the girls heard her raised voice and had become more interested in the confrontation between Saylor and Ruston, so Frankie and I exchanged knowing looks and she'd offered to take them inside.

I said I'll be in shortly but I want to make sure Saylor's okay. She doesn't look it as she drags her feet, crossing the park at a snail's pace. When she nears, I raise my hand in greeting, giving her the option to ignore me or come talk. Thankfully, she chooses the latter.

I'm shocked to see tears in her eyes as she nears me. It could be hormonal, a pregnant woman upset by a simple tiff, but from that argument I just witnessed I think it's more. I'd have to care about someone to cry if they offended me, and the depth of feeling required means there's something going on between these two as I've previously suspected.

She stops in front of me, her fingers curled into her palms, her arms rigid, like she's trying to stay in control. "Did you hear all that?"

I pat the bench beside me and she lowers herself wearily, like she's nine months pregnant rather than five and a half. "No, but your raised voice did carry."

She winces. "Sorry about that. Everyone tells me I have a loud voice and when I get annoyed it's even louder."

"Everything okay?"

"Yeah."

There's a world of untold pain behind that one syllable and I wait, giving her time to speak if she wants to.

"Have you ever done anything on the spur of the moment that you later realize is the dumbest thing you've ever done?" She's asking the right person.

I'm filled with regrets for all the times I've let my impulsiveness get the better of me. "Of course. None of us are infallible."

"What's the worst thing you've ever done?" she asks and I feel like she's testing me; if I give her some semblance of truth she'll open up to me. Not that I want to be this woman's confidante, but I'm concerned for her wellbeing. That baby she's carrying needs a relaxed mother and doesn't deserve to be flooded with cortisol; she needs to get her stress hormone levels under control.

"I've lied to someone close to me," I say, my voice barely above a whisper, regret choking me. "And not just small lies, a whopping great one that would tear his world apart if he knew."

"*His* world? Are you talking about your ex?" Her question startles me and I shake my head, but my nonverbal denial isn't enough as her eyes widen. "Is he not the father of Violette?"

"We're talking about you, not me," I say, needing a change of subject, pronto. I can't have anyone delving into my past and the subject of Violette's paternity.

"I'm in over my head," she mutters, paling a little, worry pinching her mouth. "I thought I had everything figured out when I moved here." Her shoulders sag with the burden she's carrying. "Turns out, not so much."

"You know Ruston from before, don't you?" I wonder whether she'll be honest this time.

She slides a protective arm across her belly, as if to stave off whatever misfortune is heading her baby's way. "Is it that obvious?"

"Well, newly acquainted neighbors don't get into heated spats, unless it's over dog poo on their lawn or unrelenting loud music until three a.m. every night."

She sighs and a lone tear trickles from the corner of her eye. "Lloyd doesn't know and I prefer he doesn't. He's already got it in his head I have a thing for Ruston."

"Do you?"

"Not really. We share a past, that's all…" She presses the pads of her fingers to her eyes and again I wait to see if she'll reveal anything more. "He's not being cooperative when I need him to be and it's threatening everything."

She's talking in riddles and I start jumping to wild conclusions, like maybe he's the father of her unborn child…

"Sounds like you have a plan." I hope she knows what she's doing.

"I do. But what's that old saying about the best laid plans going astray?" She presses her other hand to her chest. "That's what I feel is happening here."

"At the risk of sounding like a nag, and as someone who has no right to, all this stress isn't good for your baby and he should be your priority now." I'd love to know what her secret is, what she's trying to do and how Ruston is getting in the way, but I doubt she'll divulge the details.

She stiffens even though I haven't asked for more information. Her shoulders pull back and some of the color returns to her face, a faint crimson staining her cheeks. "You're absolutely spot on." She looks me straight in the eye. "You have no right and I'd appreciate if you mind your own business."

I bark out a laugh. "Saylor, you came up to me. I'm just lending you a friendly ear if you want to offload." I hold up my hands like I have nothing to hide. "No judgment here at all."

She grimaces. "I know. Sorry, I'm just feeling like I'm sinking, a mix of hormones and bad judgment. I'll be fine."

She stands and I do too, offering one last word of advice. "It gets easier, you know."

"What does?"

"Watching someone you care about not returning your affection."

The color in her cheeks deepens and I wonder if I'm right, that her baby's paternity is in question, that Ruston is the father of her child and she's desperate to make sure her husband doesn't find out.

"Thanks, Celeste." She touches my hand then she's gone, heading toward her house with stronger strides than before.

I hope I helped. But I know problems like that aren't easily dealt with.

CHAPTER FORTY-SEVEN

SAYLOR

Everything is unraveling.

I almost blurted the truth to Celeste in the park, an indication of just how rattled I am. Nothing is going right, I don't have the money yet, and with every passing day I feel like I'm drowning in deceit.

I barely make it inside when my cell rings and as soon as I see an unknown number on the screen my hands start to shake.

He said he wouldn't call yet. That he'd give me some time to gather the funds.

I could ignore it but he'll keep calling and I'd rather speak to him now, with Lloyd not at home.

I answer on the third ring, knowing he won't like being kept waiting.

I hear the crackle of static before he asks, "What took you so long?"

My bladder convulses at the sound of that electrically distorted tone I sometimes hear in my nightmares. I wish I knew who was doing this. I've listened for clues, hoping for a phrase or word to jog my memory, but nothing. Heck, I don't even know if it's a man, the voice is so heavily disguised.

"I was vomiting. Food poisoning." The lie slides glibly from my lips like so many others before. I want him to feel sympathy for me. He won't.

"Do you have my money yet?"

"I'm working on it."

"Not hard enough. Maybe I should pay you a visit? Introduce myself to that dopey husband of yours? Tell him how it really is? Then make a call to your parents' church? I'm sure their loyal followers would be very interested to hear about their fallen angel."

Nausea washes over me and it has nothing to do with an unexpected bout of second trimester morning sickness. This idiot can tear my parents' world apart if I let him.

"I told you this is going to take time. That kind of money can't materialize out of thin air."

"How much have you got?"

I can't tell him zero, that I'm counting on my blackmail scheme to pay him off. So I conjure another lie. "Five grand."

"So why is it in your bank account and not mine?"

"Because I can't make a withdrawal of that amount without Lloyd asking questions. Don't worry, I'm good for the fifty grand." I hope he can't hear the terror in my voice.

"You have another month and then I'm done. Got it?"

Four measly weeks? I'm pressuring as much as I can but it still doesn't feel like I'm any closer to the money.

"I need more time—"

"A month and that's final."

He hangs up, leaving me staring at my cell, my stomach still churning with dread.

There's another way out of this. Tell the truth.

And ruin my family in the process.

But I can't do it. They're innocent in all this. I'm the one who made a mistake. I'm the one who needs to fix it.

I've contemplated going to the police and after this latest phone call I'm tempted. But a police investigation won't make what I've done go away, it will bring it to light and my folks will get humiliated in the process and lose everything they've worked so hard for. No matter how discreet the police are, stuff like this has a way of making it to the press.

I am so screwed.

CHAPTER FORTY-EIGHT

FRANKIE

THEN

Ever since the disaster on my eighteenth birthday, I've never been one for celebrating dates. Though considering I met Walter, my way out of Gledhill, on the same night I guess it hadn't been all bad.

He's been on my mind today. It's our anniversary and as I stare at a sleeping Luna, her eyelashes fanning shadows across her baby-soft cheeks, her lips pursed like a rosebud, I'm filled with gratitude. Andre is away for work and I've been reminiscing, thinking about the past, mulling over what I've been through to get to this point: a happy mother and wife who counts her blessings every day.

On impulse, I pick up my cell and call Walter. Predictably, he answers on the fourth ring as always, or like he's been expecting my call.

"Francesca. How are you?"

"Good. You?"

"Can't complain."

Patient Walter never whines about anything. He's content, making the most of every day, and bears no grudges despite how I once tipped his world upside down. He sounds genuinely happy to hear from me. We make it a point never to ask about each other's spouses. I never ask about Julia—who he reunited with not long after our divorce—and he never questions me about Andre.

It's better this way. We were always honest with each other and feigning interest in each other's partners isn't our way.

I'm unsure whether to tell him about Luna or not. He's not a fool and once he learns of her age, he'll put two and two together. Not that it matters. Andre is her father and Walter will never have any involvement in her life.

"Something's wrong," he says, a statement not a question, and I smile at how well this man knows me.

"Not really, but I do have some news. Wonderful news, in fact." I take a deep breath and blow it out. "I have a daughter. Luna."

"Congratulations, Francesca, that's wonderful." He sounds genuinely happy and I lower my guard, when he asks, "How old is she?"

I'm tempted to lie for a moment but what would be the point? I've got nothing to hide.

"Two months."

I almost hear the wheels turning in his mind as he does the math. But he won't ask me. Walter is an upstanding man, a throwback to days when men were honorable and did everything they could to protect their women.

"She's the spitting image of Andre," I add, to fill the growing silence between us. "I love her to bits. She's my world."

"Uh-huh."

We lapse into silence again and I regret calling him, when he says, "I'm setting up a trust fund for her."

My blood chills. I don't want his money. How on earth will I explain it to Andre?

"Your husband doesn't need to know. It will be an account at my bank, held in trust until she's eighteen."

"Walt, you don't have to do this. She's not—"

"I don't care if she's mine or not. She's yours and that's enough for me. I care about you, Francesca. I know I was never enough for you but we did our best to make it work. I will always love you and keep the promise I made on our wedding day to protect you."

Tears clog my throat and I swallow. Only Walter could say something so heartfelt and genuine and mean it, making me feel warm and fuzzy after all this time.

"You're a sweet guy and always have been."

"I try."

He's back to his bashful best and I smile, pushing the cell against my ear. I'm not in love with Walter and haven't been for a long time, but he comforts me in a way Andre never can. Andre is vibrant and spontaneous and I love him for it, but there's a reason I was drawn to Walter in the first place and that dependability is a quality that hasn't waned over the years.

"Francesca?"

"Yeah?"

"Let's make this an annual thing. You calling me on our anniversary."

"You really are a sentimental fool," I say as if brushing off the idea, but I'm smiling and I like the thought of us doing a brief catch-up once a year.

"I am but I think you already knew that." The warmth in his voice makes my smile widen.

"Okay. Then I guess I'll speak to you in a year?"

"You will." He pauses, and I think he's about to put down the phone, before he adds, "But if you ever need anything, please don't hesitate to call."

"Thanks."

I hang up, knowing I won't do that. I'm okay with a once a year call for old times' sake but I have no intention of turning to him for anything ever again.

Look what happened the last time I did that.

CHAPTER FORTY-NINE

FRANKIE

NOW

I love this time of evening, around nine, when Luna has been asleep for an hour, Andre is usually gaming or scanning the latest gadget releases online upstairs and I'm in the living room with a glass of wine surrounded by packages.

I may be tiring of having to come up with fresh content for my lifestyle vlog but receiving freebies will never lose its appeal. I'm sitting cross-legged on the floor, a chilled Riesling on the coffee table in front of me, with a stack of unopened packages on my right. I have a system where I open them individually, record the date, item and sender in a journal so I know who to promote.

I always feel like a kid at Christmas as I tear the tape off the first parcel and discover a stunning silk scarf inside from a local designer. It's handmade, in a vibrant emerald with slashes of turquoise through it. I drape it around my neck, savoring the luxurious feel of it sliding against my skin.

The next package isn't as exciting, hand-poured soy candles from a newly opened home wares shop in Manhattan. But as I raise them to my nose one at a time and inhale, I'm transported to an imaginary island by the lemongrass and coconut, frangipani and vanilla. These will definitely get a workout the next time I feel like escaping; which is pretty much all the time at the moment.

The simmering dissatisfaction Celeste picked up on last week hasn't diminished. If anything, with every passing day I envisage doing something different with my life. Shutting down my vlog so I don't have to be so perfect every time I step in front of the camera. Taking on a new challenge.

The only problem is, I have no idea what that is. I've spent my entire life living up to other people's expectations. First my parents, being the model daughter, then Walter, being the doting wife, and now Andre and Luna, the perfect wife and mother. It's not like I resent them; far from it. But I want more and damn if I know what that is.

I've ripped open my third package when Andre comes downstairs. "Did you check the mail today?"

I gesture at the packages and he rolls his eyes. "I meant the mailbox?"

"No. I was too fixated on this pile outside the front door I forgot. Are you expecting something?"

"A new catalogue from that design place near our old apartment."

"You do know you can subscribe to catalogues online, right?"

"Smart ass. I like the feel of paper in my hands sometimes, the same way you like buying exorbitant numbers of paperbacks rather than e-books."

"Touché." I smile and wave him away. "Go. You're interrupting my fun."

"Any good stuff today, other than that swank scarf around your neck?"

"Some nice candles."

He wiggles his eyebrows. "Maybe you can bring those into the bedroom later?"

"They have to be new when I light them live online, not used."

"Too bad." He blows me a kiss. "Back in a sec."

He lets himself out the front door and I become engrossed in opening the next few packages: a label maker for the pantry, a set of newfangled fruit peelers, a halter top and sequined skirt, sun visors in various colors and a beautiful journal. As I flip the pretty pages, I realize Andre hasn't returned. I've lost track of time but he's been outside for at least fifteen minutes while I've been opening and recording the freebies.

I pick up my wine glass and move to the window looking out on the street. He's standing at the bottom of our steps, with his arms around a woman.

It's Celeste.

I stiffen and take a healthy slug of wine. It burns my throat as I watch them. Her cheek is resting against his chest, her arms around his waist, too tight. His cheek is resting on the top of her head and he looks way too comfortable, like he's done this before.

I try not to jump to conclusions because Celeste and I have grown closer and I don't want to ruin our friendship by reading too much into what could simply be a comforting hug. But there's nothing in Andre's hand so he didn't go outside to check the mailbox.

Had he gone outside to talk to her?

Violette skips down the steps next door and she joins them, and I'm relieved when Andre releases Celeste as they lean down to talk to Violette. Celeste takes hold of her hand and Andre ruffles her hair, and in that moment they look more like a family than we do.

I gulp the rest of my wine, draining the glass. It does little to ease my rising suspicion.

I know Andre's infidelity six years ago plays into my inherent insecurities. But I need to tread carefully. I don't want to cause a rift between us over something that probably has a simple explanation.

I want to look away, to dismiss this as meaningless, but I can't.

I'm transfixed.

Then Celeste glances up and spots me. For a second I think I glimpse triumph on her face before she waves, beckoning me to join them.

Celeste and I are friends now. I have got to get over this. But as I slip out of the front door, I can't help wondering: what did I just see?

CHAPTER FIFTY

CELESTE

I rarely show weakness. It's not my style. As a single mom, I have to be strong, and I want to be a good role model for my daughter. So when Vi had a temper tantrum a few minutes ago because she misses her father and blames me, it wasn't her yelling or sobs that affected me as much as her labeling me a bad mom. That hurt, because moving here has been about protecting her and I want for her to believe in me so badly, but the longer she glared at me with tears streaming down her cheeks, the more I felt the pressure building in my chest and I knew I had to get out of the house.

I'd barely closed the door and walked down the steps before the tears I'd been holding back started flowing, and to my embarrassment Andre saw me fall apart. His hug had come out of left field and I would've normally resisted, but he caught me at a rare vulnerable moment and I welcomed his comfort.

Vi must've been watching from the window because she came bounding outside, contrite and sweet, and I almost started bawling again. Until I saw Frankie watching us and realized she may misconstrue this.

She does, because I see her tight expression as she descends the steps toward us. I tell Vi to head inside and am relieved she does, because I don't want my daughter privy to this conversation, especially if Frankie's determined to think the worst of me again. She looks like she caught us naked and going at it in the park.

"Did the catalogue arrive?" She stares pointedly at Andre's empty hands and he stuffs them into his pockets.

"No, unfortunately." He sounds like a chastised little boy and I'm struck by an inane urge to laugh. "I'll see you inside."

He can't get away fast enough and I call out, "Thanks, Andre."

"No worries."

But as he closes the front door to his place there's a giant worry and she's glaring straight at me.

"Everything okay?"

I nod and glance over my shoulder to make sure Vi can't hear me. "Yeah, it is now. I'm ashamed to say I lost my cool with Vi earlier and came out here to get away from her for a few minutes so I could calm down, and Andre saw me." I point to my cheeks. "I was crying and I have to say, you have a keeper there, because most guys would run a million miles in the opposite direction at the sight of tears but he gave me a hug."

"I'm glad he could help," she says, not sounding glad at all. "Anything I can do?"

"Not unless you can miraculously produce a sibling for Vi, no."

Her eyebrows rise and I shrug. "She was bugging me about not having a dad anymore, how it's my fault we left, how she doesn't have a brother or sister, a general blame game that makes me a bad mother apparently."

"You're not a bad mom." She sighs and my honesty has gone some way to defusing her tension. "She's young and believe me, I know they can say the most outrageous things at this age."

Her understanding means a lot, especially when she appeared ready to throttle me when she barged out here. "She doesn't understand I moved here to protect her. I get that she misses Roland but it's for our safety…"

Frankie's eyes widen. "Was it that bad?"

I'm glad she's sympathetic, though I'm not willing to confirm or deny her suspicions of abuse. "I made the right choice and Vi will come to realize that in time."

She nods, her gaze sympathetic. "We all do what we have to do to protect our kids. It's instinctual."

"Yeah, though I can't do much to placate her when it's true, I have robbed her of her father." It breaks my heart, because I'd like nothing better than for us to be a family, but courtesy of Roland, I had no option but to flee in the end. "I blame TV. She's obsessed with some pony show that features a family of six and she's started bugging me about her dad and siblings ever since. Does Luna ask you about it?"

She barks out a laugh. "Rarely. She's too used to being the center of attention."

"What about Andre?"

I know I've asked the wrong thing the moment the question leaves my mouth. Her expression blanks and she stares at some point over my right shoulder. "No. We talked about more kids years ago but neither of us want to disrupt the lives we've got."

It's an odd thing to say, equating another child as a disruption, and I remember how fragile she appeared last week, a woman on the edge.

"Maybe I should send him back out? Perhaps I'm not so good at this comforting thing?"

There's bite behind her words and I have to reassure her.

"Don't be silly. We're friends and your husband happened to catch me at a vulnerable moment, that's all. In fact, I'm quite ashamed he got to see me bawling like a baby when I usually never cry."

She's not pacified as her eyes narrow, assessing, speculative. "Is Violette okay? I saw her out here with you."

She's implying I'm lying, that if Vi joined me outside I couldn't have been that upset. Damn this woman and her suspicions. I hate having to justify myself to her.

"Turns out she was contrite for her behavior, but I think it had more to do with her wanting a snack before bed."

"What's her usual bedtime?"

Considering it's now nine-thirty, she's judging my mothering skills too.

"Earlier, usually, but she wanted to finish a jigsaw with me so I was lenient tonight." I wrinkle my nose. "After how the evening turned out I won't make that mistake again."

She mumbles an agreement and that's when I notice Andre is watching us from the same spot Frankie stood not long ago. I wasn't exaggerating when I said he's a keeper. Vi would be lucky to have a full-time father like him in her life.

"I think your husband is waiting for you."

She turns, sees Andre and gives a half-hearted shrug. "I guess I better head in. You sure you're okay?"

"I'm fine. We all have our moments."

I eyeball her and she realizes I'm referring to her little meltdowns a few weeks ago, first at Saylor's dinner party, and later at my place. We're nothing alike, she and I, but women can usually sympathize with each other when we admit life isn't rosy all the time.

"If you ever want to chat, call me," she says, and I'm surprised when she reaches out to touch my arm. "What else are neighbors for?"

I can say so much but I settle for a grateful smile, before she turns and skips up the steps again.

She doesn't see my judgmental glare.

I don't need her help.

But very soon, she may need mine.

CHAPTER FIFTY-ONE
FRANKIE
THEN

Whoever said the years fly by faster after you have kids isn't wrong.

I take to motherhood surprisingly well, considering I've never been one of those women who thought having kids was the be-all and end-all. I was more of the mindset "if it happens it happens." And when it did, I still wasn't sure about being a mom. But breastfeeding Luna, watching her smile and laugh and rollover for the first time, seeing her learn to crawl then walk, cuddling her when she teethed, listening for the sound of her breathing over the baby monitor, changed me in ways I never expected. She became my world and I've never loved anyone so much.

Andre takes to dad duties instantly and could win any father of the year award. He's a hands-on dad, doing everything from changing diapers to late-night strolls with Luna in the stroller to help her fall asleep.

I adore my daughter and can't imagine my life without her, but when she's fourteen months I feel like I'm missing something. I need more than reading stories and cooking organic vegetables. I feel like I'm losing self-worth—my entire identity has become wrapped up in motherhood. While my body rebounded well after Luna's birth, I'm still feeling unattractive, and though Andre is attentive in the bedroom, on the rare occasions we make love, it's robotic. This can't be good. I'm... languishing.

So I start losing myself in watching videos online, anything from crocheting to interior design. There are a lot of videos about motherhood online too and soon I become hooked. One day, for fun, while Luna's napping, I set up my cell and I film myself making a kid-friendly lasagna. I upload it and am staggered when I check the next day and see my video has had over one thousand views. Who'd be interested in boring old me?

I try it again, demonstrating how to make the perfect lemonade. My hits rise to two thousand. Then I try filming myself live and I'm stunned by how many tune in to watch me recycle a few of Luna's dresses by sewing sparkly brocade and spangles on them. Andre is supportive but I can tell he thinks my online vlog is a hobby, something to indulge. He doesn't think that when, eighteen months after I start my vlog, I pull in my first significant bank deposit.

As one month blends into the next and Luna grows into a delightful girl—I even survived the terrible twos with only the occasional tantrum—I start to thrive in my new job. Not that I see filming as work. I have fun seemingly chatting to myself while I do everyday tasks or promoting stuff people have sent me. Christmas has always been my favorite holiday because of the surprise aspect of gifts and receiving freebies makes me feel like it is Christmas every day.

After Luna turns five, Walter sends me a text, asking me to call. It's out of character because we never talk other than our yearly anniversary chats. I do it out of obligation, not for any real desire to talk to him. My ex-husband saved me at a time I needed him most. He gave me a new life. He supported me. But he also let me go and didn't put up a fight when I wanted a divorce, so I know him reaching out to me like this means there's something seriously wrong.

I call him back an hour after he texts, when Andre is at the grocers picking up fresh berries for my live stream tomorrow. Walter always picks up on the fourth ring so when he picks up on the second I realize he must be desperate to talk.

"Thanks for calling me, Francesca. How are you?"

Polite to a fault. "All good here. How are you?"

He hesitates, followed by a long sigh. "I'm exhausted."

My heart skips a beat. "You're not sick?"

"No, nothing like that." By his flat tone, I'm not reassured. "I know this may seem out of line, but I don't have anyone else I trust enough to confide in," he says and I experience a momentary pang of anxiety. Being the only person he trusts makes me uncomfortable. I can't be his support person, for anything. We don't have that kind of relationship, not anymore. But then I remember how he was there for me when Andre cheated and I know I can't turn him away.

"You can talk to me," I say. "What's up?"

"It's Julia."

Now I'm even more uncomfortable. Having him offload about his girlfriend, being his sounding board, isn't ideal. But he's so forlorn in the way he said, "It's Julia," that I can't shut him down.

"What's going on?" I ask tentatively.

"I'm worried about her. She's behaving erratically and I'm concerned for her mental health…"

"That doesn't sound good."

"It's not." Another drawn out sigh. "She's becoming irrational and demanding. Harassing me with phone calls at odd hours. Turning up at the bank when she knows I'm working and can't be disturbed. Planning vacations I have no intention of taking with her. She acts like she owns me, when we're not even a serious couple."

"What does that mean?" I'm confused. I thought they were in a committed relationship.

"We're not together, not really, and haven't been for years. We catch up regularly but that's where it ends."

"I don't get it. Are you friends or more? Because if you're just friends it sounds like you should cut her off."

Easier said than done because if Walter couldn't cut me out of his life completely and I'm his ex-wife, I can't see him doing it with Julia, who he's dated on and off for years.

"We're friends… with occasional benefits."

I snort. "Walter, she was your first girlfriend. Then you reunited with her after we split. And you've been sleeping with her since then? Of course she has the idea you're a couple."

"But we're not. We don't live together. It just happens sometimes."

This surprises me. The Walter I know is reliable and committed and caring. For him to have this kind of casual relationship with Julia is unlike him. It makes me wonder if I hurt him so badly he's now afraid of commitment. I hope not. He deserves happiness.

"Is she wanting more?"

"Yes. Way more than I'm willing to give."

"Then you have to tell her if your heart's not in it. She deserves that."

"Don't you think I've tried?"

He sounds so anguished I wonder if there's more he's not telling me.

"Walt, if something else is going on—"

"There's nothing."

He cuts me off so quickly I'm left staring at the cell in my hand in surprise. The Walter I know is never impolite.

"I'm sorry, Francesca. I'm just on edge and at a loss."

"That's okay. But I'm not a mind reader and I can't really advise you unless you tell me what's going on."

He takes an eternity to answer. "I wish I could. But she's…" He trails off and a startling thought enters my head out of left field.

"She's not violent toward you?"

"No." I'm relieved there's no hesitation. "But the way her mind works… I'm seriously floundering, unsure what to do."

It's not my place to tell him but I hate hearing this kind man sound tense, so I say, "You have two options here, Walt. You either try to reconnect and work it out or you end it. But from what I've just heard, if she's making you this miserable, give it to her straight and distance yourself."

"I wish I could but it's not that simple."

"Then make it simple. If you want to make a go of it, maybe recapture the magic? Do something sentimental. Take her somewhere that's special for you both and talk it out? And if you don't want to do that then you owe it to the both of you to be upfront with her."

Though simplifying things is easier said than done, as I know all too well. I almost ruined my life by running into the arms of Walter for comfort when Andre betrayed me. We don't always do the sane thing or make the rational choice. We're flawed.

"Have you been back to Gledhill since you left with me?" Walter asks.

"No. Why?"

"There's a secluded beach with this rocky outcrop that creates a cave, near a bunch of small cottages built on the outskirts of town. Did you ever go there?"

"No, but I vaguely remember reading about a murder taking place in one of those cottages." I shiver involuntarily, trying to remember the details of what I read at the time. "A young pregnant girl came to town looking for the father of her child and he silenced her…"

"I don't know about any of that but the first day I arrived in Gledhill, a day before I met you at your eighteenth, I took Julia to that beach and she's loved it ever since. We've visited a few times over the years. That cave is our go-to place. Maybe you're right and I should try the sentimental approach and talk to her there? Figure things out? Soften the blow?"

From what he's told me I doubt sentimentality or a trip down memory lane is going to cut it with this woman, especially if he's going to break up with her. But he sounds like he has a plan and I want him to be happy.

"Walt, you know her best. Do what you have to do because you know what? Life's too short and you deserve to be happy. You're a good guy."

"You sound like you're spouting advice on one of your videos."

"And how would you know that?"

"I tune in occasionally."

He sounds embarrassed by the admission and I laugh. "That's sweet. But seriously, Walt, I hope you sort this out."

"Me too. And thanks for listening. Though you know this call doesn't count toward our annual chat, right?"

"I think it does. But we'll see."

I hang up, not sure I really helped but feeling okay about it anyway. I wasn't lying when I told him he's a good guy. But he's not my guy anymore. I hope he sorts his life out because I'm at a peaceful place in mine. I'm finally happy.

CHAPTER FIFTY-TWO

FRANKIE

NOW

I can't dislodge the image of Andre comforting Celeste out of my mind for the next few days. Celeste explained it away and I felt foolish for assuming anything more, but I can't forget it.

She's invited me over for coffee so the girls can play twice since then and our conversation has been easy. But since she mentioned her ex again, my concern for Luna's safety has flared, a deep-seated niggle I can't ignore. It makes me wonder if I should start keeping them apart a little more.

The girls have ballet class today and I'm tempted to drop and run, but Celeste spies me trying to make a subtle escape and she waves me over. She's sitting close to the glass separating the studio from the parents' waiting area, like she can't take her eyes off Violette for a second. I've witnessed a few helicopter parent moments: she never lets Violette out of her sight at the park, even when the girls want to ride around the perimeter sidewalk, and she hovers when Violette eats, like she's afraid she'll choke and require the Heimlich maneuver.

I used to be like that a tad when Luna was younger, probably borne of having only one child. But I've learned to relax over the last few years as she grows more confident in her own skin.

Perhaps I can say a quick hi and make polite chit-chat for a few minutes before escaping. But Celeste has dragged a chair next to hers and I know I'm stuck.

"Hi," she says, staring at my bag still clutched under my arm even when I sit. "Do you have errands to run?"

"A few, but they can wait."

Stupid. Why did I say that? She'd given me the perfect opportunity to leave. Andre says I'm a people pleaser—probably par for the course with my job—but today it's not doing me any favors.

"Good, because I want to ask you something. How do you feel about helping me throw Saylor a baby shower?"

If I want to distance Luna from Celeste and Violette, I should say no. But I'm hopeless at thinking on the spot and can't come up with an excuse fast enough. There's an awkward pause and when she raises an eyebrow, questioning my hesitation, I say, "Sure, I can help. But I'm a little surprised. I didn't know you two were close?"

"We're not, but I feel sorry for her." She sounds genuine but I'm unsure of her motivation. "If I tell you something, will you keep it confidential?"

"Of course." I don't add, "Who am I going to tell?" It says a lot about me that one of my closest friends these days is a neighbor I don't fully trust.

"Remember that day we heard her arguing with Ruston, while the girls were in the park, then you took them inside and I waited for her?"

"Yeah?" It slipped my mind and I hadn't asked Celeste about it.

"I didn't expect her to open up to me at all, and technically she didn't, but I think she's involved with Ruston somehow and it's stressing her out."

"What do you mean?"

"She knew him before and hasn't told Lloyd."

She's staring at me, waiting for me to make the connection I'd rather not. "You're not saying… is he the father of her child?"

Celeste shrugs. "She didn't spell it out but she didn't need to. It was pretty obvious."

"Hell." I wrap my arms around my middle, an instinctive protective reaction against the shock of learning a woman I'm growing to like is caught up in something so nefarious.

"I'll never understand how a woman can dupe a man she loves like that, passing off some other guy's kid as his." Her mouth twists in disgust. "It's appalling."

My arms tighten so she can't see my hands shake. It's easy for women to pass judgment when they have no idea how they'd react in the same situation.

"Is she keeping it from Lloyd?" I ask.

"I don't know. But I hope she's going to tell him. He seems like a nice guy and he deserves to know the truth."

A thought pops into my head. "Do you think she moved to Hambridge Heights to be near Ruston?"

Celeste nods, somber. "Looks like it. Pretty damn convenient otherwise. And living opposite means she can keep an eye on him."

"I wonder if they're even over," I mumble.

"That could be what they were arguing about." Celeste gives a little shake, like she's trying to clear her mind. "Anyway, if our supposition is right and Ruston is the father of her baby, she's holding up remarkably well under the stress of keeping it a secret. But it may be taking its toll from what I saw that day in the park and I think a baby shower will help take her mind off it."

"A lovely idea, and I'm happy to help any way I can."

"Great. I'll make a list of tasks. Do you think you could get a guest list from her?"

"Sure, no problem."

I end up staying for the rest of the class and I'm glad. Celeste is chatty without being overbearing and we soon slip back into the friendship we've established. I really need to get a grip on my jealousy when it comes to Andre because I'm pretty sure

I'm seeing things that aren't there and I don't want to be one of those women.

Celeste is doing a nice thing for Saylor and I'm glad they seem to have bonded if Saylor opened up to her about Ruston. It takes the pressure off my friendship with Celeste and gives me the perfect opportunity to back away a little, so Luna and Violette don't have to see each other so much; a way of keeping my daughter safe if there is some vague threat from Celeste's ex, yet preserving our friendship.

In a way I'm glad Saylor didn't choose me to confide in. The last thing I need is for Andre to think I'm sticking my nose in Ruston's business. I've seen him a few times since the dinner party, mostly to wave at across the park, and once when Luna had been riding past his place and he'd been coming home. We'd exchanged pleasantries, nothing more, and he seemed perfectly nice; especially when he didn't mention my embarrassing behavior at the dinner party.

It's disappointing to learn he may be involved with Saylor beyond being neighbors. So many secrets in this little neighborhood of ours.

So many lies.

CHAPTER FIFTY-THREE

CELESTE

I'm glad Frankie agreed to help me with the baby shower for Saylor because I'm not a great planner. I have grand ideas—like creating signature non-alcoholic cocktails, a onesie decorating station, and a diaper cake—but when it comes to the execution, I'm hopeless. I've always been like this. I wanted to be an actuary; I ended up being an accountant. I wanted to live an exciting life in Atlantic City; I ended up here. I wanted four kids with a loving husband in a big house in Connecticut with room for the kids to ride bikes and play baseball in the backyard; I'm a single mom in a brownstone with barely any furniture.

I shouldn't have built fanciful scenarios in my head. When they didn't come to fruition, it added to the noxiousness of my relationship with Roland. Our breakup wasn't pretty and I had to escape. But on occasions, usually in the dead of night when I'm lying on my side, curled in a fetal position, and rehashing all the ways I could've done things differently, I wish I could call him. Rant at him for how badly he hurt me. Rage because his inexcusable behavior has resulted in Vi losing her father. But I can't. I won't.

I'm sitting on Frankie's comfy couch with my laptop, a spreadsheet open. They comfort me, the order of listing everything in those small rectangles, and I'm making a list of party supplies while the girls are engrossed in a new jigsaw at my feet. Frankie's working at the kitchen table, doing some final editing on a video she shot earlier. It's time sensitive so she needs to get it done, then she'll join me in here and we'll do some planning together.

I want to get as much of this done as possible so we can present it to Saylor as a fait accompli, because I know she'll refuse if we give her a choice. That day in the park when she'd been discussing Ruston she'd seemed defeated, like she can't take much more, and I want this to be a nice surprise, with her not having to do a thing.

I type "paper plates, plastic cups, napkins, cutlery" into the boxes, when I become aware of the girls' conversation.

"Will you be my sister?" Vi asks Luna and I swear my heart stops. My poor girl yearns for a sibling the same way I yearn to give her one.

"Won't that be weird?" Luna's face scrunches up. "Because our moms and dads are different, how can we be sisters?"

I watch Vi ponder this for a moment before tapping Luna on the nose, like she's a fairy godmother granting a wish. "Well, you don't have a sister and I don't either, but I really want one, so why can't we pretend?"

"I guess we can do that." Luna hands her a puzzle piece. "I sometimes wish my mom would have a baby, then I wouldn't be alone."

I realize I'm leaning forward, hanging on Vi's response. "I want my mom to have a baby too. But my dad isn't here and she says she'll think about it."

Vi glances up and I quickly drop my gaze to the computer screen on my lap so she can't tell I'm eavesdropping.

"But I think she's lying."

My heart sinks and I wish I could go to my daughter and comfort her.

"I don't think she wants another baby. If she did she wouldn't have left my dad."

Luna tilts her nose in the air. "Don't be silly. Haven't you heard all the fairy tales? They'll get back together and live happily ever after and you'll get your baby sister then."

My chest aches with suppressed emotions, with the simplicity of children solving the problems of the world, with me wishing it were that easy.

"Yeah, but that might take forever, so in the meantime, you be my sister, okay?"

"Okay."

Vi holds up her pinkie finger and Luna intertwines hers with it, and I know these two will be friends forever.

CHAPTER FIFTY-FOUR
SAYLOR

I'm dealing with a nasty case of heartburn after scoffing one too many leftover fajitas for lunch when there's a knock at the door. My heart leaps but when I peer through the curtains it's Frankie, not Ruston.

I'm not in the mood to socialize with anyone at the moment but she knows I'm home. We waved to each other about half an hour ago as I returned from a walk and she was putting out the trash. Left with no option, I open the door and paste a welcoming smile on my face.

"Hi, Frankie. How are you?"

"Great. You?"

I pat my growing belly, which has popped more in the last week. "Still incubating."

When I make no move to open the door further, she asks, "Can I come in for a moment? There's something I want to discuss with you."

I'd rather slam the door in her face but I say, "Sure," and open the door wider. She enters and when we go into the living room she stands there, uncomfortable, glancing around, and I realize the last time she was here was the night of the dinner party when she got drunk and flirted with Ruston.

It had been a game to him. I know because he's done it in the past to make me jealous. But the way she reacted I'm embarrassed for her.

When she doesn't seem to be forthcoming, I ask, "What can I do for you?"

She blinks, as if refocusing. "Celeste and I want to throw you a baby shower."

I want to say hell no. I don't have the backbone to fake it much longer. With every passing day I don't get the money to pay off the blackmailer I'm increasingly panicked. He gave me a month and it's like I hear a giant ticking clock every second of the day, reminding me how seriously I've messed up and how much worse this will get if I don't pay up.

"That's nice, but I'm pretty tired these days—"

"You won't have to lift a finger. We'll take care of everything. All I need from you is a guest list."

These women are so nice. Frankie welcomed me into the neighborhood and Celeste listened to me moan after Ruston threatened to turn my world upside down. While I organized that share-a-plate supper at the park and the dinner party here, I feel like I haven't made much of an effort to get to know them, considering how consumed I am by my problems. They're offering to do something incredibly generous and maybe I should take advantage before my life is upended.

Tears sting my eyes and I try to blink them away, but not before a few trickle down my cheeks and I swipe them away.

"Oh, honey, come sit down." She guides me to the sofa like a mother hen marshaling a chick. "Can I get you anything?"

"A redo of my life," I say before I can censor the words, and she pats my back.

"We all make mistakes."

"Yeah? What have you done lately that's so bad?" I ask, irritated by her condescension.

Rather than laugh it off, she pales and glances away for a second. "Like I said, nobody's perfect and if you want to talk, I'm here."

I wish I could. I wish I had somebody to unburden my secrets to, someone who won't judge me. The sad thing is, I do—Lloyd—but I can't confide in him about any of this. Not yet.

"I'm assuming Celeste told you what we discussed in the park. Is that what this shower is about?"

Sheepish, she nods. "She's worried about you and feels you deserve something special to cheer you up."

The only thing that will cheer me up is the money I'm expecting so I can put this all behind me.

"When did you have in mind?"

"Maybe two weeks from today? That gives us time to invite people."

I want to refuse. I can't summon the energy for this or anything else these days. Lloyd has noticed and he's worried. He's been especially attentive, cooking dinners, doing the washing, buying my favorite choc-chip ice cream. He even sits beside me on the sofa and listens to soulful eighties ballads when I know he hates them. He's an amazing husband and every day I'm living a lie with him, my guilt increases exponentially.

Perhaps this shower will be a welcome distraction. And a way to get the money I'm owed sooner rather than later…

"Sounds good," I say, rising to my feet in a blatant hint I want her to leave. Because the longer she stays, so sweet and solicitous, the more likely I am to blab my secrets for the simple fact I'm desperate for somebody to talk to.

Thankfully, she does the same. "So you'll text me a guest list?"

"Absolutely. I'll get onto it now." I walk her to the door, eager to get rid of her as the burn of tears prickle my eyes. "Thanks, Frankie. And thank Celeste for me too."

"Our pleasure," she says, but she's studying me like she knows I'm on the brink.

As I battle tears I close the door quickly. I don't deserve her understanding or sympathy. If things don't go to plan and the truth comes out, everyone will hate me.

CHAPTER FIFTY-FIVE

FRANKIE

THEN

A week after Walter's unexpected call, he's still on my mind. I'm busy during the day, taking Luna on a surprise trip to Manhattan, planning my content for the next month, and spending as much time with my daughter as I can because I know these early years will fly all too fast. It's at night when I'm lying in bed, staring at the ceiling because it always takes me at least an hour to fall asleep, I think back to Walter's call and how out of character it was. How worried he was about Julia.

I love Andre but Walter is the most capable man I know. He's unflappable, the type of man you can depend on in a crisis. So for him to sound that rattled... I'm worried.

I didn't like how he has concerns about Julia's mental health. For staid, dependable Walter, the zombies of the apocalypse would have to invade earth for him to remotely be concerned about a girlfriend behaving erratically. Even when I'd told him about my parents and their lifestyle, he'd merely quirked an eyebrow though I know it had shocked him because we'd discussed it later. When a gas bottle for our barbecue had exploded in the garden shed and set the whole thing alight, he'd calmly called the fire department while trying to battle the fire with an extinguisher. When I'd freaked out after practically slicing my palm in half while chopping peppers one night making dinner, he'd reacted quickly, wrapping my hand in a dishcloth and driving fast, yet safely, to the ER department.

So that phone call and his uncharacteristic panic is bugging me. A lot.

With sleep elusive, I slip out of bed. I have to pass Luna's bedroom on the way to the stairs and I pause, peeking through the gap. She's barely moved since I tucked her in two hours ago, lying on her back, her arms spread-eagled on top of the covers, her golden plait at right angles on her pillow. Her night light casts the faintest stars around the room and I lean against the doorjamb for a moment, content in a way I never thought I could be before I had her.

She's my world, bringing me a joy I never expected when I got pregnant. Luna is unpredictable and spontaneous at times, cloyingly affectionate at others, and I love every adorable inch of her. Not that we're perfect all the time. She's not so pleasant to be around when her demands aren't met and she gets her obstinacy from me, but she's amazing and I adore her.

She stirs, mumbling something in her sleep, and I ease away, not wanting to wake her. I tiptoe down the stairs, skipping the third from the bottom because it creaks loud enough to wake me when Andre has to leave for work early sometimes. I pad into the kitchen and fill a glass of water, before sitting at the dining table and flipping open my laptop.

I've never been one to look back on my past so I've never searched on social media or elsewhere for my parents or Walter. I prefer living in the present but with Walter's weird call still making me edgy, it's time I did a little digging on Julia.

I'm blessed with a good memory so I remember Walter mentioning her full name to me way back when we started dating. I type Julia Skelke into a search engine and wait as the hits pop onto the screen. However, a B-grade movie producer in Toronto, a teacher in London, a college student in Hamburg and a chef in Sydney don't fit the bill. I scroll through a few pages, surprised there are no hits on social media either.

Puzzled by a lack of online presence—almost everyone has some kind of digital footprint these days—I take a different tack and check out if Walter has a social media profile. He does, on one of the more obscure sites, and it looks like he hasn't updated it in years. On the upside, he hasn't been clever enough to fully protect his privacy either, so I can look through his photos. There's none of me and I don't know whether to be relieved or insulted. There are a few of him at work and at conferences and this is when I finally find what I'm looking for.

It's a photo of about twenty bank employees and their significant others, taken about six months before I met Walter, at a banking conference in Chicago. Walter has his arm around a blonde woman who's identified as Julia Skelke in the fine print under the photo taken from some financial journal, but she's mostly hidden by some guy with big hair in front of her.

That pesky third step creaks and I shut my laptop. The last thing I need is Andre asking questions why I'm looking at my ex-husband's out-of-date social media profile. I sip my water as he enters the kitchen, rubbing his eyes, his hair sticking up at right angles all over his head.

His eyes are bleary with sleep. "What are you doing down here?"

"Couldn't sleep so thought I'd grab a drink, maybe a snack."

"Want me to make you cheese on toast?"

I smile. My husband thinks all the world's problems can be solved by cheese on toast at any time of day or night. "No, I'm good. I might grab one of those oatmeal cookies I made earlier today."

He wrinkles his nose but grabs the cookie jar regardless. "I don't like those white chia seeds you added to them."

"If Luna couldn't taste them, I doubt you can."

He places the cookie jar on the table in front of me and pretends to pout. "I'll have you know I'm a cookie connoisseur and

I can detect the slightest hint of healthy crap you try and hide in otherwise delicious cookies."

"Well then, I'm surprised you didn't figure out I put wheat germ and powdered greens in those cookies you demolished so quickly last week."

"What?" He clutches his stomach. "That's plain unfair."

"Hey, I have to get the healthy stuff into you guys somehow."

"You need to be punished," he says, pulling me to my feet and patting my butt.

I laugh and widen my eyes in false innocence. "Oh really?"

"Yeah. Upstairs. Now." He growls a second before he nuzzles my neck and I wrap my arms around him, thankful for this man every day.

We got through the tough times and despite my insecurities causing a few minor hiccups every now and then, and my general dissatisfaction with my work, we're doing okay.

"I love you," I whisper, pressing my cheek against his chest, comforted by the steady beat of his heart.

"Right back at you."

As we ease apart and he stares into my eyes I realize I need to stop worrying about my ex's problems and concentrate on my marriage. I have enough going on in my life to fret about anyone else's.

But the next evening, Walt calls again. I can't give him advice about how to handle his deranged girlfriend and I don't want to lend a sympathetic ear again. I need to nip this in the bud because I can't have him calling me so often. There's a vast difference between an annual call for sentimentality and being his go-to person for relationship advice. It's all kinds of wrong.

But when I answer and hear a subdued sob, I'm so shocked I don't say anything.

"Francesca, love of my life."

Hell, he's drunk. A confirmed teetotaler, life must be really bad for Walter to contemplate taking a sip of alcohol let alone drinking so much he's slurring his words and saying he loves me.

"Walt, you have to stop calling me."

"Can't. You're the only person I can talk to."

"That's not true. You've worked at the bank for years and you have college buddies. You've got plenty of friends to talk to."

I hear a sniffle. "But you're the only one who understands me."

This isn't good. After our divorce, Walter never gave any indication he has residual feelings—apart from that one slip-up when I escaped to the beach house after Andre cheated. I'm concerned that the alcohol has loosened his inhibitions and his tongue, and his true feelings, long buried, are emerging.

If that's so, I feel sorry for him, as I can never be anything other than a distant friend. I know why I indulge him in our annual chats. Because I still harbor incredible guilt that I turned to him in an hour of need and I used him to get back at Andre, even if my husband doesn't know it.

I never should've taken advantage of Walter like that. It was wrong on so many levels. At the time, I'd justified it in ridiculous ways: telling myself that Andre slept with someone so this would be payback and we'd be even, I needed to feel attractive rather than spurned, I knew Walter would make me feel good for a short period of time when I really needed the validation. But no matter how much I dressed it up or how many excuses I told myself, I had used him and I hope this isn't the result.

"Francesca? You still there?"

"Yeah, I'm here."

"Why didn't you tell me wine is so good? I've drunk a bottle and I feel so much better. I swear I can hear the waves much clearer through the living room window. I love this beach house. So many memories…"

I know I'll regret asking this but the sooner I get to the bottom of this phone call, the sooner I can hang up.

"Why do you need to feel better?"

"Because I need to break up with Julia and I know it's going to be awful."

"So you've made the decision yet haven't done it?"

"I'm a chicken."

He starts making clucking noises that end up sounding like a duck quacking and I stifle a laugh. Walter is so honorable and upstanding I can't imagine him tipsy, let alone drunk.

"Maybe if I drink some more, I'll pluck up the courage?"

"No!" I almost yell, before lowering my voice. "You need to be sober to have a conversation like that with her. You owe her that much."

"I guess… This is a disaster. Her. Me. Everything is screwed up. It wasn't supposed to be this way. Why wasn't I good enough for you?"

Uh-oh. It looks the wine has already given Walter false courage because he's dredging up the past and asking questions he should've bombarded me with back then.

"You were a great husband, Walt, and I cherished our time together. But we're too different and ultimately, that led to us drifting apart."

I can never tell him the truth. That I doubt I ever truly loved him. That he was a means to an end, a way for me to escape Gledhill and my parents, a way to never look back. When we married I cared about him a lot, may have even loved him a little. But I was never in love with him the way I am with Andre.

"You broke my heart."

I wince and sorrow makes me tear up. He sounds so plaintive I wish I can offer him some comfort, but I can't. It's not my place.

"Walt, the wine is making you maudlin. It has the same effect on me. Why don't you have something to eat, drink some coffee—"

"Is Luna mine?"

I freeze as a chill sweeps over me, raising the fine hairs on my arms, making me shiver. I sway a little and grip the table in front of me for support.

It's taken him five years to ask the question and I should be prepared to answer. I've expected this long before now. And I hate the thought he's been stewing over this for years and has only asked now because he has false courage from a bottle.

"No, Walt, Luna is Andre's."

He starts sobbing and I clench the cell so hard my fingers ache.

"I never wanted to make life difficult for you, Francesca, that's why I haven't asked before. But I've been thinking about it for a long time, hoping it's true, because that would mean we'd have a chance…"

Appalled by how much he's clinging to the past, I say, "This is the alcohol talking. Please, eat something. Take a painkiller and lie down. You'll feel better in the morning."

"I won't. I was really hoping Luna is mine—"

"She's not," I snap, my patience wearing thin at his rambling persistence. "I'll send you a copy of the paternity test if that's what it's going to take to get you to believe me. I had one done not long after her birth because of my slip-up with you and I wanted to be sure."

"Whatever," he mumbles, sounding like Luna at her recalcitrant best. "I'm sorry for laying all this on you. You're right. I'm never drinking again."

"Just take care of yourself, okay?"

"Hmm…"

The dial tone buzzes in my ear and I put the phone down, surprised to find my hand shaking. I have no idea if he'll remember any of this in the morning but I know what I have to do. Seeing tangible proof of Luna's paternity will put an end to any fanciful daydreaming.

I can't send it to the house we used to live in because I'm not sure if Julia still has access, so I'll send it to the beach house. I could email but I only have his work one and I don't want to attach private stuff to an address that can be scanned by antivirus software and possibly alerted as spam for others to see.

Sending a copy of the paternity test alone is too heartless, so I flip open a notebook and start writing.

Dear Walt,

I have no idea what to say. I value our friendship, but I wonder now if keeping in touch, albeit annually, has done you a disservice. It sounds like remaining friends, even if we usually only chat once a year, has given you some kind of false hope. Perhaps the alcohol made you say a bunch of stuff that isn't true or it could've dredged up feelings long buried, but whatever the reason, this needs to be addressed.

It was never my intention to hurt you. Our marriage was good but we grew apart and when it ended, you were upset but stoic and understanding too. It's in the past but from what you just said on the phone, you've been clinging to memories and wishing for things that will never be between us.

I consider you a friend. And as a friend I'm going to give it to you straight.

If you've been holding back emotionally from Julia because of some misguided hope for us, that has to end. Our relationship is in the past and there's no going back. You say you want to break up with her but you need to re-evaluate why. Is it because you can't give her what she wants or is there more to it? Women are intuitive and you've been dating a long time. It's not surprising she may want some kind of commitment. If your doubt over Luna's paternity has held you back, you need to move forward. Now.

Luna is not your daughter and I've attached the test results. I'm hoping that seeing cold, hard proof will free you and enable you to move forward with your life. I just wish I'd done it sooner.

This is the last time I want to speak about this with you. I encourage you to talk to Julia and whether you ultimately break up or not, make sure it's what you truly want in your heart.

I'm not sure it's wise we keep doing our annual phone call?

Take care,
Francesca

I don't sign off with "love" as I need to establish clear boundaries now. I'm saddened beyond belief that the man who'd once given me a fresh start has been dwelling on the past. I hope this letter and the paternity test will give him the closure he needs.

If anyone deserves all the good things in life, my kind-hearted ex-husband does.

CHAPTER FIFTY-SIX

FRANKIE

NOW

I'm checking off the RSVPs for Saylor's baby shower when my cell rings. It's an unknown number and I usually ignore those but it could be an invitee who prefers to call rather than text an acceptance, so I answer.

"Hello, Frankie speaking."

"Is that Francesca Forbes?" The woman's voice is cool yet professional.

"Yes."

This can't be a baby shower guest, because I hadn't given my full name on the invitations, just Frankie and my cell number.

"This is Betty Egmont from the Regional Bank."

My confusion increases. Why would someone from the bank where Walter is the manager call me? "What can I do for you, Betty?"

"I'm calling because you're listed as Walter's emergency contact."

My heart skips a beat. Something has happened to Walter. I knew there had to be a reason why he hasn't returned my calls. Though in my moment of panic I'm slightly annoyed he hasn't removed my name as his emergency contact.

"Is he okay?"

"That's why I'm calling. We don't know. Walter was due back at work a few days ago and he hasn't shown. We've reported him to the police as a missing person."

I stumble and make a grab for the nearest chair before collapsing into it. I scramble to think. How long ago did I first call him? A few weeks? Has he been missing that long?

"Do the police have any leads?" Even asking the question is surreal. I've watched countless police procedurals on TV; I never thought I'd get caught up in a real missing person case.

"I'm afraid not, but they advised me to notify you. They may want to interview you over his disappearance."

A cold clamminess washes over me. "But I don't know anything. He's my ex-husband and we haven't seen each other in years."

"Oh. Right." She sounds surprised, and I don't blame her—I'm his emergency contact, but I have no idea why. Then again, considering our last conversation about two months ago, when he'd been concerned about Julia and intent on breaking off their relationship once and for all, it makes sense he'd remove her. But surely he has someone else closer than me?

"If you hear anything at all, can you let me know, please?"

"Yes, I'll keep you posted," Betty says, and her voice wavers a little. "Walter was extremely well liked here at the bank. He's a great boss and everyone respects him."

I hate that I notice she uses past tense when describing how well-liked Walter is. There has to be a logical explanation for this. I refuse to consider any other outcome.

"Thanks for letting me know, Betty."

She hangs up and I'm left reeling. I'm worried about Walter. It's totally out of character for him to disappear without telling anyone, let alone miss work, which means there's something seriously wrong.

I remember watching the news with him nightly in the early days of our marriage and one evening a story about a father who'd disappeared had come on. The reporter had gone on to say he'd been found safe and sound a few days later and that the man had wanted some timeout from the stress of his work and family. Walt had been appalled at the man's selfishness and had assured me he'd never do something like that on a whim, that people who put their loved ones through the torture of not knowing what had happened to them should be made an example of.

So I know Walt would never walk away from his job, his life, which means it's a big deal if he's missing, and I'm terrified something awful has happened. But I'm at a loss what to do. I suppose I'll have to wait for the police to contact me.

While I'm desperate for news of Walt, I'm concerned about the police coming around here asking a bunch of questions. Questions that will lead to answers I'd rather not give in the presence of my husband; like how I converse annually with my ex on our anniversary, how we've spoken to each other more frequently lately and why.

I can't risk them finding my letter and the paternity test. Walt is so methodical I know where he keeps important documentation, which means if the police do a thorough search of the beach house, they'll find it. I can't let that happen.

I need to be proactive. Pre-empt them coming here.

To do that, I may need to take a trip.

CHAPTER FIFTY-SEVEN

CELESTE

The conversation I overheard at the last play date, when Vi told Luna she wanted a sibling, is haunting me. At the time I considered calling Roland, a silly move that won't end well, before pushing it out of my mind and busying myself with work, Saylor's baby shower and spending as much time as possible with Violette.

I know she's lonely at times with just me for company but I try to fill her days with online educational shows and new toys. It feels like I'm buying her affection sometimes and that I'm overcompensating somehow, but I want my darling girl to be happy. She misses her dad and maybe I need to push aside my qualms about contacting him and suck it up for my daughter's sake.

I wait until she's asleep before heading downstairs to pour myself a glass of wine. I gulp half the Chardonnay before picking up my cell and bringing up Roland's number.

I mentally rehearse what I'm going to say. Crazy, because I know when I hear his voice I'll probably break down in tears. My thumb hovers over the number and I end up draining my wine glass before I tap it. My chest is tight, my palms slick with sweat, as I count the number of dial tones, belatedly realizing he won't answer once he sees my number on the screen. He'll let my call go through to voicemail. I'm not sure whether to be disappointed or relieved when it does.

"Hi, Roland, it's me. Considering how we ended things, I'm the last person you want to hear from. But Violette misses you. And no matter how bad our relationship turned, I'm sure you're sorry for what you said the last time we saw each other and I'm sorry for taking Vi away. She needs you. I hope she can visit one day soon when we're both ready. In the meantime, we've settled into a new home and we have great neighbors. Vi's good friends with the girl next door, who's the same age. I sometimes wish you were here to see how your daughter is thriving." I realize I'm getting carried away and try to refocus. "I guess we both have to take responsibility for how badly we ended... I know you love Violette but we had to get away. I hope you understand why."

I hang up, tears coursing down my cheeks, the pain in my chest expanding to unbearable.

He won't call me back. I know because no matter what I say now, nothing will change the vile way things ended between us.

But at least I've called and given him some hope of a possible visit. He'll want to see Vi even if I'm the last person he wants to acknowledge.

As soon as Saylor's baby shower is done, maybe it's time I instigate steps for Vi to visit her dad.

CHAPTER FIFTY-EIGHT

FRANKIE

NOW

I'm so worried about Walter that I can't sit around waiting for the police to call. I'm going out of my mind, envisaging worst-case scenarios, and I need to do something proactive. It's crazy to even contemplate going back to the beach house but it's the one place Walt would go if something was wrong and the last place he'd been seen.

I wait until Andre gets home from work mid-afternoon to give him a heads up about my plans and explain why I'm compelled to visit the one place I think Walt may be, but as he walks in on me packing, he overreacts.

"What the hell are you doing?"

"I need to leave—"

"You're leaving me?" He swears under his breath and drags a hand through his hair, tugging so hard the strands stand up. "I can't believe this. After all we've been through, you're giving up so bloody easily."

He storms out, leaving me stunned as I hear his boots clomping down the stairs.

I can't believe he actually thinks I'm leaving him. It's bizarre and doesn't make sense. Unless he's done something to give me reason to, but I can't contemplate that now. I won't let my latent insecurities interfere with the task at hand: discovering if Walt is okay.

I zip my suitcase, pick it up and head downstairs to try and reason with my crazy husband.

I find him standing at the bottom of the stairs, looking so devastated I don't know whether to hug him or chastise him for doubting me and thinking the worst, that I'd ever walk out on him and Luna.

"If you'd let me finish up there, I was saying I need to leave to check in on Walter at the cottage, you big jerk." I whack him softly on his chest. "Where we first met, remember?"

He winces, before enveloping me in his arms and squeezing so tight I can barely breathe. "Sorry for overreacting. It really freaked me out seeing you packing, then hearing you were leaving."

"Glad to know you care."

He squeezes tighter and I yelp, so he releases me. "I love you, Frankie. You're my world and I'd be nothing without you."

I have no idea why he's so panicked, but I don't have time to delve now. "Maybe I should pack a suitcase more often?" I try to lighten the tone.

"Don't you dare." He kisses me, a hard, possessive kiss branding me as his. "You're not going anywhere. Apart from chasing after your ex apparently," he says, still somewhat rattled.

"I know it's odd, but an employee at his bank called me because I'm his person to contact in an emergency and they're worried."

"This is nuts." Andre starts pacing the living room before stopping in front of me, confusion furrowing his brow. "Why the hell are you the emergency contact person for your ex-husband? And why are you compelled to go looking for him?"

"I can't answer your first question because I wondered that too. And I'm not looking for him—"

"The hell you aren't. You're running off to that beach house in New Haven." Anger turns his eyes flinty. "I don't get this. Why would you go chasing after some guy you haven't spoken to in years?"

I want to tell him the truth and I will, but now isn't the time. I'm seriously worried about Walter and I can't ignore a sliver of guilt I may be responsible for this. I didn't sleep last night and have been mulling over it all morning, wondering if Walter has been unstable and that's what his rambling phone call had been about. And worse, if my subsequent letter and the paternity test result drove him over the edge.

"Honey, you know I love you and I've told you about my past." I take hold of his hands, hoping to convey my sincerity. "Walter helped me escape all that and I owe him."

"You owe him nothing," Andre mutters, but I glimpse a softening in his eyes. "Besides, if he's a missing person, who knows what he might be involved in? It could be dangerous for you to go traipsing down there."

Considering Walter only tried alcohol for the first time recently, I seriously doubt he's involved in anything untoward. But I can't tell Andre, not yet. If he learns about my yearly conversations with Walter, and our more recent phone calls, he'll freak and leaving will be impossible.

So I reach for a little white lie. "The police want to interview me at the cottage. That's why I'm going."

His eyebrows shoot up. "You didn't mention anything about the police?"

"He's listed as a missing person. Of course the police are involved."

"I don't like this." He shakes his head and slips his hands out of mine. "I should come with you."

"And drag Luna along with us? She'll ask a million questions and I don't want to put her through it. I'll drive up now and be back tonight. I only packed a few things in case the police questioning takes longer than expected."

"This is crazy. It's a four-hour round trip." He glowers at me for a moment, before enveloping me in his arms and squeezing tight. "Promise me you'll be careful."

"I promise," I murmur, against his chest.

I know I'm probably on a fool's errand but I need to do this.

As for my ulterior motive—finding my letter—Walter isn't the kind of guy to leave something like that lying around. He's too orderly for that, but I can't take the risk. The police will search the beach house at some stage and I want to make a preemptive strike, because if they find that letter and its contents, my interrogation will be lengthy and Andre will learn the truth the hard way.

I will tell him, all of it, but I need to get ahead of this.

I need to leave ASAP.

I choose a playlist from the 2000s for my drive to New Haven but I barely hear a word of the lyrics filtering through my car. Despite my bravado in front of Andre, I'm unsure what I'll find when I get to the cottage. What if my outlandish supposition is right and Walter has done something silly to harm himself? No way do I want to walk in on that.

Turns out, I needn't have lied to Andre about the police wanting to interview me. Betty at the bank must've given them my information because they call about half an hour after I leave Hambridge Heights and want to talk to me. They've thoroughly searched Walter's home in Hartford and are moving onto the cottage, so I say I'll meet them there early evening. Which means it's imperative I get there before them, regardless of what I may find.

Ninety minutes later I park under a makeshift carport on the left of the cottage. Memories swamp me: Walter bringing me here for the first time and carrying me over the threshold, barbecuing steaks on a small grill out the back, long walks on the beach when we didn't have to talk because we were so comfortable together.

I blink back tears as I get out of the car and inhale, allowing the familiar briny tang to comfort me. There has to be a logical explanation for this. I hate to contemplate anything else.

I'm counting on Walter's predictability as I lift the third conch from the left in a bed of shells near the front door. I turn it over and press the spring-loaded flap. It reveals a key. Not that I need it. I still have mine from years ago but I want to make sure it's there because I know the police will ask how I got in and I don't want to raise any suspicion about why I'm still holding onto mine.

If I can find that letter, they'll never know about the paternity test and what happened between us. But if they do... I'll become further embroiled in this when it's the last thing I want.

I'd wondered if he ever told Julia about what happened. Highly doubtful, considering he'd already dumped her once to marry me, and if those accidents before we got hitched had been linked to her... no, he wouldn't have revealed he'd cheated on her again because they'd been in a relationship at the time.

So many mistakes in the past... I shake my head as I jiggle the key in the lock, lifting the handle as I turn, knowing its intricacies. It finally gives and the door swings open. I'm holding my breath as I step inside, forcing myself to move forward.

I sneeze and relief filters through me as I acknowledge there's no horrid smell that could indicate the worst possible outcome I'd been envisaging. I move through the living room, casting an eye around, but everything seems in order. The remote controls are lined up on the coffee table, the cushions perfectly plumped and in place. I enter the kitchen and head to the fridge. If Walter has been here, it will be well stocked. It always was. But apart from several jars containing pickles, pesto and olives, and a few bottles of sparkling water, it's empty, which means he hasn't been here for a while.

It doesn't make sense. When I called the bank initially after he hadn't returned my calls, I'd been told he was on vacation. And Walter is such a creature of habit he never vacations anywhere but here. He'd told me many times why spend money to fly to some resort destination when we have our own better beach here. And when he'd drunk-dialed me, he'd mentioned being here.

Increasingly worried that he may be genuinely missing, I head for the main bedroom. The moment I open the door, memories assail me of the last time I was here, the two of us entwined on the bed, knowing it was wrong but filled with rage against my cheating husband and desperate to lose myself for a few hours in the comforting arms of my ex.

I blink rapidly to erase those traitorous memories as I move toward the closet. Walter didn't have a safe at the cottage, but he'd made a special hiding place for any valuables whenever we came here. Mostly the jewelry he'd given me. I open the doors and squat down, feeling for the panel he'd cut out of the wood. I rely on muscle memory, my fingers finding the groove quickly and the tiny knob at the top. I pull on it and the panel falls to the floor.

Holding my breath, I feel around the tiny space, encountering nothing but the crackle of paper. I exhale in relief when I bring out the envelope and see my handwriting.

I'd been right. If Walter had hidden this away, he hasn't told Julia or anyone about it.

I carefully replace the panel, wriggle backwards and stand, before closing the closet doors. I fold the letter and slide it into the back pocket of my jeans. At least now I can answer the police questions without having the complication of Luna's paternity dragged into it and muddying everything.

It'll be easier if I wait in the car for their arrival so I head toward the front door. To do so, I pass the spare room. The door is open and I'm about to walk past the room when something on the bed snags my attention. A stuffed pony.

Maybe Julia likes stuffed animals but it's not displayed proudly against a pillow, it's thrown haphazardly at the foot of the bed, like a child in a hurry would do. Curious, I enter the room. I'm not sure where to look first. At the pile of neatly folded laundry on a chair, girl's dresses and tops and socks, or the children's books on a shelf. At the board games for children under eight or the solar system night light exactly like Luna's.

Confusion makes my head ache. Not once during our conversations over the years has Walter mentioned Julia having a child. Then again, he never discussed anything to do with Julia until recently and I'd never asked. I'd been glad he'd found happiness with her again after our divorce. It alleviated some of my guilt at ending our marriage because he'd never been enough for me.

But surely this child warranted a mention? Something in passing? Especially when he knew I had Luna. What possible motivation could he have for keeping her hidden?

Perhaps Julia's daughter isn't his but considering the size of the clothes and the age range of those books and games, the girl would have to be between four and six, so he'd been back with Julia then.

Yet another mystery for the police to solve. On impulse, I pop into the room Walter had laughingly labeled his den. Considering how tiny it is, the space is barely bigger than a mudroom and I assumed that's what it had been built for, to take off sandy shoes and clothes after returning from the beach and before entering the house. But being the manager at the bank meant Walter had to work at times, even when we were relaxing down here, so he'd set up the world's smallest office; a chair tucked into the existing bench, where he'd place his laptop or documents. It had a penholder filled with black, blue and red pens, and a plastic holdall with a stapler, scissors, glue stick, stuff he never used because he did most of his work online.

There's a photo frame near the penholder, a white plastic frame embedded with seashells, like it had been bought from a local souvenir shop. I might get to see the reclusive Julia at last.

But as I move closer and pick up the frame, I realize two things at once.

It's not a woman in the frame, it's a child.

The child is Violette.

CHAPTER FIFTY-NINE
CELESTE

I'm making Vi one of her favorite dinners, tomato soup and toast, when there's a knock at the door.

"The soup's nearly ready, sweetie, so hang tight, okay?"

Vi rolls her eyes and I get a glimpse of what she'll be like as a teen. "I'm right here, Mom." She waves the electronic tablet at me. "I'm hungry but I want to finish watching this."

"Cheeky." I tug on her ponytail and she swats me away, already engrossed in the princess show again.

I wipe my hands on a dishcloth as the knock sounds again. I'm not expecting anyone but with a little luck it'll be Frankie wanting to arrange a play date with the girls so we can finalize the baby shower details.

I open the door, surprised to find Andre and Luna on the other side.

"Hey, you two."

"Can Violette play, Celeste?" Luna brandishes a backpack that's bulging. "I've brought loads of stuff because Daddy says I won't get bored that way."

I'm at a loss with what this means and Andre shrugs, sheepish. "I hate to do this to you, but could you watch Luna for a few hours? I've been called in to work on an urgent job and I can't take her with me."

"Sure, no problem." I smile down at Luna, who's craning her neck to look past me, already searching for her bestie. "Violette's about to have dinner. Have you eaten?"

Luna claps her hands before pressing them together in a pleading gesture. "No, and I'm starving."

I laugh and point at the kitchen. "Why don't you go join her while I chat with your dad for a minute?"

"Yay! Thanks, Celeste."

She runs past me, her backpack banging my leg but she doesn't break stride. I love how close the girls are. It's exactly what I'd wanted when we first moved next door.

"I don't expect you to feed her," Andre says. "I've packed fruit and crackers and juice in her backpack."

"It's no problem at all. I always make extra so I don't have to cook every day."

"Great. Thanks for this." He flashes me a grateful smile. "I'm not sure what time I'll be back but it shouldn't take more than an hour or two."

"Take your time. The girls love playing together and it keeps Vi out of my hair for a while."

"I'm not sure when Frankie will be home but I doubt it'll be before me. But I'll let her know Luna's here just in case."

"Is she having some much needed mom time?"

"I wish." He grimaces. "Apparently her ex-husband is missing and the police want to interview her at a beach house they had in New Haven."

I hear what he says but I can't compute as there's a faint buzzing in my ears, like a million bees have been let loose.

Frankie can't be at the cottage.

Because she might figure out the truth and it's too soon.

"Celeste? You okay?"

"Yeah, just hungry, got a little woozy for a second." I pat my stomach that's churning so badly I fear I may vomit. "I get low blood sugar sometimes."

"I better let you eat then. Thanks again. My number's on my business card tucked it into the front pocket of Luna's backpack so if you need me for anything, just call, okay?"

I manage to nod and smile, while clamping down on the scream building inside me. It clamors to get out, deafening and unrelenting if I let it.

As he heads down the front steps, I close the door and take the stairs two at a time.

There's no time to lose.

I need to pack.

The girls and I have to leave. Now.

CHAPTER SIXTY
SAYLOR

I'm at my usual spot at the front window, spying on Ruston and the rest of my neighbors, stressing over my money turning up, when I see Celeste. She's stuffing overnight bags into the trunk of her SUV and glancing over her shoulder repeatedly, like she's being followed.

Her behavior is odd and when I see her run up her front steps and return holding Violette and Luna's hands in each of hers, it's even odder.

Where could she be taking the girls at six thirty? They should be eating dinner or winding down before bedtime. Then again, I know nothing about kids or their evening routines.

But why the bags?

I'm relieved the girls don't look particularly upset, though Luna keeps glancing at her house with a puzzled frown. When they get to the car, Celeste releases their hands. Vi climbs in the back seat but Luna balks. She tugs at Celeste's sleeve and points to her house. Celeste appears panicked for a moment and almost bundles Luna into the car.

That's when I make a move. I open the front door and call out to her. Either Celeste doesn't hear me or she chooses to ignore me because she slides into the driver's seat, guns the engine and tears up the street with a squeal of tires.

Unease ripples down my spine and I give a little shake. Something about what I saw jars and I should tell Frankie what I've seen. But I saw her leave earlier with a suitcase, and Andre only dropped off Luna at Celeste's not that long ago, so he's probably the logical person to call.

He doesn't pick up and I'm not surprised. He ignores most of my calls these days. When the dial tone stops and diverts to voicemail, I leave a message.

"Hey, Andre, it's me. I thought you should know I just saw Celeste tear out of here like a madwoman, and she had Luna with her. I'm assuming she's minding her while you and Frankie are out, but there was something off about her. And she had bags in the trunk. Anyway, call me."

I barely hang up when my cell rings and it's him.

"Hey, did you get my message—"

"Quit bugging me," he yells so loud I have to move the phone away from my ear. "Stop calling me. Stop leaving me messages. Just stop."

I can't. I won't. Not until he pays me the money, but that's not why I'm calling this time. "Listen, I—"

"I don't have to listen to anything you say, Saylor. I'm done. I've had a gutful. Why can't you leave me the hell alone?"

I hate that he's jumped to conclusions and won't give me a chance to explain, and I'm tempted to hang up on him. Then again, I have been hassling him. Trying to get him alone when we socialize. Calling incessantly. Making demands. But he insists on ignoring me, and it won't end well.

"Before you yell at me some more, I'm calling about Luna."

"What about her?" His tone instantly shifts to one of concern and I like that he's a good dad.

"I'm assuming you and Frankie are out and Celeste's minding her?"

"Yeah? So?"

"It could be nothing, but I saw her bundle the girls into the car a few minutes ago and drive off like she had demons on her tail."

"Maybe she had an errand to run," he says, sounding uncertain.

"She had overnight bags in the trunk."

"What the…" He swears. "I'll reach out to Celeste. You didn't call Frankie, did you?"

"I said I wouldn't, and I haven't. Yet," I add, as a threat I've held over him since I first moved in next door to this infuriating man who turned my world upside down. Between him and Ruston, little wonder I'm a mess.

"Thanks for the heads up on Luna. As for your petty attempt at blackmail, save it. I'm done playing games. I'm telling Frankie the truth."

Before I can say anything else he hangs up. He's lying. He won't tell Frankie a goddamn thing. He's gutless. He would've already revealed everything to her when I first moved in if that was the case. He's bluffing and I don't appreciate it, but I'm glad I called. From his reaction, he knows nothing about Celeste taking his daughter on an overnight jaunt. In which case, he has every right to be worried.

Celeste has been nothing but nice to me and while she's reserved, I respect her. She's good with her daughter and has been pleasant to Lloyd and me. For all I know, Frankie called her and asked her to bring the girls to her, but I doubt it. Andre wouldn't have sounded so panicked.

Whatever happens, I've done the right thing for once.

CHAPTER SIXTY-ONE
FRANKIE

Reeling, I pick up the photo and study it. I'm sure it's Violette when she was younger. Maybe as a toddler of about two. And there's a woman in the background that vaguely resembles Celeste. Different hair color and style, with bangs that cover half her face, but I think it's her.

It doesn't make sense.

Is Celeste Walter's Julia? And is Violette Walter's child?

My mind is spinning out of control with too many outlandish scenarios, so I call Andre. It goes to voicemail so I leave a brief message asking him to call me ASAP. Not that he'll be able to shine any light on what I've found here but I want to let him know I arrived safely and as soon as I'm done with the police I'll be on my way home.

I replace the photo and go back into the spare room. The closet has a few jackets on hangers, with some jeans and sweaters. Winter clothes for the beach, which means Celeste and Violette are regular visitors here in all seasons.

None of this makes sense. From what Celeste has told me, it sounds like she fled a toxic relationship and is hiding out in Hambridge Heights. She had to leave her ex to protect herself and her daughter. And there's no way in hell Walter can be that ex. He doesn't have a mean bone in his body.

As for Violette's father being lousy as Celeste implied on many occasions, that's not Walt either. He wanted kids more than anything. Heck, that was a catalyst for our marriage ending, so if Violette was his daughter he'd dote on her. Besides, why would Julia change her name to Celeste and turn up as my neighbor? What game is she playing?

I feel like I'm missing something, like trying to figure out one of Luna's puzzles and discovering a piece has vanished.

That's when I remember Walter's call.

If Julia and Celeste are the same person, my husband and daughter are next door to a madwoman right now.

I call Andre again and it still diverts to voicemail. Damn it. I could call Celeste but what would I say? "Hey, I think you may be my ex-husband's girlfriend so why didn't you tell me? Oh, and are you crazy for perpetuating this sham? And do you know what's happened to Walter?"

In that moment, an awful, insidious thought slithers into my subconscious.

Did Walter try to break up with Julia, and she did something to harm him?

I try to rack my brain for snippets of conversation about her partner who she called Roland. How she'd left him because he was a threat. How Violette missed her dad and how she wished she could take her for a visit. How Roland had been a deadbeat dad.

None of that sounds like Walter. Maybe I've got this all wrong and Walter has been seeing Celeste recently, after she broke up with Roland? Maybe Roland was abusive as Celeste intimated and she's been in hiding with Walter? Heck, for all I know they could be colleagues from work. Celeste is an accountant, Walter has worked in the bank for ages. Maybe they've been holed up here away from Roland? That fits Walt to a tee, rescuing a damsel in distress, being a protector.

I know I'm clutching at anything to excuse her lying. But if she is Walter's friend and was sheltering here, she hasn't been lying at all. She'd have no idea Walt is my ex-husband so why would she feel compelled to tell me anything? She's protective of her child and I understand that. If she has been in hiding with Walt, she'd want to protect his identity from Roland too. And if that's the case, she just hasn't shared much of her past and we're all guilty of that.

But my logic doesn't calm me and increasingly agitated, I call Andre a third time, and he finally picks up.

"Frankie, thank God. I just got off the phone from Saylor and was going to call you."

"I've been trying to get through."

"Sorry about that. Listen, have you been in touch with Celeste?"

I'm instantly on guard. How could he know anything when I'm still trying to piece it all together myself? "No, why? How's Luna? Is everything okay?"

"Shit…" Andre makes a weird choking sound that chills my blood.

"Andre, what's going on?"

"I'm so sorry, Frankie—"

"What have you done?"

"I got an emergency callout to that last job I did, some problem with the graphics for the Times Square billboard, so I—"

"Where's Luna?" My hands are shaking because deep down, in a place I don't want to acknowledge, I know what he's going to say and it's going to kill me.

"I asked Celeste to mind her."

The ache in my chest expands, filling me so I can barely breathe. Spots speckle my vision and I sway, light-headed. "You need to go and get her right now and take her home."

He's silent and I can't take much more of this.

"What aren't you telling me?"

"Saylor called me a few minutes ago. She was concerned because she saw Celeste bundle the girls into her car and take off, with overnight bags in the trunk."

A piercing keening fills the air, a hair-raising scream I belatedly realize is coming from me.

"Frankie, I'm sorry. I'm sure she's fine—"

I hang up on him, the stupid, irresponsible man who left our precious daughter in the care of a lying manipulator.

I can't breathe and I tear at the neck hole of my T-shirt, gasping for air. I want to bawl. I want to smash something.

As I scream again, two police officers rush into the bedroom with their guns drawn.

CHAPTER SIXTY-TWO
CELESTE

"Where are we going, Celeste?" Luna's wide-eyed with excitement as she leans forward, the seat belt straining slightly.

"On a grand adventure, sweetie, like that video you and Violette watched the other day," I reply.

"Wow," the girls say in unison from the back seat and my heart swells with so much love I fear it may burst. Luna is the perfect sibling for Violette. My beautiful daughter has always wanted a sister and now she has one.

I know it's not going to be easy but I've planned for this scenario, though I expected our departure when it eventuated to be leisurely, not a mad panic. I wanted the girls to become inseparable over time and for Luna to completely trust me before I made my move in a calm, orderly fashion when Frankie and Andre least expected it. I had envisaged the police taking longer to track me down. Even if they'd searched Roland's house and the beach cottage, they wouldn't find much connecting me to him beyond Violette's room; we hadn't been to his house for six months as things between us deteriorated, he always came to us. But Frankie visiting the cottage and seeing any evidence Roland left around of Vi, probably photos, has expedited my departure and I need to stay focused.

There'd been a moment back at the house when I thought it might all fall apart, when Luna hadn't wanted to get in the car. But I'd soothed her with talk of Frankie and Andre joining us soon on our adventure and she'd been appeased.

If I have my way, she will never see those two liars again.

It's been incredibly difficult for me to maintain a friendly façade around Frankie and Andre. But I've hidden my loathing well, as they never suspected the only reason I moved next door was to reunite Violette with her sister. I hate Frankie for lying to Luna, pretending Andre is her father, and I detest Andre for usurping Roland as Luna's rightful dad.

Luna deserves to meet her real father and by this time tomorrow, she will. But first, we need to change cars.

"The city is so exciting," Vi murmurs, and when I glance in the rearview mirror both girls are craning their necks to look out the window. "Look at all the lights."

"It's like a fairyland," Luna says, a moment before she squeals. "Look at that. A real live clown walking on stilts!"

I let the girls' chatter wash over me, going over the plan in my head. I'll be at the parking garage soon, where I'll change cars. From there, I'll head out to Long Island tonight. I'll stop at a fast-food drive-thru and get the girls a snack, and with full stomachs and the motion of the car, they'll sleep for hours.

I can't risk staying in a motel overnight so I'll drive straight to the cottage, the one I rented in advance for this very outcome. Then I'll wait until morning so we can visit Roland.

I assume I have an hour's head start at least, probably more. I'm certain Andre will be home by now and wondering where Luna is. He'd implied he wouldn't be at work long, though what kind of father doesn't specify a time he'll pick up his child?

My cell has been buzzing with incoming calls I assume are from Andre but I've ignored them. I have nothing to say to him.

As for Frankie and what she's done… no, those liars are a good match and they don't deserve to parent a darling like Luna.

She'll be much happier with me.

And her biological sister Violette.

CHAPTER SIXTY-THREE

SAYLOR

The situation next door is dire.

Three police cars pull up, sirens blaring and lights flashing, then uniformed officers and plain-clothed detectives go into Andre's place. They don't stay long, before he gets into one of the cars with several officers and they drive away. The other officers and detectives force their way into Celeste's.

That's when I know this is serious.

Police don't break down doors unless there's real danger and from what I saw earlier, it looks like Celeste has kidnapped Luna.

Disbelief makes me tremble and I clutch at the windowsill for support. Why would Celeste have taken Luna? What would propel a perfectly nice woman to do something so despicable as rob another mother of her child?

One of the officers catches me peering out the window and I ease the curtain back. I know they'll want to question me, but I need some time to pull myself together. I glance across the park but Ruston's house is in darkness. Not that he's a man to depend on in a crisis but with Lloyd not due back home until tomorrow, I need someone to comfort me.

Before I'm tempted to barge across the park in search of Ruston, I force myself to relax. I tidy up the living room, check online pregnancy sites and try to watch some mindless reality TV for an hour or two, but I'm still worried about what's going on next door.

I'm making a cup of chamomile tea when I hear a blood-curdling scream. It sounds like Frankie and my heart breaks for her. It's the anguished cry of a mother whose child has been taken.

I'm torn between wanting to go next door and comfort her and staying away because I'm the last person she'll want to see if Andre follows through on his threat to tell her everything.

A few minutes later there's a pounding on my door. I expect it's the police but when I open the door, a disheveled, wild-eyed Frankie is staring at me like she's seen a ghost.

"Andre told me," she says, and bursts into tears.

I'm stunned and at a complete loss, filled with guilt and regret. What a complete and utter bastard Andre is to tell her the truth about us at a time like this. I wish I could deny it but she's distraught and the least I can do is apologize.

"I'm so sorry, Frankie. I never meant to hurt you." I focus on my shoes, unable to look her in the eye. "It was a one-off thing, something stupid I did to make Ruston jealous." I give a self-deprecating laugh. "I've always been a tad obsessed with Ruston, him being my first love and all, and I used Andre, but I never expected this."

My hand splays protectively over my belly. "I know Andre is wealthy, and with him being the father I need the money desperately…"

I still can't meet her eyes and the enormity of the situation sinks in. If Frankie knows, then I have no leverage against Andre, and he has no reason to give me the fifty grand I need so desperately to pay off the blackmailer. It's over. The blackmailer will go public with what I did and my folks will lose everything.

"What the hell are you talking about?"

I look up to find Frankie's tears have dried and she's staring at my belly in absolute horror.

Shit. *Shit, shit, shit.*

She'd said, "Andre told me" and I thought he'd followed through on what he'd said on the phone earlier, about telling his wife everything. But now I realize that isn't what she's referring to and probably has to do with what I saw earlier when Celeste left with the girls.

Her eyes are bulging as her gaze swings from my face to my belly and back again. "Are you saying Andre is the father of your baby?"

It's too late to lie.

This is a mess of my own making. And I seem to be digging myself into a deeper hole with every passing day.

While I'm not certain, I bite my bottom lip and nod.

Frankie crumples. There's no other word for it as her face collapses into a mess of lines, her shoulders slump and her knees buckle. She leans against the doorjamb, gasping for air, and intense remorse stabs me, like someone has plunged a knife between my shoulder blades.

"Do you want to come in—"

"I want nothing from you," she hisses through gritted teeth, her glare feral. "Just tell me what you saw when Celeste took Luna."

CHAPTER SIXTY-FOUR

FRANKIE

Numbness floods my body as I stumble up the steps leading to my house. I barely make it halfway and sit before I fall, my butt landing on a step with a painful thud that jars my spine from my tailbone to the base of my skull. I barely feel it.

My veins have turned to ice, my muscles to liquid and I know I can't take much more.

Learning my husband has fathered a child with Saylor has taken my already tilted world and flipped it on its axis. I can't think straight let alone comprehend the enormity of it and what this means for our marriage. But right now, I don't give a damn. All I care about is Luna.

The police questioned me at the cottage, and I told them everything I know: how Walt's love of routine makes his disappearance out of character, how our divorce was amicable and we chat occasionally, how confused I am by seeing Violette's photo as she's the child of my new neighbor Celeste. Stating facts, answering the police officers' questions, calmed me, but I couldn't wait to get back to Hambridge Heights to see for myself what the hell is going on. The police mentioned they'd put out a BOLO on Celeste, but I can't wait for them to be on the lookout. I need action.

Andre is at the station giving a statement and Saylor doesn't tell me much more than what she'd told Andre. It had taken every ounce of self-control to listen to her faux concern when all I wanted to do was slap her for turning my world upside down even more.

My eyes are burning but I know that crying isn't going to help right now. I'm not sure what will at this point. That numbness is invading every cell of my body, making rational thought impossible.

I barely see Ruston until he's climbed the first two steps in front of me, his brows drawn together in a worried frown. "Frankie, are you okay?"

"No." The simple act of speaking hurts my throat, tight with regret and recriminations. "Celeste has kidnapped Luna."

"Fuck," he mutters, sinking onto the step next to me. "Are you sure?" My glare is scathing and he says, "Sorry, that's a dumb thing to ask. I'm just shocked. You two are pretty close, and your girls are too. Are you sure they're not off on a play date or something?"

"No, she's taken her." I can't fathom it and the ache in my chest expands like a balloon. "It's complicated but it looks like a kidnapping, and the police are already involved."

"Do you need me to take you to the police station?"

I look at this man who I don't know that well, and I'm so grateful I want to blubber all over him. It was bad enough driving back from New Haven, trying not to break the speed limit to get home and see for myself my baby is gone, but now I've also learned about Andre fathering Saylor's baby, I'm in no fit state to drive. And I can't depend on my husband; Andre has already gone with the police. Not that I want to be anywhere near my lying, cheating husband after what I just learned. But my devastation over another betrayal must be pushed aside because all I can focus on now is getting Luna back safely.

"Actually, that would be great."

As I stand and take a step, my legs wobble, and he braces my elbow. "I'm really sorry you're going through this, Frankie."

His sympathy surprises me again and I allow him to lead me down the steps. I studiously avoid glancing left or right. I can't cope with getting the merest glimpse of Celeste's or Saylor's places right now.

"I can't believe she'd do this," he says, shaking his head. "She seemed so normal when we spoke at the dinner party."

I nod, hating how she duped me. "Since I heard she's kidnapped Luna, I've gone over every conversation with Celeste in my head to try and remember if I missed something… a sign…" The guilt in my gut solidifies, that I unwittingly let a monster into our lives and have put Luna in jeopardy because of it. "I know this is a long shot, but did she say anything to you that might help me locate Luna?"

His face screws up, like he's trying to remember. "We made small talk mostly. About her job, about mine. How she likes the neighborhood. She asked if I had a girlfriend, I asked about her partner."

I latch onto that. "What did she say?"

"Not much. How Violette liked spending time with her dad at the beach. How they had a favorite spot, how they liked collecting shells, visiting the lighthouse, general stuff."

My heart sinks. Celeste was talking about the beach house, but there's no way she'd take the girls there. She knows it's one of the first places the cops would look.

But there's no lighthouse anywhere near Walter's cottage in New Haven. In fact, the only lighthouse I can think of is the one at Montauk on Long Island.

Something niggles at the edge of my conscience, something Walter had said about a favorite spot…

"I'm sorry I can't tell you any more than that," he says, his expression downcast. "Let me take you to the station—"

"I'm not going to the police station." I break into a run, heading to my car.

"Where are you going?" he yells after me.

"Home."

CHAPTER SIXTY-FIVE

CELESTE

As expected, the girls are angels and fall asleep as I soon as I hit the highway. I love driving at night: the lack of traffic, the lights, the chill in the air. I lower the window slightly and inhale, filling my lungs with the crispness of freedom.

Have I ever felt this free?

I've always been controlled by other people. Told what to do and who to be, even when I was a child. Because my mom had me in her teens and my dad married her out of necessity, once I hit puberty they feared I'd end up making the same mistake so they were watchful and suspicious all the time. They rarely let me out of the house except to go to school and I always felt like a prisoner.

The fire that killed them and devoured our home was unfortunate but necessary.

I'd been sixteen at the time and put into a foster home; I thought things would be better, but I was placed with an equally controlling monster I could never call mother. I'd run away, been found, and placed in another two homes before I turned eighteen and escaped. I should've felt free then, but my lack of finances imprisoned me into a life I didn't like in another way. I drifted from job to job, menial stuff mostly, at the mercy of cruel bosses who looked down on me because of my lack of a college education. When I finally saved enough money to put myself through community college, doing an accountancy course was the smartest thing I ever did.

I met Roland at twenty-five, at a deli counter of all places. He'd been ordering olives, salami and Parmesan, I'd been buying a takeout pasta salad for one. He commented that was one of his favorites, we shared a smile, and from that moment I knew he was the one. Reveling in my freedom to make my own choices, I chose him, and for the first time in my life I'd been truly happy. I loved him so much I gave him my virginity, my heart, my devotion.

Then he dumped me.

I'd seen it coming. He didn't know I'd snuck into Francesca Mayfair's eighteenth birthday party. I'd feigned a migraine because I didn't want to go to a party filled with rich kids intent on drinking their body weight in alcohol. But when I'd looked out the upper story window from his godparents' house next door and seen him talking to some girl in a secluded part of the garden, I'd had no option.

I'd slipped into the party along the fence line, staying in the shadows, listening, watching. I'd thought Roland adored me, that he'd never do anything to hurt me. I'd talk about the future and he'd listen intently, nodding in all the right places. He'd take me to banking conferences and I saw the pride on his face when I conversed with his colleagues as an equal, my love of numbers matching theirs.

But the night of that stupid party changed everything.

I saw him chatting with her and didn't think much of it until later, when he came in to check on me. I knew in an instant he'd changed. His eyes had been shining and he'd smiled more in the fifteen minutes discussing the party than he had in the previous month. I never would've picked my stable boyfriend to be smitten with a woman so quickly but that's exactly what happened and it terrified me.

I insisted we leave the next day, expecting him to follow. Instead, he called my bluff. For the next twenty-four hours after I got home, I alternated between wanting to slash his suits or throw his clothes on the lawn. I did neither, taking my frustration out at the local gym in a kick-boxing marathon that left me three pounds lighter.

When he walked through the door the next day, I was beyond relieved. He wouldn't have come home so soon if anything had happened with that girl. He would've stuck around. But then he started talking about how he hadn't been happy for a while, how our relationship had become stagnant, how he wanted to be on his own to do some thinking. BS clichés, all of it, because I knew in my gut that *she* had caused this.

That stupid, young, naive upstart with her big blue eyes and glossy blonde hair, who'd taken one look at my man and wanted him for herself.

I wanted to hurt Roland but I couldn't. I loved him too much.

So I watched from a distance as he brought her home. As she moved in with him. As they strolled every evening after he finished work, holding hands, gazing into each other's eyes, grinning like idiots.

I couldn't hurt Roland but when I heard he asked her to marry him, I toyed with her. I keyed the car he bought for her. I left a gutted squirrel on her doorstep. I smeared dog crap over her shoes by the front door. Yet she stayed and the day I saw them come back from City Hall and he carried her over the threshold of the house that should've been mine, I realized I'd lost.

She'd won the grand prize, Roland, and I got nothing.

I wanted to move away, to make a fresh start, but my obsession with the only man I'd ever loved was too great. I kept my distance from them but I watched. For years. Until my opportunity came.

She left.

And my Roland had a broken heart only an old friend could mend, and I finally had a chance to win back the love of my life.

I orchestrated a few chance meetings—at the supermarket mostly—pretending I didn't know about the separation until he told me. I had sympathy down to a fine art by the time I asked him out for coffee and while it gutted me to sit there and listen to him drone on about how much he missed her I knew being patient would earn me a second chance.

It came a year later when his divorce papers were signed, sealed and delivered. That night, Roland lost himself in me. Our friendship slipped back into relationship territory and rather than shove me away again as I half expected, he continued to date me. But I never moved in and I got the feeling he considered me as a friend with benefits. It was enough. Until it wasn't.

So I did what I had to do.

I got pregnant.

Surely a baby would bind us and I'd get the wedding ring I'd coveted for years?

But marriage had changed Roland. *She'd* changed him. And while he said he'd support me and would be as involved in our child's life as I wanted, he didn't make our relationship official let alone propose. I got the feeling he was still pining for her, even though he'd told me she'd remarried. She'd moved on, why couldn't he?

When I asked how he knew about her marriage, he got evasive. Worse, he looked guilty, like he'd seen her. I pried but got nothing out of him. Until not that long ago, when I'd pushed and he'd exploded, spilling the god-awful truth.

It should've destroyed me.

Instead, the truth set me free.

CHAPTER SIXTY-SIX

SAYLOR

I haven't touched alcohol since I got pregnant but after Frankie leaves my house I pour myself a glass of wine and barely make it to the sofa before I collapse, my legs wobbling as much as my resolve to keep this farce going.

Now that Frankie knows the truth, I've lost my leverage. I can't hold the baby's paternity over Andre any longer. Even though I don't know he's the father for sure, I haven't told him that. The threat of exposing his one-night stand with me and the resultant pregnancy to his wife had been enough to ensure he'd pay up to buy my silence. Or so I thought.

I stare at the wine, a rich red from Napa, and swirl it around and around, craving a sip but worrying I'll hurt the baby. I may be a horrible person but the bigger my belly gets, and the more kicks I feel, the more protective I become. I never wanted a child so soon. I can barely look after myself let alone a baby and the responsibility is enormous. And now… I'll have to tell Lloyd everything. He needs to hear it from me before my blackmailer tells the world and my husband's and parents' lives are ruined. I owe him that much.

I hear a key in the door and I push up into a sitting position. He isn't due home until tomorrow and I'd been counting on that time to compose myself, to try and come up with a way to tell him that doesn't make me look like a monster.

As the door swings open and he catches sight of me, his lips easing into a grin, I burst into tears.

"Hey, what's wrong?" He closes the door, drops his wheelie suitcase in the hallway and rushes to comfort me. "Not quite the greeting I expect when I come home early from my trip as a surprise for my expectant wife."

I can't speak past the lump in my throat and he bundles me into his arms, only pausing to take the wine glass from my hand and place it on the coffee table, one eyebrow raised before he pulls me close.

I sob my heart out, my eyes stinging and my nose clogged until I can barely breathe. He still holds me, smoothing my back, pressing his cheek to the top of my head, and his consideration makes me cry harder.

"You're going to make yourself sick," he murmurs, easing me away, concern creasing his brow as he pushes my hair out of my face. "Tell me what's wrong."

"Everything," I say, punctuated by a hiccup, and I'm surprised when the corners of his mouth twitch in amusement.

"At the risk of you hitting me, you sure this isn't the result of a hormonal surge?" He pretends to duck. "And you're making a catastrophe out of something small?"

If only.

I scoot away from him, needing to establish some distance between us if I'm to tell him the truth. I need to see the disgust on his face, to see him recoil from me, to reinforce how badly I've hurt this caring human being.

Lloyd is nothing like Ruston and Andre. He would never cheat or lie or take advantage of anyone. He wouldn't obsess over an ex or marry an upstanding person on the rebound. He wouldn't have a one-night stand and lie to his partner about everything.

How can I tell him any of this?

He'll never understand.

I'm almost as afraid of his reaction as I am of what the black-mailer's going to do when I tell him I can't pay him. I'll have to warn my folks, see the confusion morph into derision in their eyes when they realize what kind of daughter they have. Worse, watch them lose everything they've spent a lifetime building: a thriving church in several cities, the devotion of their followers, the respect of a community. It's gut-wrenching.

"You're scaring me." He reaches for my hand and I snatch it away, earning another raised eyebrow.

"I've been lying to you from the start," I say in a rush, the words tumbling over themselves, harsh in the silence of the room. "Lying about our relationship, the baby, why I wanted to move here, all of it."

My breath hitches as I wait for his reaction and I wrap my arms across my belly. I can't do much to save myself but I can protect my unborn child.

His expression is eerily blank, his eyes glassy.

"Did you hear me? You, me, this baby? All of it is a lie."

That's when the oddest thing happens. He shrugs, like my deception hasn't torn our world apart.

"I know," he says, his flat tone as scary as the strange smile on his face.

"How——"

"Because I'm the person blackmailing you."

CHAPTER SIXTY-SEVEN
CELESTE

The cover of darkness is perfect when we arrive at the cottage. Not that anybody's around. I found this place, not much bigger than a studio apartment really, when I first followed Francesca here after she left Roland.

I wanted to make sure their separation wasn't a ruse, that I had a real shot with him again. But I guess the joke was on me when she didn't stay here long. I think her parents had moved or they were estranged, because when Francesca returned to Gledhill she stayed in a B&B in the heart of town. She did a lot of walking, mostly along the promenade in town and she spent the afternoons sitting on a bench near a path leading to the beach, staring at the ocean.

I half expected her to have second thoughts, to crawl back to Roland begging for another chance. I'd been worried when she left Gledhill and returned to the beach house in New Haven, but they had zero contact before she headed to Manhattan. I'd never known relief like it.

My cottage is the last one on a dead-end street. The housing in this estate, about fifteen minutes from town, all looks alike, short-term rentals for people who want to get away from it all and can't afford the exorbitant Hamptons' prices. I know the three cottages nearest to mine are empty. The realtor had pointed out nobody liked to be stuck down the end of a road that led nowhere.

Nobody except me.

I need the privacy. Long enough to decide what to do.

I've come here to visit Roland, so Violette can see her father. Luna too.

Though I'll have to tread carefully with Luna. I can't tell her the truth—that Roland is her biological father too—until she's really bonded with Violette and accepts her as her sister. I don't want to terrify the poor girl.

The girls don't stir as I park the car around the back and unlock the back door. I carry each of them inside and lay them on top of the covers in matching beds. Pink, with fairies dotted over the white pillowcases and the blankets I carefully place over them. After switching on a night light, I close the door but not fully shut. I don't want either of them waking in the middle of the night and being scared.

Once I've unloaded all the bags from the trunk, my arms are aching and I'm unsteady on my feet. Must be the adrenaline wearing off.

I can't believe I'm here.

And tomorrow morning, we'll be seeing Roland.

Initially, I'd hated that Francesca didn't know him as well as me and had no idea of his second middle name—Walter Charles Roland White, such a majestic name—but it's become invaluable in the ruse I've perpetuated. She has no idea my Roland was once her Walter.

I just wish I'd had more time to prepare Luna to be absorbed into our family, but once I heard Frankie had gone to the beach house looking for him I couldn't take the risk of sticking around.

I had to escape.

Once I see Roland tomorrow, I'll know what to do. I'm in a precarious position. Kidnapping charges can be laid, but technically I took the girls on a trip to see their father. I can lie and say I had every intention of returning. That this whole thing is one giant mix-up. Besides, when the truth comes out, Frankie will be the one who looks bad for lying to everyone, especially her husband and daughter.

At least, that's what I hope. All I want is to bring our family together. We can't stay here, and once I get some clarity after seeing Roland I'll know where to take our newly formed family.

I've never had a proper family and it's all I've ever wanted. A mom, a dad, and kids sitting around a dinner table, sharing anecdotes from our day, passing the beans and mashed potato, basking in the warmth of security.

That's Roland's only flaw. He never understood how much I craved to belong. Even though he didn't ask me to marry him or move in, I know once I present him with his other daughter and he sees how close Vi and Luna are, he'll have no option but to ask us to become a family.

When he'd flung the horrible truth at me the last time we met, using it as a weapon to drive me away, I'd been furious. I'd overreacted. But when the enormity of Vi having a sibling sunk in, I saw the positive side, even if it meant I had to play nice with Frankie so I could have the family I've always wanted.

I've never met a more self-absorbed, shallow person in all my life. All she cares about is her precious bloody image online, creating the perfect persona. How would her followers feel if they knew the truth? That she cheated on her husband and lied to him about the paternity of their daughter?

I've resented her for so much over the years. For stealing Roland from me, for using him then dumping him, for hurting him, for ruining my life. Now she'll feel what it's like to lose a person she loves, to have her world ripped apart.

Luna is my only concern in all of this. I love Vi with all my heart so as a doting mother I know Luna is going to miss Frankie. I can only dress up this situation as a grand adventure for so long before she starts pining for her parents. I'm hoping Roland will help with that too.

I know him. He'll think I'm crazy, that I need to return Luna immediately. But I know my Roland better than he knows himself. He may be upstanding and law-abiding, but once I explain the situation and accentuate the dream of us being a family, he'll come around.

All I've ever wanted is to give Vi the sibling she wants so badly. That's what this entire escapade has been about. It's what had driven the final confrontation with Roland. When I'd begged him to have another child with me, for Vi's sake.

Our argument had been ferocious. I'd never seen him lose his temper like that, and when he'd flung in my face that he'd never have another child with me because he already had another daughter with his ex-wife, I'd lost it too.

Because of his precious bloody Frankie, Vi wouldn't get the sister she deserved.

Until I realized she could.

She already had a sister.

Luna.

And bringing the girls together has been my number one objective since.

One of the girls cries out in her sleep and I hope it's not Luna as I tiptoe toward their bedroom, determined not to wake them. It will be hard enough facing their relentless questions in the morning.

I peek through the gap in the doorway and sigh in relief when I see they're both still sleeping, though Luna is tossing a little. I want to rush in there, to soothe her, to reassure her that everything will be okay.

It has to be.

CHAPTER SIXTY-EIGHT

FRANKIE

When I refuse to go to the police station to meet up with Andre and have him come with me to Gledhill, Ruston insists on driving me. I'm resistant but he's adamant and in a way I'm glad. It would've been difficult concentrating on the road when my mind is mush and the adrenaline coursing through my body is making me tremble intermittently.

He doesn't ask why I don't want Andre to accompany us, though when I initially yelled at him for suggesting it he cast me a knowing look. That's when I remember that scene between him and Saylor, and how Celeste had said Ruston had fathered her baby. If so, why was she pointing the finger at Andre? Not that it makes me any less angry; Saylor has admitted they've slept together, so whether Andre is the father of her child or not is irrelevant. He's cheated on me, again.

When I first figured out Celeste is Walt's Julia, I wondered if Andre might be Violette's father and that's why he warned me against befriending Celeste initially. What I'd thought of as a huge coincidence at the time he confessed, his first one-night stand being in Hartford where I'd once lived with Walt, could be significant as it's also where Celeste/Julia resided as it turns out. And if Saylor's unborn child is Andre's too, my seemingly devoted husband has fathered two illegitimate children.

Appalled at the thought, my throat constricts. And while it won't change anything if Andre isn't the father of Saylor's baby—I still hate him for betraying me again—I must ask, "Did you have an affair with Saylor?"

He doesn't take his eyes off the road but his hands clench the steering wheel tighter. "Where did that come from?"

"When you found me having a meltdown on my front steps, I'd just learned my husband is the father of Saylor's baby."

He's silent but his knuckles are now so prominent they appear translucent in the dimness of the car. "I'm sorry."

"You've got nothing to apologize for. But you didn't answer my question. Did you two have an affair?"

It's stupid, that even now when Saylor's shattered my trust in my husband, a small part of me hopes her baby isn't Andre's, and that if she slept with Ruston too, maybe there's a chance it's his?

"No, she's my ex-girlfriend. We've been on and off for years, broke up last year. I didn't know she was married let alone pregnant, so when she turned up in Hambridge Heights I wondered if she'd followed me. She's always been a tad obsessed."

He hesitates, as if unsure whether to tell me more, and gut instinct tells me what he has to say has to do with my husband.

"Go on," I prompt, needing to hear it all, no matter how hard it'll be.

"About six months ago I bumped into her at a job. Later that night at the wrap party she went a little nuts when she saw me with another woman. Next thing I know, she was all over your husband."

I'm stunned. I had no idea Andre had worked with Saylor and Ruston. "So you were on an advertising job with them?"

"Yeah. One of the big marketing firms was doing a shoot for designer watches. I was doing the photography, Andre the graphic design, and Saylor coordinated the shoot."

I don't know what to say at yet another example of my husband's treachery, and Ruston shoots me a sideways glance. "You didn't know?"

"No."

"Sorry, Frankie. When Saylor asked me to keep our connection a secret I didn't realize it'd affect you too."

"It's not your fault." It's Andre and Saylor I blame and I'm sick to my stomach.

Saylor repulses me. She wouldn't have been married for long when she slept with my husband because she was infatuated with her ex and wanted to make him jealous?

But it's nothing on my abhorrence for Andre, who I learned to trust again after he first cheated on me six years ago, only to discover he's betrayed me a second time.

"I didn't mention she's my ex because I actually feel sorry for her." He shrugs. "I told her once she should come clean to her husband as we had nothing to hide, and she lost it."

I realize that must've been the argument Celeste and I witnessed that day in the park, when we'd wrongly assumed Ruston could be the father of her baby. Now I know the truth, how I wish that was true.

"The thing is, I understand why she acts out. Her parents are religious zealots and have high expectations. She always felt pressured by them to be perfect and I get the feeling she rushed into marriage on the rebound, got pregnant, and has no idea how to deal with any of it."

I don't want to sympathize with Saylor for a second, but I think Ruston's right. I'm a textbook example of someone dealing with the pressures of faking perfection. Not that I want to excuse Saylor, far from it, but she's young and if anyone knows the silly decisions one can make in their early twenties, I do.

I don't want to talk about Saylor but it's providing a welcome distraction from the stomach-churning panic of wondering if Luna is okay. I can't see Celeste hurting her; from observing their interactions she's been nothing but sweet and caring with my daughter. I keep telling myself this to stave off the disabling terror that threatens to strangle me with every passing minute as I try to figure out why the hell she's doing this.

"Let's not talk about Saylor anymore—"

"Actually, while I hate what she's done to my family, talking about this is distracting me from panicking about Luna." His expression is dubious, but there's one thing I have to know. "Did Andre come on to her or was it the other way around?"

"You sure you want to hear this?"

Bile rises in my throat, but I swallow and nod.

"After Saylor saw me with that other girl, she targeted him. He resisted at first, but they were both pretty wasted and he ended up flirting back."

I hate asking questions when I know I won't like the answers, but the more informed I am, the better I can deal with Andre's dishonesty when we get Luna back and I confront him. Luna is my priority but the constant nausea plaguing me is a symptom of my disgust at my cheating husband too.

"How wasted were they?"

He's quiet for a long time and when I glance at him, I can't discern his expression. But his jaw is clenched so tight it juts.

"It's the norm for big clients to host a party on the last night of a shoot after it's a wrap. The brand we were shooting for is huge and they threw a few thousand dollars on a bar tab and left us to it. Everyone who worked on the job stuck around. Most of us got drunk, high, or both. There were hookups all over the place…"

And one of those hookups had been Andre and Saylor. My husband had sex with another woman that night. After the last time, he knows how I feel about sleeping around.

I'm not hypocritical. My one-off had been an aberration, something I've regretted every day since. But it looks like my husband is a serial cheater and if I know about two, how many more women have there been?

"So what do you think Celeste wants with your daughter?"

He's trying to change the subject and I appreciate it. But the thought of Luna god-knows-where with Celeste is so much worse than discussing my husband's rationale in betraying me.

I know this could be a wild goose chase but I have to do something proactive. I couldn't sit around at home, waiting for the police to follow procedure and I lose my daughter in the process.

There's a small chance I'm right about where she is, and if I am I might get to find out what Celeste wants, and hopefully get my daughter back.

"Honestly? I don't know. From what I've seen she's a good mom and loves Violette. The girls have bonded since she moved in and I've encouraged their friendship." It doesn't matter if I tell him the rest. It's going to come out anyway and our close-knit community of Hambridge Heights will be buzzing with this news for years to come. "But it turns out she has ties to my ex-husband and I think he's Violette's father."

"What the… how on earth do you figure that?" Shock deepens his voice.

"My ex is missing. Apparently I'm still listed as his emergency contact so his employer reached out to me. We keep in touch sporadically and he hasn't been returning my calls either, so I got worried and went looking for him."

"That's awfully nice of you." Ruston's tone is off, like I've been having an affair, and I resent the implication.

"My ex is a good guy but he's clueless, one of those guys anyone can take advantage of. Last I heard he was vacationing at the beach house we owned so I went there. He wasn't around but I saw evidence of a child living there. And a photo of Violette and a woman I think is Celeste."

He makes a low whistling sound. "Okay, you're right, this is weird…" He pauses. "It still doesn't explain why she took her…"

I have a theory and I hope it's wrong.

If Walter had told Celeste about how he thought Luna's his after our night together, she'll think our daughters are related. Does she hate me for stealing Walt from her and taking Luna is some kind of warped revenge to get back at me?

My panic rises. In my wilder suppositions, I wonder if Walter is in on this outlandish plan and imagines them being one big happy family. Until I remember he saw the letter and the paternity test result so he knows he isn't Luna's father.

"Frankie?" Ruston's voice is soft, tentative.

"I have no idea why she took her."

"You're contacting the police when we get to Gledhill, yeah?"

I'm sure he regrets driving me to Gledhill where I think Celeste might be without the police knowing anything about it. But having the police storm the area where I'm hoping to find my daughter isn't ideal, especially as I can't help but remember the alarming things Walter once told me about his ex. If Celeste is unstable, the slightest thing will set her off and Luna may get caught in the crossfire. I want to approach Celeste myself, give her a chance to explain, before the police potentially scare her into doing something rash.

"Yeah, but I want to see if I'm right first, if she's at the place I think she is. Once I find her, I'll talk to her and you can call the police—"

"Whoa. What do you mean, you'll talk to her?"

"I need to make sure Luna's okay and I'm terrified she'll do something crazy if cornered by police, so I want to have a face-to-face conversation with her first."

He mulls this for a minute before grunting in approval. "That makes sense. I'll be nearby if you need backup."

I should be reassured but I'm not. Because if Celeste is as unstable as I think she is, all the backup in the world won't stop her from potentially harming my daughter.

CHAPTER SIXTY-NINE

SAYLOR

Disbelief makes me lightheaded as I stare at the man I thought I knew but haven't really known at all.

"What do you mean you're blackmailing me?"

"Exactly that." He shrugs, like his mind-blowing revelation means little. "From the moment we met, you've put me in a box. Mr. Nice Guy. Dependable Lloyd. Charitable Lloyd who works with kids in the youth ministry and would never do anything wrong. Stupid, gullible Lloyd—"

"I don't think of you like that." I lie, because he's right. I have labeled him as nice, dependable and sweet; but not once since I've perpetuated this sham have I thought of him as gullible.

"Then tell me, dearest wife. How do you think of me?"

"I love you—"

"You've got a funny way of showing it, cheating on me after we've been married for three months."

Heat flushes my cheeks, a testament to my mortification. I knew we'd need to have this conversation at some point, but now the time has come my chest is tight and my throat dry, and it's difficult to get the words out. How does he know?

"That night was a mistake. But to explain, I need to tell you about Ruston."

His eyebrows shoot upward. "What's that pretty boy got to do with it?" Fury lights his eyes. "Don't tell me you slept with him too?"

"Not recently—"

"What the hell does that mean?" He leaps off the couch and starts pacing, shaking his head and muttering something I assume are nasty names for me under his breath.

"Please sit and listen. I should've told you this at the start, when we first met, but I didn't want to ruin the best thing to happen to me."

I'm not sure if it's my plaintive plea or hand wringing or tears slowly trickling down my cheeks that get to him but he finally takes a seat on the sofa. His arms are folded, a deep frown grooves his brow, and he can barely look at me.

I know what I say next will make or break us.

"You know my parents. How upstanding they are and how revered in the church. To them, Ruston was their biggest nightmare. He was my first boyfriend, my only boyfriend, as a senior and beyond. I wanted to move to the city with him and they were horrified." Shock widens his eyes and I continue. "You've met him, you know what he's like, has to be the center of attention, expecting every woman in a room to fall at his feet and, sadly, I did for too long."

I'm explaining it clinically, but what I can never tell my husband is how consumed I was by Ruston, how he was the focus of my every waking thought and most sleeping ones. It irks that, even now, seeing him again has affected me when it shouldn't. Not that I love him—he's still the same jerk he always was—but it's only a year since we broke up that last time and he's like a persistent virus I can't get rid of.

"Did you know he lived here when you insisted we move to Hambridge Heights?"

His narrow-eyed skepticism implies he won't believe me whatever I say.

"No, I swear." I press my hand to my heart. "I was shocked to see him and wanted to avoid him."

"Then why did you invite him to that bloody dinner party? You could've said no when I insisted we ask him." He flushes an angry puce. "I had that prick in my house and I had no idea he's already screwed my wife."

"Ruston and I were finished before I met you."

"How long before we met?"

"A week."

That's when the truth dawns and he visibly recoils. "Your parents set us up, didn't they? You just said they hated Ruston and they wanted you in a relationship pronto so you wouldn't fall back into old patterns." He grits his teeth, his jaw clenching. "What I don't get is why you went along with it, me being rebound guy and all."

"You weren't—"

"Don't lie to me!" he yells and I jump. "Haven't you done enough of that to last a lifetime?"

"You weren't my rebound guy. Honestly? I was prepared to dislike you because the more my parents insisted I meet you, the more I rebelled. But then you turned up and… how could I not love you?"

Some of the anger drains from his face but his back is rigid, like he's sitting on a poker. "This is seriously messed up. All of it."

I agree, but the most messed up thing is my husband blackmailing me.

"It is messed up. I shouldn't have been fixated on Ruston at a wrap party one night after a job, but I was, and seeing him all over another woman made me go a little crazy. That's why I slept with Andre, to make Ruston jealous, which is truly awful, and something I'll never forgive myself for, but you have to know, there's nothing going on between Ruston and me now."

The softening I glimpsed a moment ago hardens. "Nothing you say changes the fact you had sex with Andre three months after we married."

I reached an all-time low the night I had sex with Andre. I don't blame the drugs, the alcohol, or the inane urge to prove I was still attractive because I felt some of my identity slip away after I married Lloyd. I blame my stupid addiction to Ruston. I'd organized that shoot so it had been easy to put forward his name as the main photographer. I'd wanted to see him, to make sure I hadn't made a mistake in marrying Lloyd. But it had backfired, because the moment I saw him I remembered how good we'd been together, so when I glimpsed him making out with one of the sound technicians I lost it, making a determined play for Andre in some crazy, party drug-fueled haze to make my ex jealous, surprised when Andre reciprocated and unable to stop what I'd set in motion.

"If I could erase that night, I would."

Shame makes me want to reach out but by the sneering curl of his upper lip Lloyd won't welcome the contact. "You can't erase it. You're a married woman, Saylor. This isn't high school where if you muck up you can take the test again. There are no do-overs."

"I know, but I need you to understand—"

"What I understand is the night of the shoot, when I popped in to surprise my wife because I couldn't get enough of you, I missed you and wanted to be with you, was the night you broke my heart." He eyeballs me, and my heart lurches when I see his agony mixed with anger.

"Guess I shouldn't be surprised you didn't see me, considering you were screwing Andre and I witnessed it."

Shame fills me. I've regretted what happened that night ever since I lost my head and slept with Andre, but to think my husband saw… I'm mortified. "Why didn't you confront me then, or afterward?"

"Because I was reeling and relied on my faith more than ever. I prayed on it for weeks, hoping to gain some clarity, and I acted my ass off so you wouldn't figure anything was wrong. Either I deserve an award for my drama skills or you're so self-absorbed you're clueless, but you had no idea how I was falling apart on the inside."

Which only makes this entire situation worse. To think I caused him irrevocable pain, and while he struggled with it I hadn't noticed. It's unfathomable. He's right. I'm selfish and I never deserved him.

"By the time I decided to talk to you about it, you'd announced you were pregnant." He shakes his head. "It changed everything and I hoped it would be a turning point for us. Until you told me your due date and I realized the baby could be his. And you didn't breathe a word of that possibility to me." His expression hardens again and he's glowering at me. "That's when I decided to teach you a lesson."

"By blackmailing me for fifty thousand dollars?" I shake my head in confusion. "I don't get it."

"I hoped you might confide in me after I first blackmailed you, that if you trusted me enough you would tell me everything and it'd prove our marriage is solid and you believe in me." He grimaces and appears sheepish for a moment. "And stupidly, I kept hoping that every time I called you, it would force the truth out of you. But you didn't tell me and it spiraled out of control… I guess it proved you don't love me enough."

"You're wrong. I do love you—"

"So whose baby is it, his or mine?"

My head dips in shame. "I don't know."

"Let me guess. You told Andre if he didn't pay up you'd tell his wife."

Shame crawls over my skin and I can't sink any lower. I nod.

He scowls and I see how much he despises me.

"What would you have done if I paid you the money?" I ask.

"Put it into an account for your baby, because that poor kid's going to need all the help he can get."

"And if I hadn't paid up?"

"I wouldn't have ruined that asshole's marriage, it's not my style, and I certainly wouldn't have dragged your folks through the mud. They're good people and don't deserve that." He shrugs and I see a glimmer of the man I love behind his anger. "I would've confessed to you to make you feel guilty. I'm not the bad guy here, Saylor. Learning my wife cheated on me three months after we got married messed me up." He makes circles at his temple. "I wanted to test you, and you failed."

This is so warped. Like something out of the B-grade movies we like to curl up together and watch. That's the moment I realize I'll never have that again with Lloyd. Our marriage is over and the sadness I feel intermingles with intense regret.

"I've really screwed this up." I shake my head.

He nods and I glimpse a flicker of sympathy.

For a moment I consider appealing to his belief in forgiveness and begging him to give me a second chance, to attend couples' therapy, to stay and try to make this work. To be with me. To raise my son. But this entire situation is twisted and we can never recover from this. I may have made some poor decisions the night I conceived but he's put me through hell and I hope to God the stress hasn't affected my baby.

"I'll sleep in the spare room tonight," he says, standing. "I'll move out in the morning. And if the baby turns out to be mine, I'll help you raise him with clear-cut custody arrangements, but you and me are done."

I nod in agreement and watch him pick up my wine glass, move into the kitchen and tip it down the sink before heading upstairs. And in that small, considerate action, even after I've proven what a lying cow I am, I realize how much I've lost.

CHAPTER SEVENTY

CELESTE

I can't wait until the morning to see Roland. I'm too wound up. And if I see him now, I can forewarn him about meeting the girls so he can prepare. Then again, maybe the element of surprise is better? *"Hey, Roland, look at this, your girls are reunited, isn't it fantastic?"*

Though I know him. He's not fond of surprises and that's why I have to talk to him tonight.

I check on the girls, relieved they're both sound asleep. I leave a note propped in the middle of the kitchen table in case either of them wake and find me gone. While Vi can't read yet, I'm glad Luna can.

Dear Vi and Luna,

Hope you're enjoying your grand adventure. I've gone for a walk along the beach, back soon. There's milk in the fridge and cookies on the counter in case you want a snack. I'm so excited to be here with you two. We're going to have so much fun together.

Mom xx

One kiss for each of them. I must remember to treat Luna as my own, even though Vi holds my heart. She's fragile and easily scared, and I'm hoping some of Luna's boldness will rub off on her. I would hate for Roland to make comparisons between the girls and like Luna better. I know all too well what it's like to be second best and I won't have my daughter tolerating the same shoddy behavior.

I hate how the world we live in these days values beauty above all else. How a trumped up nobody like Francesca Mayfair can reinvent herself as Frankie Forbes and become famous. How looks are prized more than intelligence. How fake peppiness garners fans when a quiet resilience is often seen as a sign of weakness.

Frankie is my opposite in every way but I won't have her daughter being Violette's opposite. I need them to meld, to complement each other. Only then can we be a true family. I won't tolerate anything less.

I check all the windows and the front door to ensure they're locked before pocketing the keys and slipping out of the back door. I hear the lock click behind me but I jiggle the knob just in case. I need to keep my girls safe.

It's an easy half-paced jog from the cottage to Roland. The wind is strong tonight, the sea spray misting my skin, the sound of crashing waves resonating in my ears. I can't believe he thought it would be easier to bring me to our favorite spot to break up with me. When he'd first mentioned we take the trip I'd been filled with hope. A nostalgic trip to our spot could only mean one thing: he was going to propose. Little did I know.

The thing is, I always forgive Roland anything. But then he'd started saying all that stuff about Francesca and Luna and…

We'd never quarreled like that. How can someone so rationally calm one moment lose it the next? I guess we all have hidden violent tendencies that explode when pushed too far.

For me, that trigger is Violette.

Nobody, not even her father, can get away with disparaging her while lauding his other child over me.

I reach our spot, a secluded part of the beach with a rocky outcrop that creates a semi-cave.

When I see him, my heart expands with love.

My man.

Mine. Not hers.

No matter how much he wished otherwise.

"Hey, it's me." I hover at the entrance to the cave so I won't be tempted to rush inside and fling myself at him. "I've missed you."

I don't expect him to answer. Besides, I have enough to say for the both of us.

"I know it's weird, me showing up here in the middle of the night, but I couldn't wait to see you. I've got news. Big news. And I hope you'll be happy for us."

I take a step closer and peer into the darkness, wishing he would hold me, knowing he won't. "The last time we spoke, when you were raving about 'Luna this' and 'Luna that' and how you'd never give me another child because you already had one and it's her, I know I lost my cool and I'm sorry for that, but I hope you'll forgive me when you discover what I've done."

I throw my arms wide like I'm expecting his embrace. "I've brought her to you. Luna. She's so close with Vi. Best friends who are actually sisters. How amazing is that? They're alike in so many ways and I'm sure you'll pick up their similarities as quickly as I did. She's sweet, but not as good as our Vi, and I hope you don't favor her because I won't tolerate that and you know what happens when you anger me."

A gust of wind sends my ponytail vertical and propels me forward a little. I should go to him. But I can't. I have to wait until the girls are with me. Only then will he be inclined to forgive me.

"Sleep tight, my love. I'll be back."

I'm pleased with how our conversation has gone, until I turn to head back the way I came, and see Frankie standing three feet away.

CHAPTER SEVENTY-ONE

FRANKIE

I always thought this was a long shot and I've been steeling myself the entire way here that Celeste may be anywhere and not to get my hopes up. But the moment Ruston pulled up and I saw her, sheer relief swamped my rising panic. I found her. And I'm one step closer to being reunited with my daughter.

Celeste isn't violent and I can't imagine her harming a child. Which means Walt was right during our call when he said he had concerns for her mental health and this could be her way of dealing with whatever she's going through.

Not that I'll ever excuse or forgive her for kidnapping my child, but as a mother I understand we're all driven to extremes at times.

My feet sink into the sand and I struggle against the headwind whipping off the ocean. The tang of brine fills my nose and I breathe deep, willing my body to relax so I can stay calm when I confront her.

The closer I get, I see she's standing at the mouth of a cave, the one I remember Walt mentioning as their spot, and I almost burst into tears. But I can't show weakness. If she's unstable, I have no idea what she's capable of.

As I edge closer I see she's talking to someone but I can't see who it is. My heart skips a beat. Is it Luna? However crazy Celeste is, surely she wouldn't bring a five-year-old out here in the middle of the night. She's a mother too. She wouldn't hurt a child, would she?

Ruston is nearby, on top of the rocky outcrop that creates the cave below. He's waiting to call the police. I asked him to give me a few minutes alone with Celeste and he almost didn't agree. But I can't risk her hurting my girl if Luna's nearby and who knows what Celeste will do if startled by police.

I have no idea what to say now I'm here. My stomach is twisted into knots, my legs wobbling, but I have to make a stand. For Luna's sake.

As I approach, I'm grateful for the crashing of the waves and the muffling of the sand beneath my shoes. I'm close enough to touch her and she hasn't even noticed that I'm here.

She half turns, catches sight of me, and screams. I leap back, stumbling and almost falling.

"Don't be alarmed, Celeste, I only want to talk." I hold up my hands like I have nothing to hide.

"You can't have her back." She's belligerent, her lips compressed in a thin line, and I'm not sure if it's defiance or insanity I glimpse in her eyes. "Luna belongs with my Violette. Sisters should be together. Even Roland thinks so. He said he wouldn't have a second baby with me, a sibling for Vi, because he already had another child." Her glare is malevolent. "With you."

I'm stunned. Why would Walter lie about something like that when he knew it would enrage her?

"That's not true. Walt knew—"

"Stop calling him that! He's Roland. Only those closest to him knew his second middle name. But you didn't. I'm the only one special enough to call him that." Her top lip peels back in a sneer. "He used Walter Charles on official documentation and always left off Roland. I even saw it on your farce of a marriage certificate. But I knew him longer than you. I loved him longer than you," she yells, her words whipped away by the wind. "He was always Roland to me, right from the start."

"So I guess that makes you Julia," I say, secretly appalled but hoping my calmness will rub off on her.

She slow-claps. "Yeah, though when I got pregnant, I wanted a complete fresh start and insisted Roland start using my middle name too and I've been Celeste ever since."

Which explains why Violette doesn't think it odd her mom's called Celeste and not Julia, though I wish I'd thought to ask Violette's surname because that would've given me a heads up to Celeste's lunacy, regardless if her daughter uses Skelke or White, Walt's surname.

"Though Roland didn't know I had a second middle name too, Reagan, so I dropped Skelke when I moved next door to you. Quite the coincidence, huh?" Her hands clench and unclench, a slow, repetitive motion that petrifies me as much as what she's saying. "Nothing like a little neighborly friendship to get you to trust me. I've been biding my time, waiting for you to let your guard down, before I took Luna." She jabs a finger at me. "You and your snooping just brought the timeline forward. Did Roland have a photo of Vi at the beach house?"

"Yes."

"I guess I should be grateful for that small mercy, seeing as he always favored Luna over her anyway."

"He didn't—"

"He did!" she roars, her face flushing puce. "I saw the proof. He set up a trust fund for your precious daughter yet hardly had time to spend with Vi."

A mother scorned is dangerous and a small part of me pities her, for waging this long battle against favoritism when I'd never been aware of it.

"Celeste, listen to me. Luna isn't Walt's daughter. I sent him a paternity test to prove it."

"You're lying. The trust fund is irrefutable proof."

I shake my head, wishing he hadn't done this when I'd told him not to. "He insisted on setting up the trust fund as a way to commemorate our marriage. He was sentimental like that."

"He was an idiot."

I focus on one word.

Was.

Past tense.

My gut churns and I want to ask her about Walter. But Luna is my priority and I'm hoping this chatter has lulled her into opening up to me.

"Are the girls here?"

I aim for casual and thankfully, I've done the right thing by mentioning "girls" and not just Luna, because in her crazy mind she considers them a pair now—sisters—and her expression softens.

"They're at the cottage, sleeping. What kind of mother do you think I am, that I would consider dragging them out here in the middle of the night?"

She doesn't want me to answer that question because a caring mother wouldn't kidnap someone else's child.

So I play along, anything to placate her and keep her talking. Ruston would've called the police by now and she's told me what I wanted to know, where Luna is. Many of the cottages we passed look deserted and even if they're not it won't take the police long to search each one to find the girls.

"From what I've seen, you're a good mother. And our friendship—"

"Our friendship was nothing!"

She's back to yelling and I try not to flinch in the face of her outrage.

"Do you have any idea how hard it was to pretend every time I was around you? To not slap you or tear your hair out for stealing Roland from me?" Her fingers curl into her palms, her fists clenched. "From the moment I saw you in the garden chatting up my boyfriend at your stupid party I knew you were a heartless tramp. Then after Roland callously dumped me, I had to sit back and watch as he brought you home then paraded you around, and you didn't even leave after I did all that bad stuff."

So I'd been right. It had been his ex.

"The thing is, I loved him so much I wanted him to be happy so when he actually married you I backed off. I left you alone. But then you broke his heart like I expected and he turned to me for comfort." She pounds her chest with a fist. "Me, the woman he should've married all along. And we were happy, until you intruded yet again. YOU SLEPT WITH HIM and you cheated on your husband. How could you?"

I don't owe her an explanation. Besides, nothing I say now will change anything. Because she's right. I was a horrible person to Walter when he didn't deserve it.

"For what it's worth, Celeste, I'm sorry—"

"No, you're not. Women like you never are. You project this perfect image all the time but you're vile, evil to the core."

I want to make a flippant comment about her looking in the mirror but it's not wise to enrage her.

"And now, even after everything we've been through, you still won't admit the truth. That Luna is Roland's."

"I have proof in my back pocket, so I can show you." I move slowly so she doesn't think I have some kind of weapon, and slide the envelope out of my pocket.

When I tucked it in there earlier today I never envisaged having to use it like this. "But first, tell me where Walt is."

The anger contorting her features eases as she points at the cave. "He's in there. I was talking to him when you showed up here uninvited. How did you find us anyway?"

I'm horrified to think she has Walt in the cave, probably captive. Or worse, and I tremble at the thought. "Something Walt said to me once, about this being your go-to spot as a couple."

"We had some special times here…" Her expression hardens again. "When he brought me here the last time I thought he was going to propose. So I preempted it with my hopes of another baby, how it's all I've ever wanted, and in response he breaks up with me and flings Luna in my face."

She's furious again, fairly vibrating with it as she gestures at the cave. "I've never seen him lose his temper but when I wouldn't listen to him about breaking up, he got mad. Really mad, and I did too. We said some awful things. He broke my heart and I couldn't take it any more so I shoved him… there."

The moment she points to the spot where she pushed Walt, I know he's dead. The low-hanging outcrop… stumbling backward… hitting his head… Sorrow wells in my chest and I stifle a sob.

"I miss him so much…" She sinks to her knees, tears streaming down her face. "I never meant to hurt him."

"I know," I say, when I know nothing of the sort. I can't believe what she's done.

Out of the corner of my eye I see several officers with Ruston on top of the outcrop and more streaming up the beach toward us.

"Celeste, the police are going to arrest you." She'll spot them herself any moment and I don't want her startling and doing something crazy, like running, and making the officers draw their weapons.

I'm not sure if she hears me, and when she raises her tear-streaked face, her gaze is scared rather than deranged. She glances up the beach in the direction of the cottages and mutters under her breath, "I want the girls to be together. Vi needs a sister like Luna. She's never had a sibling and she deserves one. I can give her this…"

Before I can say anything, she skewers me with a stark stare that raises goosebumps on my arms.

"You have to take care of Vi for me. Even if Roland lied and he's not Luna's father, she's close to Luna and you're a good mother.

I may hate you but that's your one saving grace, your maternal instincts." She's rambling, panicked. "Please look after Vi for me."

I'm stunned by her request and before I can process what she's asking me to do, she continues, "I don't want her in foster care. She can't be raised the way I was, unloved and unwanted. I want her with you." She reaches out, palms up, beseeching. "I'll sign anything. You can adopt her, raise her like your own."

I can't believe what she's saying, but I'm relieved the panic is making her give up both girls unharmed. But every conflicting emotion is evident in her eyes—desperation, fear, sorrow, and regret—and it makes me cry.

We're both sobbing when the police arrive and she offers no resistance as an officer places the handcuffs on her wrists and the others enter the cave after I mention Walt is probably in there.

Ruston slides an arm around my shoulder. "You okay?"

I nod and I can't stop crying as I watch the police take Celeste away. But I must pull myself together. I need to find my daughter. "Luna's in one of the cottages. I have to find her…"

"The police have already found the girls. They're safe. A social worker is with them." Ruston squeezes my shoulder before releasing me.

I breathe a sigh of relief. "Take me to them, please."

"The police have questions—"

"Now, Ruston. I need to see my daughter."

To his credit, he doesn't hesitate. "Okay, let's go."

As he helps me up the rocky path to the road above, I hear a plaintive cry. I glance over my shoulder and my gaze locks with Celeste's.

"Take care of my girl," she shouts, her tears running unabated.

I should be furious at her for putting me through this, for making me live every mother's worst nightmare.

But she's a mother too, so I offer a brief nod.

For now, it's enough.

CHAPTER SEVENTY-TWO

FRANKIE

Despite imploring Ruston to take me to Luna immediately, the police interviewed me on the beach for forty minutes, so it seems like an eternity later when I reach the cottage, the last one at the end of the street, and I'm ready to ram the front door and burst through it to get to Luna. But as we pull up in the driveway, a well-dressed woman in her late forties comes out to meet us.

"That must be the social worker the police mentioned," Ruston says, and I turn to him, wanting to thank this man for standing by me in a way I never expected.

He must see a look in my eyes because his smile is self-deprecating. "I know. I surprise myself sometimes. Who knew I can add hero to my CV?"

I smile for what feels like the first time in forever. "Thanks, Ruston. You've been amazing."

"I try." As the woman approaches the car, he says, "Go. Do you want me to stick around and take you back?"

"Thanks, but I think I'll be here for a while. I'm not sure of protocol but the police may want to get the girls examined, then there's the custody issues for Violette." I grimace, hating how much that poor girl will go through now her mother will be locked up. "Best you head back."

"Okay." He slips something out of his back pocket and I see it's my cell. "You left it in the car. Andre has called a hundred times so I texted him where we are and he left immediately."

I can't imagine what our first confrontation will be like but I'm too bone-deep exhausted to worry. All I care about now is Luna and Violette.

"At the risk of sounding like a broken record, thanks again." I take the cell, a quick glance at the screen confirming Andre has called. A lot. I may hate him for sleeping with Saylor but he's Luna's father and he must be beside himself with worry too. "Does he know Luna's been found?"

He nods. "Yeah. I texted him that too."

"You are definitely one of the good guys," I say, flashing him a last grateful smile as I get out of the car and walk toward the woman.

"That's not your husband?" she asks, an eyebrow arched in surprise.

"No, a neighbor. My husband was with the police in Brooklyn when I hightailed it up here. He's on his way."

She's obviously a woman used to assessing the unsaid and not asking unnecessary questions, because she nods and holds out her hand. "I'm Marisa, the social worker from the Gledhill Help Centre. The police call me when there are children involved in cases like this."

I shake her hand, somewhat comforted by the firmness of her grip. "Thanks for being here. I'm desperate to see my daughter. Is she okay? How's Violette?"

Her smile is reassuring. "Both girls are fast asleep. I think they've had quite the adventure but I'm glad you're here. It'll be nice for them to wake to a familiar face."

I'm not sure how to broach the subject of what happens to Violette from here, but I settle for the direct approach. "Celeste

Reagan, Violette's mother, asked me to look after her daughter. She doesn't want her to be placed in foster care. She'd rather Violette stay with my family and she's willing to sign whatever documentation to support this."

Marisa appears confounded for a moment. "This is highly unusual. Is she mentally capable to sign legal documents?"

"I think so. She was perfectly logical when we spoke, just… resentful and caught up in wrongs of the past."

I leave out the part about Celeste talking to a dead Walter because I want to do what's best for Violette.

"Okay then. I can call a private attorney we use and get the ball rolling—"

"Can I see Luna please?"

"Of course." Marisa briefly rests a comforting hand on my shoulder. "For what it's worth, this is a good outcome. Not all parents are so lucky."

I don't want to contemplate for one second what could've happened to Luna if Celeste had been seriously unhinged or what those other unlucky parents have been through.

"Take me to her." It comes out a soft plea. I can't wait one second longer to see for myself Luna is okay.

The moment we set foot inside the cottage I want to run to the bedrooms and fling open doors until I find my girl. But I follow Marisa as sedately as possible as she heads down a short hallway, to a room with the door partially ajar.

She glances inside and, apparently satisfied, steps aside so I can look in.

When I see Luna curled up on her right side with her shoes poking out from beneath a blanket, I almost lose it. She looks so innocent, so peaceful, and the fact Celeste obviously carried her in from the car and took the time to cover her with a blanket, makes me want to do the best for her daughter despite what she put mine through.

When I glance across at Violette in the single bed opposite, I'm surprised to find her sleeping position mirroring Luna's, like two halves of a whole, and my chest aches for what this poor child will have to endure.

Marisa touches my arm and points to a doorway I assume leads to a kitchen, and I nod and back away from the door. I follow her and when we reach the kitchen, I see a note propped up in the middle of it.

"Celeste left the girls a note in case they woke," she says.

"Because she didn't want them to be afraid," I murmur, not wanting to like anything about that woman but grateful her maternal instincts were strong.

"Yes. Now, I have a lot of questions. Shall we start?"

By the time Andre arrives I'm exhausted after a lengthy chat with Marisa, who's outlined a lot of the legalities regarding taking custody of Violette, and another interrogation by the police. I want to hate Andre but the moment I see his face, and the ravages stress has inflicted while worrying about Luna, I relent a little.

"Is she really okay?" he says, practically falling into my arms.

I stiffen, unwilling to embrace him, but knowing what I have to confess to him shortly means I'm not totally blameless.

I wrap my arms around him for a moment before pulling away. "She's fine. Both girls are still sleeping. There was concern for a moment they'd been drugged but a doctor has been and reassures us they're merely exhausted."

"None of this makes sense." He collapses onto a seat at the kitchen table, his head dropping into his hands. "Why did she do it?"

I'm preternaturally calm now the moment has come to reveal the truth.

"Because she thinks Luna is Violette's sister."

His head snaps up, confusion clouding the eyes I thought I'd gaze into forever. "Why on earth would she think that?"

"Because when you cheated on me the first time, I went to Walter for comfort and we had a one-night stand."

His mouth drops open and he presses his palms to his ears like he can't quite believe he's heard right. When he does the math, he slumps forward, a beaten man.

"Is Luna mine?"

I consider torturing him for a second after all he's put me through, but I need this ordeal to be over.

"Yes. I have a paternity test to prove it."

Relief shimmers in his eyes before he blinks, and it's replaced by shame. "I'm sorry."

"For knocking up Saylor? You should be." I snap my fingers. "But turns out, you only have a fifty-fifty chance of being the father, considering she has a loving husband who's been cuckolded like me."

Regret renders him pale. "I wouldn't have paid her the money. I would've told you the truth."

"Lucky me."

"Frankie, I know I've mucked up, again. But we need to present a united front now for Luna's sake—"

"Violette's coming to live with us. And you're right, for now the girls need stability after their ordeal. But beyond that, I don't know."

"About us, you mean?"

"About everything."

"Frankie, I love you."

It's a plea from a desperate man trying to cling to something he ripped apart.

"Sometimes love isn't enough."

It wasn't for Walter and me. If I'd never left him, if I'd never gone back to him for that one night, he would still be alive. Grief crushes my chest in a vice and I want to bawl, but I'll mourn in private later, remembering our good times, honoring a man who deserved so much more than he got. Sadly, my love for him wasn't enough and ultimately, it got him killed.

Not that I could've anticipated the depths of Celeste's jealousy and how far she'd go, but this guilt is something I'll have to live with for the rest of my life.

EPILOGUE
FRANKIE

Two months later, the residents of Vintage Circle in Hambridge Heights are gathered in the park again. I'm hosting an impromptu get-together as a way to facilitate healing.

Gossip has been rife for the last eight weeks and I don't want it following the girls around whenever they come out to play. All it takes is an offhand remark or careless comment and this way everyone can see the girls are fine.

At least, Luna is. She thought Celeste had taken them on an adventure to the beach and she would've seen us the next day. When she woke in that cottage and saw Andre and me hovering, she'd flung her arms around us, then promptly demanded what's for breakfast. Now she's back to her exuberant best, bossing me around, rolling her eyes at Andre, but interestingly she's softer with Violette, like she senses she needs to be handled gently.

These days, Violette asks for her mother less. Though shy, she's laughing more spontaneously and is eating better. When she asks where her mom is, we tell her the version of truth Marisa advised us to say: that Celeste is sad about her dad dying and she needs some help to recover. We don't mention the J word as jail will terrify a girl who's already fragile. Violette is seeing a renowned child therapist and I'm hopeful she'll make progress.

As I watch her now, running around and playing tag with some of the kids from the neighborhood, I can't help but be optimistic for the future. Luna is close by, protective and intuitive. I love that about her. I like to think she gets her nurturing side from me.

There's a touch on my arm and I turn to see Ruston balancing a giant store-bought croquembouche. "I come bearing gifts."

"So it's true. Size does matter."

He laughs and does a deliberate jiggle, like he's about to drop it. "I know it's over the top but there's a lot of people to feed. Big turnout today."

"Yeah. Most are curious, I think."

"And you wanted to show you're all okay."

"There you go again, impressing me." I've already thanked him numerous times for his support the night Celeste kidnapped Luna but I still feel indebted. What he revealed about Andre and Saylor that night in the car on the way to Gledhill has helped me release some of my resentment toward my husband. They hadn't been having an affair. It had been one drunken, drug-fueled, crazy mistake. Not that I'll ever completely trust my husband again but Ruston's insight has helped me work toward forgiveness.

"Don't be too impressed. I'm no saint."

"Considering how you've been supporting Saylor, I beg to differ."

To my surprise, he blushes. "I feel bad for how I treated her all those years and it's tough to see how she's struggling now. It's the least I can do, lend a helping hand when she needs it."

"Whatever your motivation, I think it's great you're assisting her."

He shrugs, his lopsided bashful grin one of the things that probably attracted Saylor to him in the first place. "I like that we've finally reached a place where we can be friends."

"I think she appreciates it. Just go easy on her, okay?"

If he hears the underlying warning in my remark—not to let her get too invested in their friendship so she starts hoping for more—he doesn't say. He nods and glances over my shoulder. "Saylor's heading this way, so I'll leave you ladies to chat. I'll see you later." He takes a step before pausing. "For what it's worth, I'm glad you and Andre are trying to work things out."

I don't correct his misconception. Instead, I smile and turn to see a heavily pregnant Saylor waddling toward me. She's eight and a half months now, wearing that weary expression of a woman who's ready to give birth.

"You came," I say, somewhat surprised.

She's barely been outside for weeks, not since I had a blunt discussion with her: namely, stay the hell away from my husband and if he's the father we'll deal with it when the time comes like mature adults. Lloyd paid her rent for the next six months before he left, thoughtful considering what she did precipitated the end of their short-lived marriage. She's unprepared to be a single mother so having her next door is convenient; if the baby's Andre's, we'll do our bit. Co-parenting, co-custody, whatever.

"Ruston said it would be good for me to come, to get out of the house for a while. Besides, it seemed right, considering we all met at my gender reveal three and a half months ago."

She's pale, without a hint of make-up, and her hair is pulled back into a low ponytail, making her look a vulnerable eighteen rather than twenty-six. But there's strength in her steady gaze, as if she's come to terms with what she's done and the potential fallout on our lives, and she's dealing with it.

"I'm glad Ruston's helping you." I gesture to where he's chatting with Andre. "Turns out he's more than a pretty face."

Her eyes follow to where I point and her smile is soft, that of a woman who's realistic yet hopeful. "He's really surprised me, stepping up to grocery shop and take me to appointments and whatever I ask." Her gaze returns to me and I'm relieved it's clear rather than smitten. "We're in a good place as friends."

"I'm glad," I say as Luna appears.

"Wow, Saylor, your tummy is huge." Luna's eyes are wide as she stares at Saylor's belly. "Do you have more than one baby in there?"

I'm about to chastise my daughter about the polite way to greet a pregnant woman, when Saylor says, "It's just one baby. A boy. He's big."

"Humungous." Luna holds her arms wide. "I think he's going to be as big as this when he comes out."

"I hope not," Saylor murmurs, and our gazes meet in mutual amusement.

I don't hate her. I don't hate Andre either.

Because I know better than most that nobody's perfect.

"Mom, can you come and cut the chocolate cake now? Us kids are starving."

"Sure thing, sweetie." As she slips her hand into mine and gives a tug, I say to Saylor, "Don't worry. Everything's going to be okay."

As my precious daughter leads me to a long trestle table laden with food, I know it's true.

It seems like fate that Luna and Violette are united.

Sisters should live together.

I'm glad I lied to Walter about Luna's paternity and falsified that test. Anything can be done on the Internet these days. The one I sent him looks so real. Even I couldn't tell the difference between the actual test and the one I forged.

At the time, I knew what would happen if Walt learned the truth. He'd lay claim to Luna. He'd want to be a parent to her. And I couldn't have my daughter's life disrupted; or mine.

So I lied.

Perfection comes at a cost and I couldn't risk being dragged through a custody battle that would put my marriage, my career, and the flawless life I so carefully constructed, at risk.

No one knows the truth but me. It's why I haven't kicked Andre out. Because we've all done things we're not proud of and I think my secret outweighs all the ones he's kept from me.

In a crazy way, I almost hope he's the father of Saylor's baby. I like the idea of having a boy as a sibling for the girls. Accepting our blended family has lifted a weight off my shoulders.

I don't have to struggle with perfection any more.

My imperfect family has completed me.

A LETTER FROM NICOLA

I want to say a huge thank you for choosing to read *The Liar Next Door*. I hope you enjoyed it and take the time to leave a review. If you want to keep up to date with all my latest releases, please sign up at the following link. Your email address will never be shared, and you can unsubscribe at any time.

www.bookouture.com/nicola-marsh

Like *My Sister's Husband*, when the idea for *The Liar Next Door* popped into my head, I had to write it ASAP and the words poured out in a crazy sixteen days. Bringing Frankie, Celeste and Saylor to life was a rush! I hope you loved *The Liar Next Door* and if you did I'd be grateful if you could write a review. I'd love to hear what you think, and even a few simple words of appreciation makes such a difference helping new readers discover my books for the first time.

I love hearing from my readers—you can get in touch on my Facebook page, Instagram, Twitter, Goodreads, BookBub, or my website.

Thanks for taking the time to read *The Liar Next Door*.
Nicola

🐦 @NicolaMarsh

🖥 www.nicolamarsh.com

f NicolaMarshAuthor

📷 @nicolamarshauthor

ACKNOWLEDGMENTS

I'm thrilled to have another of my domestic thrillers published with Bookouture and bringing a book to life is a team effort. Huge thanks to the following:

Jennifer Hunt, editor extraordinaire. We make such a great team and I love working with you.

Kim Lionetti, my agent, whose support with every book is invaluable.

Noelle Holton and Kim Nash, publicists at Bookouture, who do a fabulous job of marketing my books.

Jane Eastgate, for her copyediting skills.

The entire Bookouture team, you're amazing and I'm so glad my domestic suspense novels are published with you.

My neighbors, most of whom have lived here as long as I have. Rest assured, everything in this story is fiction.

My parents, who moved so often when I was growing up that I'm sure they were just helping me gain neighbor fodder for this future plot!

Martin, who likes to joke that he's the inspiration for my dark and twisted books where the wives want to do bad things to their husbands. LOL!

My beautiful boys, for being you.

Soraya Lane and Natalie Anderson, my writing support duo.

Nic's Super Novas, my reader group on Facebook, who helped me come up with Hambridge Heights as the suburb for this suspenseful tale.

Janelle Marsh, my cuz, who put the name Frankie into my head for the main character, and April Naomi Lin on Instagram for suggesting Saylor and Luna.

For the bloggers, reviewers, librarians, and bookstores that take the time to read my books and spread the love.

Last but not least, my loyal readers, for buying my books. Every purchase enables me to keep writing more books and I'm so thankful!

Made in United States
North Haven, CT
23 August 2023

40637530R00189